SELECTED WRITINGS

GÉRARD DE NERVAL

SELECTED WRITINGS
GÉRARD DE NERVAL

TRANSLATED WITH A CRITICAL
INTRODUCTION AND NOTES
BY
GEOFFREY WAGNER

Ann Arbor Paperbacks
THE UNIVERSITY OF MICHIGAN PRESS

ACKNOWLEDGMENT

Some of the material presented in the Introduction was
originally published in *The Adelphi,* and is reprinted here
with the permission of Professor B. Ifor Evans.

CONTENTS

INTRODUCTION

Il n'y a qu'un problème philosophique vraiment sérieux: c'est le suicide. Juger que la vie vaut ou ne vaut pas la peine d'être vécue, c'est répondre à la question fondamentale de la philosophie.

ALBERT CAMUS, *Le Mythe de Sisyphe*

M O R E than most writers Gérard de Nerval has suffered from failing to fall into any very definite period or genre. His influence has been wider than his appeal and he has not always come off well in the rather arid region of literary history for his work, like the work of any mystic poet, resists classification. André Gide, of all writers, has lately been referred to as a mystic and in the sense that his work was always concerned with spiritual values this surprising judgment is just enough. But if Nerval is anything, he is that rarity, a natural French mystic poet, and it was this aspect of his genius that demanded from him that withdrawal from what we call the social ego, that attempt to mount higher "pour nous isoler de la foule," as he put it, which has meant much to the surrealist writers of our century.

Although a poet like Yeats refers to Nerval with the obvious affection of affinity, he has too often been handicapped by the stereotype of him as the gentle dreamer, which developed in the latter half of the last century. In his own time he meant a great deal. Baudelaire, we believe, was introduced to both Petrus Borel and Nerval by Edouard Ourliac; [1] he paid tribute to Nerval in his article on Hégésippe Moreau [2] and borrowed his well-known gibbet image in *Un Voyage à Cythère* from Nerval's *Voyage en*

---

[1] Charles Baudelaire, "Réflexions sur mes contemporains," *l'Art Romantique, Oeuvres Complètes,* Pléiade, II, p. 518.

[2] Baudelaire, *OC,* II, pp. 562 ff.

Orient. Beyond this Nerval's translations from Goethe, Bürger, and other German authors, persuaded many French scholars and writers to further efforts in this field and he himself was one of the first major French poets to assimilate fully into his work the influence of the *blaue Blume* school of poetry. His whole erotic orientation is deeply indebted to Hoffmann. His appreciation of Ronsard, Du Bellay, and their contemporaries, considerably affected his successors, while his work on the legends of the Valois, which he loved so much, awakened a living interest in the literature of the French provinces. Nerval seems to have been read consistently in France throughout the Symbolist movement and his influence there to have been pervasive. But if for Henri de Régnier his voice was like a silver bell, it is more to the somber notes of *Aurélia* that our century has responded. There have been, of course, notable exceptions. Even Jean-Paul Sartre has confessed to being seduced by *Sylvie*, the "divine Sylvie" as Maurice Barrès called it. Proust, in whom we find perhaps the happiest and most confident elaboration of the implications of Nerval's work, referred to *Sylvie* in *Le Temps Retrouvé* as one of the masterpieces of French literature and likened its method of involuntary memory to his own.

But it has been Nerval's visions, particularly those of *Aurélia*, that have chiefly fascinated our century, especially in the attempt of surrealism to find a new freedom in the casuistry of the dream. Nerval's own life, moreover, has seemed important to those artists of our time who have seen the material world as a sham and the outbreak of scandal, on literary as well as on other levels, the only sign of authenticity. Before judging Nerval's work by its influence, however, it is as well to see it against the background of its time.

* * *

Nerval's real name was Gérard Labrunie and he was born on May 22nd, 1808, at eight o'clock in the evening, the son of an Army surgeon then stationed in Paris. As soon as he began publishing Nerval changed his name, a fact that has rather inevi-

tably been seen as opposition to a father who was as usual un-
sympathetic to a literary career.   Actually, although Nerval had
the customary poet's struggle against his male parent, the fact
that he never signed his work Labrunie [3] puts an undue emphasis
on his relationship with his father who was by no means what
General Aupick was to Baudelaire.   Nerval was to use a variety
of pseudonyms, such as "Cadet Roussel," "Louis Gerval," "Fritz,"
"Lord Pilgrim," "M. Beuglant," "Ex," "M. Personne," and a host
of pseudo-initials like "G." or "G. de L." or "G. D." which has
made the task of assembling his work unusually difficult.   Between about 1844 and 1845 he took the name "Nerval" from a field
(Clos de Nerval) belonging to his uncle's family near Mortefontaine in the Valois, rather in the same way that Restif de la Bretonne, who considerably influenced much of Nerval's writing, took
"de la Bretonne" from the little group of farm buildings of that
name which his family owned in the village of Sacy.

Nerval then used his new name for the rest of his life, only
pausing to prefix to it the aristocratic "de" in common with so
many French writers of the Nineteenth Century, most of whom
sprang from the middle classes.   We find Nerval, for instance, pro-
testing in a love letter that he is a "descendant d'un châtelain du Périgord."   He liked to imagine himself a son of Joseph Bonaparte,
as well as a descendant of the twelfth Roman Emperor, Nerva,
whose coins we later find him assiduously collecting in Egypt:
the former association would confer on his mother not only the
beloved name of Julie but also the Neapolitan crown.   Restif claimed
ancestry from the Roman Emperor, Pertinax.   If this sort of thing
was at one time a happy spoof for Nerval (rather like the rumor
of Apollinaire's father being the Pope), it provided much material

---

[3] Gautier Ferrières (*Gérard de Nerval*, Paris, 1906, p. 97) is unusual in believing
that Nerval used Labrunie.   These pseudonyms have given rise to endless controversy,
the most celebrated of which converges on the name Aloysius Block.   In general
terms it seems certain that Nerval wrote twice under the name Aloysius, but that
Aloysius Block, attributed to Nerval by Gautier in his *Histoire du Romantisme*, was
used by other writers as well as by Nerval, and is therefore an "attribution suspecte."

to carry over with him into illusions of grandeur in his later insanity and as such it is important to mention these references. Indeed they haunt his work.

In the December of the year Nerval was born, his father, Etienne Labrunie, was posted to the Army of the Rhine and his wife went with him, leaving the child in the care of a peasant woman, a wet-nurse, in the village of Loisy, near Mortefontaine. Two years later Mme Labrunie was taken ill in Silesia and died, a fact which Nerval records with compassion in *Aurélia*.

As a result of her death the boy went to live with an uncle or grand-uncle, called Antoine Boucher, in Mortefontaine, a period which gave birth to his undying love for the French countryside and especially for the Valois, "où, pendant plus de mille ans, a battu le coeur de la France." It did more than this, however, for nearby was the last home of Jean-Jacques Rousseau, at Ermenonville, and if there is one writer who led Nerval to confessional literature it is Rousseau. The two spirits are strangely close in some respects and Nerval was one of those who liked to believe in the theory of Rousseau's suicide. And this uncle Nerval also invested with an exotic ancestry, giving him the Seventeenth-Century Flemish painter, Olivier Béga, as a forebear. It is likely that the poet now formed a boyish attachment with a young peasant girl of the district, to be personified in his writings as Sylvie, possibly a Sylvie Tremblay who died at Loisy in 1852, who gives a kind of pagan balance to the other friend of these years, "la religieuse," his "sainte" in *El Desdichado*, Adrienne.

It has been said that Nerval re-created and romanticized Adrienne from the Duc de Bourbon's daughter, living not far away at Chantilly. This is a confusion, though an understandable one. Louis Henri Joseph de Bourbon, the last Prince de Condé—though he superstitiously disliked using the title being without heir himself after the Duc d'Enghien's death—did have a daughter who came occasionally to Chantilly when not residing at her house in the rue Monsieur in Paris. This was the Comtesse Adèle de Reuilly, an illegitimate daughter of the Duke and a dancer at the Opéra called Mlle Michelon, or Mimi to her intimates. The Duke himself had been married at the age of fourteen to Louise Marie Thérèse Bathilde d'Orléans, sister of Philippe Égalité whose memory he naturally detested. The Duke did not see much of his illuminist wife after the Bourbon restoration of 1814/1815, but he brought back with him from his English emigration a young girl of luminous beauty, judging from two miniatures in the Salle des Gemmes at Chantilly. For convenience sake he married her off to an un-suspecting aide-de-camp (later to be created a Baron) Adrien de Feu-chères. This was the lady Nerval tells us he saw, after 1815, riding "en Amazone" through the woods around Chantilly and Morte-fontaine and whom he called Adrienne, not knowing her real name. Few knew it, in fact. Certain memorialists of the time, including Chateaubriand, speculated on the origins of the Duc de Bourbon's incomparable Montespan; it seems that she was an English girl of the lower orders, daughter of a fisherman, whom he had met in London, possibly having won her at a wager of whist from the Duke of Kent, a successor in this way to La Murphise or Louise O'Murphy, mistress of Louis XV and Boucher's favorite model. All this is mentioned in detail because, by a will of August 30th, 1829, the Duc de Bourbon left "Adrienne" a pile of properties including those of Boissy, Montmorency, and Mortefontaine where Nerval was living. "Adrienne" was, in fact, co-legatee of the cele-brated Duc d'Aumale, son of Louis-Philippe, then (1822) Duc d'Orléans. Alexandre de Lassalle has gone to some pains to prove "Adrienne's" connivance, both with Talleyrand and the Duc d'Or-léans, in the adoption of the Duc d'Aumale by the Duc de Bour-bon. However that may be, the shadow of suicide was once more flung over Nerval's literary associations by this personification, for on August 27th, 1830, shortly after Louis-Philippe had accepted the Lieutenant-Generalship of the kingdom, the Duc de Bour-bon was found hanging from an espagnolette in his château at Saint-Leu. Neither M. de Lassalle nor the milder Louis Blanc are happy with the verdict of suicide given for the last of the Condés by the Court doctors Marc and Marjolin, but as such it has gone down in history. Suffice it to say here that the Duke's bedroom was connected by a secret passage with that of "Adrienne," in a manner described by an eyewitness visitor, the Duchesse de Gontaut. Two final points should perhaps be mentioned. In his projection of this femininity figure, Adrienne, Nerval usually saw her as blonde, and, ironically, as a blonde descendant of the nobility of the Valois. Secondly, there is the religious side, the counterbalance to his paganism. And this symbolism can be found in the Bourbon-Condé affiliations also. For Louise Adélaïde de Condé, the Duke's sister, was an intensely pious lady who later became, as Soeur Marie-Joseph de la Miséricorde, Abbess of Remiremont. Moreover, the sacred ground of Saint-Sulpice-du-Désert, mentioned in *Sylvie* (see my note 9 thereto), came into the possession of Mme de Feuchères-Adrienne, as did Antoine Boucher's house in Mortefontaine. All in all, this lady, whom Albert Béguin believes to be the Delphine of *Angélique*, an earlier story than *Sylvie* in *Les Filles du Feu*, meant a great deal to Nerval. He inscribed her name on his "family tree," and in his madness had delusions of marrying her.

To return to Nerval's life, however: in 1814 Dr. Labrunie came back to France, troubled by a wound received at Wilna. He asked for, and was granted, his discharge from the Army and settled in Paris. He brought his son back from the provinces and sent him to the Lycée Charlemagne, though allowing him to spend his holidays at Montagny. It was now that Nerval first met Gautier who was to prove a lifelong friend. And it was now that he published in Paris his first precocious poems, *Napoléon et la France guerrière* (1826), *Élégies nationales et satires politiques* (1827), while a year later his miraculous translation of the first part of *Faust* made Goethe write to him, "Je ne me suis jamais si bien compris qu'en vous lisant." By this translation alone Nerval's name would stand today. 4

---

4 A brief bibliographical warning is perhaps in order here. The first edition of Nerval's *Faust I* was published in Paris by Dondey-Dupré père et fils in 1828. The translator is "Gérard." This edition is referred to by Aristide Marie in his bibliog-

As soon as he left the Lycée Nerval began to mix more freely with the youth of the day. He was presented to Victor Hugo. He became friendly with Petrus Borel and Célestin Nanteuil. Nodier and Paul Lacroix saw to it that his articles appeared in the *Mercure de France au XIXe siècle* between 1829 and 1832. In 1830 he assembled selections of German poetry and the poetry of the Pléiade, the two major influences on his own work. But on that memorable evening of February 25th, 1830, he proved his allegiance to the early French Romantic group by attending the première of Hugo's *Hernani*, along with Gautier and his friends, although, typically, he did not forget to slip out at nine o'clock to say good-night to his father. Nevertheless, despite this homely action, Nerval was well primed for the occasion, his pockets filled with the paper squares, each of which was inscribed with the blood-red password of the evening "Hierro." "Tu réponds de tes hommes?" he is said to have asked Gautier, to which, according to Maxime du Camp, Gautier replied, "Par le crâne dans lequel Byron buvait à l'abbaye de Newstead, j'en réponds!" And his men echoed him, "Mort aux perruques!"

As is well known, the play, wittily heckled all through, resulted in a victory for the new writers whose colorful and spectacular ranks Nerval now joined. This period, delightfully described for us by Gautier and Maigron, proliferated in figures like Borel who held orgies in his aptly chosen establishment in the rue d'Enfer of the type made familiar by Balzac's *Peau de Chagrin.* Here many young people assembled, not all with talent, but some genuinely gifted, like Philothée O'Neddy (the pseudonymous anagram of

raphy of Nerval's work forming the first volume in the Champion edition, at p. XII, and the editions of Nerval's translations of *Faust* are correctly collated between pages 61 and 69 that follow. Unfortunately M. Marie's printer has not been so faithful and at page 67 a cover of this edition (Bibl. nat., Réserve m Yh 4;—Yh 2528) is reproduced with 1828 become 1823. I would note one other error here in this excellent bibliography. At p. XXXV M. Marie writes that Nerval's adaptation of Goethe's work under the title *Damnation* was given, under Berlioz's direction, at the Opéra-Comique on November 29, 1856. The year should be 1846.

Théophile Dondey, who wore glasses in his sleep so that he might see his dreams), [5] Gautier, Hugo, and Nerval himself.

Borel, with his feline teeth, his melancholy eyes fixed on a spaniel at his feet, his full beard faintly perfumed and his mouth like an exotic flower, as Gautier tells us, well crystallizes the oddities of dress, fashion, and morality of this era. At Borel's house, with Ourloff in his Cossack boots, Eugène Devéria dressed like a Spanish grandee, Bouchardy in a bright blue Maharajah's coat with gilt buttons, and Nerval dressed like Werther, there was danced the famous "galop infernal," a measure taken so literally that after a round or two the floor was littered with the bodies of unconscious participants and the time had to be given by the cracking of pistol shots. Potent rum punches were served, and ice-creams in skulls. Borel subsequently took a house on the outskirts of the city where his group, which called itself "le petit cénacle," sat and discussed the questions of the day stark naked in the garden. The neighbors grumbled but, Parisians, most openly complained, it seems, when the clique began to blow concerted music through brass wind instruments which none of them had any idea how to play. The name they acquired at this time, when they included six significant poets, Gautier, Nerval, Borel, O'Neddy, Alphonse Brot, and Auguste (or Augustus) MacKeat, and which has come to stand for a movement of protest of the time, was "les bousingos," or rowdy fellows. [6]   One legend claims that it came to them from the police who arrested them for running through the streets one peaceful night, singing "un refrain peu attique: Nous avons fait, ou nous ferons, du *bousingo*." Certainly, as a result of this evening, the

[5] Even contemporaries were confused by the anagrammistic changes of name then in vogue; the third edition of Nerval's *Voyage en Orient* replaces the previous dedication "A Thimothée O'Neddy" with "A Un Ami."

[6] The name was variously spelt then as now. In *La Presse* for September 11, 1839, Gautier (who was to deny many of these early associations) promised an article on "les *Bousingault*" by Nerval. Nerval's own most usual spelling is the one given here. This group, with defections and additions, is roughly the one known as *Les Jeunes-France* which was the name given by Gautier to a collection of sketches, first appearing in *La France littéraire*, *Le Cabinet de lecture*, and *Annales romantiques*, from 1832 on.

ringleaders were locked up and it was at this time, lodged with political prisoners, that Nerval underwent his short, but apparently unpleasant, stay in Sainte-Pélagie prison, to which his poem *Politique* refers.

Nerval was in no way outdone by these eccentrics. Although, like Hugo, he is said to have attended such gatherings carefully and formally dressed, there are several stories told of him at this period; it is hard to substantiate them all, but the two most common are, first, of the skull he carried with him as a drinking vessel, telling his audience that it was his mother's and that he had been forced to kill her to obtain it (again, he would say it was that of a drum-major killed in battle), and, second, of the wigwam —actually, the conical tepee—he took with him whenever invited to spend the night away from home. This he would set up and sleep in on the guest-room floor, scorning the more comfortable bed offered him. It was in this mood that, in 1832, he published what he called a "histoire macaronique," called *La Main de Gloire*, warning us that it had been extracted from some *Contes du Bousingo* by a certain "camaraderie." A letter from O'Neddy to Asselineau in 1862 reveals that this collection was an abortive effort to give the bourgeois "une leçon de bien écrire."

It was no doubt now, too, that Nerval met the talented bousingo sculptor, Jean (or Jehan) du Seigneur, who in his room in the rue Vaugirard brushed his hair into twin peaks to simulate the flames of genius, and to whom we are indebted for the charming young likeness of Nerval, dated 1831, a head on a "médaillon" of which he speaks in a love letter to Jenny Colon.

It is interesting that, although Nerval flung himself with gusto into this movement of revolt, his talent remained remarkably untouched by it. Apart from romantic blasphemy, there is not even a phase in Nerval's work that might be traced to the "divine Marquis" or to such text-books of eccentricity as *Madame Putiphar*, which with their reiteration of indecency and horror are mostly minor, reflected as they are later in the pages of *Le Décadent* and in the strange novels of P.-J. Toulet. Nerval was influenced by the bousingos in his occasional choice of a violent and shocking title, such as *Les Filles du Feu*, or *Contes Fantastiques* with its inevitable *Sonate du Diable*. Yet both Borel and Nerval were to share the same fate, for it seems likely that Borel killed himself in North Africa by self-inflicted sunstroke.

In 1834, at about the same age as Baudelaire when he came into his money, Nerval was left a legacy and at once went to Italy. It is possible (though the dates are contested) that he now met on his travels a young English girl, to whom he was to refer as Octavie in his writings, and to identify by the way in which, on one occasion, her teeth sank into the rind of a lemon (as in the poem, *Delfica*). It may be that Nerval did not see her swimming in the blue waters of the Mediterranean until later, but what matters is that, under the name of Octavie, she forms part of his conception of womanhood. Significantly, he visited the Temple of Isis at Pompeii with Octavie.

In 1835 Nerval returned to Paris and set up house next door to Gautier with Camille Rogier, a firm friend, and Arsène Houssaye. Soon afterwards he became Gautier's associate on *La Presse*, but for all Gautier's generous references there can be little doubt that Nerval could not acclimatize himself temperamentally to a regular job and often shirked his duties.

It was perhaps unlucky that at this moment, still with a future in front of him and with a reasonable fortune at his command, Nerval met Jenny Colon. She was a natural blonde with dark eyes, an indifferent singer at the Variétés when he first saw her (she had made her début at fourteen with her sister Eléonore at the Théâtre Feydeau), and she had been born the same year as himself. She was of scant significance in the dramatic world and would only exist today beyond Nerval's devotion to her by such slender references as Gautier's, in *La Presse* after the performance of one of the many Dumas-Nerval collaborations, *Piquillo*. [7] Jenny

[7] The extent of this collaboration remains controversial. Nerval and Dumas are said to have agreed to split their output, each signing alternate works; Dumas is generally considered the author of *Piquillo*, and Nerval of *Léo Burckart*.

was the vehicle for a whole attitude of mind in her lover and her inspiration runs through Nerval's dream writings, *Aurélia, Les Chimères,* and *Autres Chimères.* From the first she had the force of an abstraction for Nerval. He saw her as the incarnation of all womanhood, and it is this conception that informs the major body of his work from now on, for Jenny is Aurélia, as well as, to some extent, Adrienne, and other figures.

From his first meeting with this ambitious actress Nerval's life was changed. He lavished money and gifts on her, he founded *Le Monde Dramatique* to swell her reputation, and he wrote unsuccessful plays for her at the Odéon, the Comédie Française, and elsewhere. Although he did some dramatic work at this time that will live, it was ironically only after Jenny left him that Nerval wrote what is generally considered his best play, *Léo Burckart,* in 1839, a play incomparably superior to another of the same year, in which he also shared, *l'Alchimiste,* graced as the latter was by the future Mme Dumas, Ida Ferrier.

Le Monde Dramatique cost Nerval dear. Among its contributors it had numbered men like Gautier, Karr (also a contributor to the projected *Contes du Bousingo*), Lassailly, and Roger de Beauvoir, while its illustrators had included names like Nanteuil, Leleux, and Camille Rogier. Nerval is said to have run through about 30,000 francs with this periodical over a short period, a very large sum of money by present standards. Moreover, he saddled himself with lifelong debts. Thus for Jenny he dissipated "en seigneur," as he tells us, the last of his legacy. He made his friends write odes to her, and he poured out his soul to her in letters she had not the sensibility to understand. Nerval, indeed, had little theatrical talent and it is unfortunate that Jenny Colon turned his attention to the theater at this moment.

It is thought that Nerval did not possess Jenny. In his love letters, published after his death, [8] there are a number of references to suggest that he made efforts in this direction. But Gautier claims that she never yielded and mentions in this connection the huge

[8] *La Revue de Paris,* February 15th, 1855.

Renaissance bed Nerval bought as a symbol of the culmination of his wooing. This bed, on which Marguerite de Valois was supposed to have slept, together with his Fragonard panels, added considerably to Nerval's housing difficulties because of its size. Balzac makes an allusion to it and it inspired a little story by Théodore de Banville [9] in which Nerval is characterized as one, Roland, whose love was "celui d'un agonisant." It was the love, too, of Lassailly for the Comtesse de Magnencourt which drove him also into the hands of Dr. Blanche.

Such it was and, as such, presents a parable of the aesthetic dictum for which Nerval was to be made responsible. For here in this love-for-love's sake attitude we find the lover, like the surrealist, loosed of convention and responsibility. We find Nerval the courtly lover, echoing the age of Guillaume de Lorris and Jean de Meung in whom he showed such interest. Throughout his letters to Jenny there is a humiliation, a self-abasement, the prostration of a Marcel Schwob (which only has relevance in the masculine feudal age), coupled with a Casanova-like speciousness while Nerval makes himself out the predestined disappointed lover. But the love letters, beautiful in their way, do help us to understand his work; in *La Nouvelle Revue* for October 15th, 1902, P.-B. Gheusi called them "ces lettres d'amour du plus délicat de nos romantiques à la plus frivole des actrices médiocres de son temps, objet indigne... d'une si chevaleresque passion."

The passion, indeed, was "chevaleresque." Every circumstance is phrased to allow this original lover to play the role of "soupirant"—even the word "pitié" is used in the sense of "pitëe" in the *Roman de la Rose*. The loss of self in spiritualized sexual love may have been a necessary homiletic eroticism for the Middle Ages, but today, as the later handlings of the Tristan and Iseult legend show, it is dangerous if carried too far. "Il l'aimait peut-être trop pour la vaincre," Arsène Houssaye wrote of the affair, and surely his remark has a certain relevance to the aesthetic movement Nerval helped to initiate. It was finality, that "amor de

[9] *La République des Lettres*, March 18th, 1877.

lonh," Mallarmé's "l'absence" in which you positively do not want your ideal to be present. Nerval constantly protests of his lack of jealousy for Jenny. It did not matter to him, he wrote, if she were unfaithful, and this is quite consistent with that unabated passion for her prolonged beyond her death until he killed himself, as he had once told her he would, for Nerval was not in love with a woman, but an idea. "Les bêtes s'aiment de près," he wrote once, "les esprits s'aiment de loin."

There is much of this kind of feeling, of course, in Marcel's relations with Gilberte in Proust's work. Again we have Marcel the devoted slave, or "fin amant," and Gilberte the feudal "belle dame sans merci." If one likes to see this relationship from the point of view of the psyche, one concludes that for writers close to the dream the subconscious must bifurcate sharply. The lover, like Nerval, becomes the hysteric or compulsive, and the beloved the absolute force of inhibition, the one who constantly says no, satyr and nymph, in fact, of the pastoral, a form that attracted Nerval more than once. Naturally this state of permanently un-satisfied desire, of contemplation of the ideal as the whole function of art, encourages a voyeuristic attitude towards woman. Such is what we find in Nerval and such, to a considerable extent, in Proust. But gratification of nostalgia as a formula for art pre-supposes a nymph-ideal; you do not possess someone you believe to be a cross between Isis and the Queen of Sheba.

However such speculations may be, in the psychology of ado-lescent love, or "sentimental education," Jenny Colon's influence on Nerval was enormous. As soon as he ceased to be useful to her, as attendant puppet to her "gloire," Jenny tired of him and in 1838 she married a flutist. Nerval ran away to Germany, a visit most fruitful to him for not only did he fall further under the spell of Hoffmann (from whose *Serapionsbrüder* it is thought that he borrowed the name of Aurélia), but wandering back through Austria he met Marie Pleyel who assumed for a moment the iden-tity of the womanhood figure in his mind, and who is the Pandora of the tale of that name he later wrote.

But in Vienna at this time Nerval must surely, as he confesses, have played the Casanova somewhat. He contracted a weakness for a voluptuous beauty he called La Katty (Caterina Colossa, as she seems to have been appropriately named), "*bionda e grassota*" as Nerval describes her, possessed of a dove-like neck, shoulders both childlike in their charm and Herculean in strength, and a skin so white it seemed to have been preserved under glass. La Katty yielded to a Slav girl, La Vhahby.

In 1840 Nerval was back in Paris and had recommenced work, this time on the second part of *Faust*—he was to see Faust's poodle almost everywhere he looked in later years. Now his friends noticed his hitherto harmless eccentricities becoming more and more pronounced. He took a trip to Belgium but when he got back it was the same. One night, in Méry's words, "nous trouvâmes Gérard en proie à une fièvre chaude ... c'était un spectacle navrant dont je supprime les détails." He was taken off to a mental home nearby and then transferred to the asylum run by Dr. Esprit Blanche in the rue de Norvins, which moved, in 1847, (under the direction of this doctor's son, Emile) to Passy. The type of mental illness from which Nerval was suffering is likely to remain controversial; cases have been made to show that it was either oneiro-phrensy or, again, schizophrenia. Quite recently a Paris *maison de santé* turned up in its register an entry for Nerval in 1852. His diagnosis in this case was erysipelas.

After eight months, in November 1841, Nerval appeared cured. He remembered all that had happened, yet did not seem to personify himself with the events, many of which he recorded in the document of his madness, *Aurélia* or *Le Rêve et la Vie*. In the asylum, he tells us, time lost all meaning for him. Past, present, and future were intermingled, and he believed that his hallucinations, seen in this condition, were moments of vision granted to him alone, and that therefore these visions were worth recording for others. The result was *Aurélia*. Possessed by his dreams, by the divine madness of the *Ion* or *Phaedrus*, Nerval became a sort of Delphic oracle, annihilating his personality, or ego, to allow the dream, or id, to erupt spontaneously. "Cette âme pure qui voltige ... comme un oiseau," is one of Gautier's descriptions of Nerval; Plato describes the one possessed of the divine madness in the *Ion* as follows, "he is like a bird fluttering and looking upward and careless of the world below."

Slowly but, it seemed, surely, Nerval began to recover, writing occasionally for *La Sylphide*, until Jenny Colon died in 1842. He at once left Paris and went to the East. Not only did orientalia provide both Gautier and Flaubert with temporary vicarious escape, but several French writers of the Nineteenth Century fled there after some personal tragedy. Borel went to North Africa. In Byzantium Nerval met Camille Rogier, who was also suffering from the death of his beloved. Nerval first, however, set up house in Cairo, and Jules Janin tells us of the impractical way he spent his days there, buying a mass of useless things, odd bits of canvas, fragments of wood, old coins, and another vast bed which he had to sleep beside, rather than in, since he lacked the money for a mattress. Nerval soon discovered that it was considered immoral for a man to live alone in Cairo in those days, and he accordingly went into the market and, out of pity more than admiration, bought a Javanese girl whose most distinctive features were the henna dye of her arms and eyelids, her richly tattooed chest, her brand marks, and her pierced left nostril. But life with Zeynab (Z'N'B') proved too much even for Nerval when she began filling the bed with onions, the smell of which, together with their religious connotations, made her sleep better. He offered to send her to Gautier, whose oriental taste in women he knew well, but Gautier refused the gift.

In the East Nerval fell in love once more. It did not matter that it was a new girl, Saléma, daughter of one of the chieftains of the Druse, for it was the old love, ideal womanhood, which he pursued all his life. Although he knew himself well enough to know that he was not fitted for a settled, married existence, Nerval went so far as to become betrothed to Saléma, but soon afterwards he took a fever and had to be moved from the Lebanon, where he

then was, to a healthier climate in Constantinople. This illness
Nerval interpreted as a decree of fate against the wedding and he
duly wrote to the chief of the Druse asking to be released from
the engagement. As a final gesture he sent Zeynab to be Saléma's
companion.

When he was better, Nerval returned to France, permanently
adopting from 1845 on the pseudonym by which we know him
today. In 1844 he travelled to Holland, landed in England for
a brief visit, and in 1848 went to Germany again. On his return
he began publishing more of his *Scènes de la Vie Orientale, Les
Femmes de Caire*, some of his most immediately popular work,
subsequently collected under the title, *Voyage en Orient* (1851).
It must be remembered that Cairo was still relatively untouched
by Western civilization at this time and Nerval has left us in this
work a really valuable, as well as entertaining, memoir of the Near
East of a century ago, especially of such oddities as slave markets
and harem customs, for as usual he seems to have been able to
get in anywhere he wished. In 1850 he collaborated with Méry
to produce *Le Chariot d'Enfant*, an adaptation from the Sanskrit
of Súdraka, an Indian poet of the First Century B.C. Despite
the fact that Marie Laurent starred, the Nerval-Méry adaptation
was no immediate success, but as luck would have it, it was later
produced with great financial rewards by Lugné-Poë at the théâtre
de l'Oeuvre, with sets by Toulouse-Lautrec, and Suzanne Desprès
in the leading role.

In 1851 Nerval was once again seriously ill and had to return
to the mental home for treatment. But the next year he was well
enough to start work in Paris again and write, again with Méry,
L'Imagier de Harlem, as well as the original prose work, *Les Il-
luminés*, which contained essays on such eccentrics as Restif de
la Bretonne, Quintus Aucler, l'abbé de Bucquoy, Jacques Cazotte
(an introduction he had made earlier for a de luxe edition of Cazotte's *Le Diable Amoureux*), Cagliostro, and Raoul Spifame. He
was doing German translations and had met Heine who was living
in the French capital. For Heine's wife, Mathilde, Nerval wrote

a charming little poem in her album. Needless to say, none of this work brought Nerval much money. Méry tells us that he used to leave the poet in the early morning shivering with cold and not knowing where he was going.

In August 1853 he was taken back to Dr. Emile Blanche who was by now the only doctor in whom he had any confidence, and who remained to the end "mon excellent médecin" with "la figure bonne et compatissante." [10] Indeed one aspect of *Aurélia* is a tribute to the care Nerval received at the hands of this doctor. By May 1854 he had recovered sufficiently to be released once more and this time he took out with him the uncompleted manuscript of *Aurélia*. It should be said, also, that another reason for his release was that he begged his friends to request it of Dr. Blanche; Nerval did not enjoy his periods in the asylum. On August 16th, 1854, *Les Filles du Feu*, that tender work with the bousingo title in which "feu" is used in the Seventeenth-Century sense of "passion", appeared, including as its central gem the previously published *Sylvie*, and Nerval's name began to have a chance of being recognized in his own day. But these lovely stories were daughters of the flame, indeed, for another crisis had caused their creator to be confined again. In October he was again discharged. It was to be for the last time.

In these final years of his life it became clear to Nerval's friends that his eccentricities, once so light-hearted, had become a serious mental disorder. Some of the incidents in which he was involved now are reminiscent of the early bousingo days. He paraded the gardens of the Palais-Royal with a lobster on a pale blue ribbon and, when asked why he did this, he replied that he preferred lobsters to dogs or cats because they could not bark at you and, moreover, they knew the secrets of the deep. This incident is often

10 Dr. Emile Blanche was later to tend, and fall in love with, the Comtesse de Castiglione. When he died, the celebrated mistress of Napoléon III came out of her retirement to attend his funeral and throw flowers on his coffin. As a result of this, she was approached by the doctor's son, Jacques-Emile, who has left us two portraits of the Comtesse de Castiglione "sur le déclin."

quoted and Joyce mentions it in *Stephen Hero*. Again, like some character from Giraudoux, Nerval would toss his money up in the air in a restaurant or throw his hat happily to a hatless hippopotamus he saw in the Jardin des Plantes.

As one would expect, his work is now fragmentary. *La Bohème Galante* is no more than a series of jottings, a literary commonplace book. He translated Kotzebue's *Menschenhass und Reue*, his version, *Misanthropie et Repentir*, enjoying a mild success at the Comédie Française after his death. Much of his time now was spent wandering around the Paris streets, hungry, cold, and ill clad. He was living in cheap hotel rooms and lodging houses, moving from one to another not only because of lack of money, but also, so he told Charles Asselineau, because of his fear of being found and reclaimed by Dr. Blanche. But, despite this fear, his letters to Dr. Blanche at the end of his life remain friendly and respectful and, indeed, form a touching autobiography in themselves. And the fact that Nerval's friends lost him for days on end now may also be attributed to his desire not to bother them with his suffering. He wrote once that he had "la pudeur de la souffrance," going on to describe himself as a wounded animal withdrawing into solitude in order not to let others hear his complaint. But the police would come across him. "Qui êtes-vous?" they would ask him, when they picked him up in Les Halles in the early hours of the morning. "Monsieur Gérard de Nerval." "Que faites-vous ici?" "Je pense," would come the reply. Béguin has suggested that in these last, lonely wanderings Nerval was seeking for communion and fraternity in his suffering, and that he found such among the poor. Certainly the district round Les Halles was not the happiest place in Paris at that time.

The eye-witness accounts of Nerval's final agony vary, but a few facts seem certain. A day or so before his death he sought out Méry and, not finding him at home, left a coin on which he had scratched a cross, symbol of his own suffering. On January 24th, 1855, he wrote a lucid and charming letter to his aunt—for Nerval's capacity for suffering seems to have been matched with an equal fund of thought for others—and this ended, "Ne m'attends pas ce soir, car la nuit sera noire et blanche."

On the morning of the following day he borrowed seven sous from Asselineau, the price of a night's lodging in a dosshouse, and he refused to take more. "Je ne sais ce qui va m'arriver," he said, as he pocketed the coins, "mais je suis inquiet." It was an icy day, there was snow on the streets, but Nerval was as usual now lightly clad. Late at night he was seen in Les Halles, and again in the rue Casimir-Delavigne. A police patrol came across him in the early hours of the morning. This must have been shortly before he knocked on the door of a dosshouse in the rue de la Vieille Lanterne, then a narrow, dirty, twisting street near the Place du Châtelet, today the site of the théâtre Sarah-Bernhardt. This street is likely to have interested Nerval since a shopkeeper had set out on the pavement there an Egyptian mummy in order to attract custom. The concierge did not answer Nerval's knock. Later she confessed that she had heard it, but that it had been too cold to go to the door. At dawn Nerval was discovered by some market gardeners. He had hung himself from a grating at the bottom of the stone stairs leading to the rue de la Tuerie, by means of an old apron-string he had taken to carrying around with him, insisting, according to Nadar, that it had once been the Queen of Sheba's garter, or, according to other sources, the corset-string of Madame de Maintenon, or Marguerite de Valois. It is said that a raven hovered over his head, reciting the only words it had been taught by its owner, "J'ai soif!" In Nerval's pockets were found the final pages of *Aurélia*. The "Extrait des Archives de la Morgue," dated January 26th, gave the manner of his death as suicide.

As with most literary suicides, a theory sprang up that Nerval did not kill himself. Actually, although few scholars tolerate the idea that he was murdered, we may at least owe to this claim the fact that the Catholic Church permitted him its sacrament. The theory, which had some currency in the Nineteenth Century and was recently resuscitated by R.-L. Doyon in an introduction to *Les Filles du Feu*, and more recently still by Francis Carco, asserts that Nerval, who in his last months had indubitably been associating with the lowest elements of Parisian life, was set on by some ruffians and hung. Those who persist in adhering to this theory support their contention by contesting Gautier's statement that the last pages of *Aurélia* were found on the body, since the first part of the work had been published in *La Revue de Paris* on January 1st of that year, and therefore the second part, which the review printed on February 15th, must have been in the publisher's hands before Nerval's death. Certain obvious arguments in reply to this theory have made it one that has had little acceptance, despite the alleged testimony of one old lady who said she saw him murdered (as in the case of Verlaine's death, a lot of extremely unreliable concierges and gossips came forward with "eye-witness" accounts, and Houssaye recounts a ghastly squabble between two of them as to whether Nerval's feet were touching the ground before he was cut down). The majority of critics, such as Paul Gautier and Béguin, agree with those of Nerval's contemporaries, like Maxime du Camp and Georges Bell, that suicide was an all too logical conclusion to his life, and accept Dr. Blanche's dictum that "Gérard de Nerval s'est pendu parce qu'il a vu sa folie face à face." [11] Nerval had taken the dream as refuge and was ready to pay the price. How sad his death was for his many friends, Janin testifies:

A la porte d'une maison borgne, par le vent de bise et la nuit profonde, à l'heure où tout dort, où tout repose, où le silence est tombé sur cette ville immense et la protège à la façon de l'oiseau qui tient sous son aile son humble couvée, il s'est tué, cet ami de nos jeunes années, ce compagnon charmant de nos travaux de chaque jour, ce rêveur tout éveillé dont on n'a jamais vu que la bienveillance et le sourire.

* * *

Nerval's first poems, published when he was still in his teens, were political verses after the style of Delavigne, rather exagger-

---

[11] Raymond Jean, "Le Suicide de Gérard de Nerval," PMLA, March 1955, summarizes this haunted necrology very thoroughly, even down to an attempt made in 1943, in the press of occupied France, to prove Nerval the victim of Freemasonry.

ated for contemporary taste, but interesting as showing the young "revolutionary" poet looking back to the heroism of a warlike France, a France now left "malheureuse et trahie." These *Élégies Nationales* were quickly followed by the translation of the first part of *Faust* which drew such praise from Goethe. To Eckermann, Goethe added that he thought the work a prodigy of style and that Nerval would become one of the purest and most elegant writers in France. Gretchen's song at her spinning wheel, *Chambre de Marguerite*, resembling the later cries of Nerval's own heart, is put into French with a simplicity that makes it a poem in its own right, and Nerval indeed printed it separately on occasion.

Content to remain for the moment a translator, and a scrupulously careful one (he produced, for instance, five versions of a ballad by Bürger between 1829 and 1835), Nerval published French versions of selections from Klopstock, Schiller, Heine, and others. He then edited a volume containing work by Ronsard, Du Bellay, and their contemporaries, whose style so influenced his own. In his comments on these writers in *La Bohème Galante*, called "Les Poëtes du XVIe Siècle," however, he is by no means uncritical and sees them, in Ben Jonson's words of the ancients, "as guides, not commanders." Referring to the "école de Ronsard" in particular, he laments "l'espèce de despotisme qu'elle a introduit en littérature."

After 1830 Nerval began writing his first plays, as was only natural for a young author who had that year witnessed the *bataille d'Hernani*, and his work became more original. His *Odelettes*, deliberately modelled on Ronsard, began appearing in various periodicals and attracted attention chiefly for their classical adherence to conventions of form, which were at that time so out of fashion among the young. However at this point, as we know, Nerval's interests were unfortunately returned to drama by Jenny Colon, and shortly after she left him, his only success came out, *Léo Burckart*.

This political piece of young Germany of the *Sturm und Drang* era, reminiscent of the early Schiller, once again shows the "revo-

lutionary" Nerval. There are some excellent scenes, particularly
where the student's court passes sentence of death on Léo, who
is actually among them behind a mask, and there is a powerful
finale where the fanatical student idealist, Frantz Lewald, sent in
to kill Léo, is driven to take his own life. The character of Léo
himself is well drawn—the theoretical revolutionary who is offered,
and forced to accept, the task of putting his theories into practice,
only to find the pitfalls of politics too much for him; while Frantz,
torn between love for Marguerite, Léo's wife, and his revolutionary ideals, though perhaps an over-romanticized character, can
still arouse our sympathy.

After his first bout of insanity and subsequent trip to the Middle
East, Nerval published his *Scènes de la Vie Orientale*, re-edited
in 1851 as *Voyage en Orient*, a work Gautier called, in a typical
phrase, "ce livre adorable, plein d'amour, d'azur et de lumière."
Apart from its interest in connection with contemporary travel,
mentioned above, it contains, in some of Nerval's best prose,
much of his deepest thinking on nature and esoteric religions, on
Swedenborg and the Cabala "qui lie les mondes" and in the heavenly correspondences of things on earth.

His poems began appearing more frequently now, and a collection came out at about the same time as *La Bohème Galante*
which, apart from its critical section referred to, is an account of
his life in Paris, in the same way that *Lorely, Souvenirs d'Allemagne*,
dedicated to Janin and published in 1852, was an account of his
experiences in Germany.

On August 15th, 1853, Nerval's first really important work,
Sylvie, appeared in the *Revue des Deux Mondes*. This enchanting
work is a frame-story with its roots in literary pastoralism. One
thinks of d'Urfé's Sylvie in what is perhaps a consummate instance
of pastoral romance, and one recalls that *l'Astrée* was, like Nerval's work, both an autobiographical compilation and a *roman à
clef* with an obdurate shepherdess and that "chagrin d'amour"
which must have drawn Heine to Nerval, and vice versa. Both
works, *l'Astrée* and *Sylvie*, reacted against prevalent philosophies

l of awakening memory, then, opened the way for
hat so triumphantly greets us in the work of Marcel
nts directly at Proust's method of involuntary memory,
hich, as Justin O'Brien puts it, "repose sur une de ces
où la mémoire affective agit sans qu'intervienne la

ove attitude, as we have seen, involved the phantasy
was with him always; this idea, like the doctrine of
ge in literature (in which our ancestors are always
er our shoulders), surely enhances the exhibitionist
under the surveillance of what we like to call the ego
is little privacy. Consequently you must put all on
are forced to confessional literature, of which *Aurélia*
nding example.
ame time Jenny-Aurélia, like Beatrice for Dante, was
' (*El Desdichado*): the poet is astrophel, guided (like
by the star, which plays a moral role. There is here,
fferent circumstances to Dante, a proximate relationship
tual and myth. To be a lover in this world is to be a
o be a poet is to love. Like Beatrice, too, Jenny-Aurélia
our levels: she is a beautiful girl, she is a living symbol
beauty, she is an incitement to virtuous behavior in this
oral meaning), and, lastly, on the anagogical level, she
ress of heaven itself. This longing for union, coupled
mission of poet as prophet (*vates*), Nerval saw as his
piration; contemplation of his "étoile" was the function
rk.
is outstanding, one has to confess, more for its subject-
an for its style. It is not one of Nerval's best-written
arred too often by the fulsome phrasing of its period,
ages show his artistic discrimination at its lowest ebb.
ure of individual man horribly alone, walking through
rld where the stones shout out at him and bodiless voices
om the shadows, is, however, like a nerve-end of our
ness contracting in advance. Just as it is impossible to

of materialism, both are covered in a patina of nostalgic reverie, with the longing of late afternoon and with a desire for the golden age. Meanwhile, the idyllic moment on an island, which we find in so many romantics, including once again Rousseau, lends itself readily to various interpretations; *The Tempest* is perhaps a supreme example of this literature which the Jungian symbolism fits so well, with the fortunate island (personality) set in the turbulent sea (unconscious).

The main theme of *Sylvie* is formed by a series of utterly simple anecdotes of the author's youth at his uncle's home in the Valois. By its sense of unusual intimacy, by the pathos of Sylvie's position objectively conveyed, and by its derangement of time in the interests of the life of the psyche rather than in those of normal chronology, the work would alone rank high among autobiographies of adolescence. But it is in manner that it is almost perfect, for here the purity of Nerval's heart was clearly reflected in the luminosity of his style.

Of course the reader must remember that the element of distortion, present here in the purposeful confusion Nerval makes of the three women, Sylvie, Adrienne, and Aurélia, was due to the fact that memories of all three were entwined in his own mind around that central conception of womanhood which stylized his amatory writing from now on. The round dance, with which the work begins, is essentially a round of his erotic trinity, Sylvie and Adrienne surmounted by Aurélia, the Blessed Virgin.

In a sense *Sylvie* is one of our last and most lovely pastorals, a lament for a vanished and vanishing world, not only, Rousseau-like, for the rural life yielding to increasing urbanization, but also for the past world of the author's own soul. *Sylvie* is singularly touching when Nerval interjects moments of humor that show us how well he understood himself. This, then, is conscious nostalgia. It is devoid of self-pity. It is a laurel wreath Nerval places on the passing of time, and its permanent appeal, especially its appeal to Proust, shows how harmoniously conceived, how deceptively well controlled, and how beautifully balanced in its antiphonal refrains from section to section, this little masterpiece is. In the light of his whole work its pantheism balances the Christianity of the last part of *Aurélia*, unorthodox as this may be.

In 1854 *Sylvie* was put together with other stories, including *Emilie*, a narrative of the Revolution in Alsace, one of Nerval's finest, if least typical, stories, and published as *Les Filles du Feu*, together with an important dedicatory letter to Dumas. *Emilie*, which is equal to the best of Merimée or Maupassant, shows another side of Nerval's genius, one that should not be overlooked, and it is as well to balance any large weight of his autobiographical writings with a plain story like this in which he showed admirable technical ability. It is not surprising that the author of this tale was the son of an Army surgeon, but it is pleasant to see Nerval fully in control of a form of writing of his day, and it is only in the old Abbé's descriptions of the countryside that Nerval here relinquished a fairly taut, direct narrative style. Again, suicide haunts the story.

Nerval's most significant prose work, *Aurélia*, did not appear complete in his lifetime. In a phrase, Gautier called the work "la Folie se racontant elle-même" and so indeed it is. It is not difficult to find Freudian symbolism, in our enlightened age, in these hallucinations. Nerval, however, warns us against the vulgarity of the purely scientific method of approach. Yet L.-H. Sebillotte has not had to be perversely ingenious to find an Oedipus complex in *Aurélia*.[12] Almost everything, ranging from Mariolatry to Orphism, could be, and has been, worked out of Nerval's hallucinations, but presumably only Dr. Blanche will ever know which of these manifestations were the outstanding signs and signals of Nerval's illness.

The basis of the book is Nerval's unrequited passion for Aurélia, or Jenny Colon, and his spiritual pilgrimage through a disordered world to this goal. The central figure is a composite abstraction of womanhood, an *Ewig-Weibliche* invested with Nerval's omnivorous reading in the Cabala, the Zohar, Egyptian religions, the

[12] L.-H. Sebillotte, *La Vie Secrète de Gérard de Nerval*, Paris, Corti, 1948.

medieval schoolmen, and
the early Seventeenth Cent
detailed by Jean Richer.[13]
Nerval presents this centra
main consisting of Sylvie a
Octavie is only a passing fl
for Egypt?—while Pandora,
Helen, as we read at the be

Aurélia herself is essentiall
she is a Schekhina, the wom
attributes of pure good who
the Blessed Virgin and the
who tells the protagonist:

Je suis la même que Marie, la
sous toutes les formes tu as touj
j'ai quitté l'un des masques don
verras telle que je suis.

Around this composite creat
and reality. On the physical le
such a special erotic role in
have the transformation—"l'act
la Médiatrice, Isis, la Vierge,"
mystical writers, like Hoffmann,
has such close affinity, occult or
emotional stimulants to the artist.
tified in his sight by the imaginati
by the conscious, and for this re
them to posterity:

Je croirai avoir fait quelque chose
vement la succession des idées par
une force nouvelle à opposer aux m

[13] Jean Richer, *Gérard de Nerval et*
d'Or, 1947.

This method
the vision t
Proust; it li
a method w
expériences
volonté."

Nerval's
that Jenny
noblesse obl
looking ov
factor. For
ideal there
paper, you
is an outst

At the s
his "étoile"
the magi)
as under d
between ri
poet, and
exists on
of God's
life (the n
is the for
with the
highest as
of his wo

Aurélia
matter th
works; n
its last p
The pict
a lost wo
shriek fr
consciou

read the city poems of Baudelaire and Verlaine today without feeling that they contain an extraordinary significance for our time, so it is hard to hear Nerval calling out from his asylum without a tremor of sympathy, and perhaps also fear at the apparently uncontrollable progress of materialism that can make a poet write:

les visions qui s'étaient succédé pendant mon sommeil m'avaient réduit à un tel désespoir que je pouvais à peine parler...
Je me levai plein de terreur...
le sentiment qui résulta pour moi de ces visions... était si triste, que je me sentais comme perdu...
je n'ai jamais éprouvé que le sommeil fut un repos...

Yet if we take a cosmic view of this suffering, we must remember that Nervial did not. For him it was simply a hellish dualism—"dualisme chronique," as Baudelaire is thought to have called it—and a "descente aux enfers" to bring back what he thought was truth. He would have agreed with Gauguin that God belongs to the dream, but this does not mean that he treated insanity as an escape. "Tendre fol," he has been called, "le pauvre Gérard," "gentil Nerval," "doux rêveur," [14] but there is something stronger about this man who, while writing to Deschamps in 1854 "je travaille et j'enfante désormais dans la douleur," could produce this epitaph on his own life, not as a plea for leniency, but as the picture of a world that he thought would help others. In some ways the words of the document Hermann Hesse's Steppenwolf left behind him in his bourgeois boarding-house fit *Aurélia* also:

These records, however much or however little of real life may lie at the back of them, are not an attempt to disguise or to palliate this widespread sickness of our times. They are an attempt to present the sickness itself in its actual manifestation. They mean, literally, a journey through hell, a sometimes fearful, sometimes courageous journey through the chaos of a world whose souls dwell in darkness, a journey under-

---

[14] This persistent phrase, used in almost any context (and out of it) with Nerval, appears to be infectious. Thus, in Jean-Jacques Bernard's *Le Secret d'Arvers*, we find Nodier talking of Michelet as a "doux rêveur," and are not surprised to hear that Nerval has been invited for the evening a few lines later.

taken with the determination to go through hell from one end to the other, to give battle to chaos, and to suffer torture to the full.

* * *

Nerval's poetry was only posthumously assembled, the collection of 1877 being the first to enable a true appreciation of his value as a poet, and to show how the three ages of the poet, of which he wrote in *Petits Châteaux de Bohème*, bear a direct relation to his work.

First, there come what he called the poems written "par enthousiasme de jeunesse." These include the early political poems, imitations of Delavigne, Béranger, and others, the best of which concern the Grande Armée in Russia, perhaps owing to his mother's death and his father's wound in these campaigns.

Second, there are the poems "faits par amour," the *Odelettes*, translations of German ballads, popular songs, and personal anecdotes.

Third, we have the poems written "par désespoir" or in a "*supernaturaliste*" state of mind—Nerval himself italicized this word, adding "comme diraient les Allemands," and he used it to describe the poems of his later years, when he was mad, the verse counterpart, in fact, of *Aurélia*.

The poems of the first group are generally unoriginal. Those of the second are largely reminiscent of his own life. Exquisitely expressed and perfectly formal they are little cameos of experience which, though less sentimental than Coppée, remind one more of him, or of Jammes, than of Baudelaire and his successors. *Une Allée du Luxembourg*, for instance, should be set beside Baudelaire's *A Une Passante* (which is said to be indebted to it) to see the essential difference between the two poets. Nerval is chiefly out to capture the atmosphere of Parisian spring, and his verse is accordingly light:

> Elle a passé, la jeune fille
> Vive et preste comme un oiseau:
> A la main une fleur qui brille,
> A la bouche un refrain nouveau.

At the end comes the poet's comment, in this case a spiritual nostalgia that is typically *nervalien*: and here the metre slows.

> Mais non,—ma jeunesse est finie....
> Adieu, doux rayon qui m'as lui,—
> Parfum, jeune fille, harmonie...
> Le bonheur passait,—il a fui!

The poem, *Avril*, too, is so perfect that it might well have come fresh from the Pléiade, simple as an act of faith. In this sort of work Nerval is not trying to produce original matter, so much as to give "What oft was thought but ne'er so well expressed." His emphasis is on manner. In *Les Cydalises*, with its delightful opening stanza, we have a characteristic instance of Nerval's use of a word to symbolize a meaning. Who are these "cydalises"? They were female camp-followers, as it were, of the *jeunesse dorée* or bohemian set of the day, and they include as their number one Camille Rogier's girl friend who, apparently unusually beautiful, was fêted by several poets of her day and caught Nerval's eye on more than one occasion. Like Jenny she died young and in the full flower of her beauty. So Nerval, in company with Ourliac, used her as a symbol of all youthful, but transient, beauty, the type of the *jeunes-France*. He mentions her several times, in several contexts, but he deliberately confuses her with Jenny Colon when he writes, in *La Bohème Galante*, "Ma Cydalise à moi, perdue, à jamais perdue!"

Here we have, then, a typical example of Nerval's cypher-like use of that personal mythology which is to fill his last poems and make some of them almost impossibly obscure. Again, in *Épitaphe*, we have another enigmatic reference to one of these word-symbols—"rêveur comme un triste Clitandre." Clitandre was a common stage name in Seventeenth-Century French drama. Molière's Clitandre is the sham doctor of *Amour médicin* who is called to attend Sganarelle's daughter but contents himself, on the basis of sympathy between father and daughter, with taking Sganarelle's own pulse, a sort of Dr. Knock in advance. Corneille's

Clitandre has, as its sub-title, *l'Innocence delivrée*, which is surely not the explanation for her sadness in Nerval's poem. There are many theories put forward by exegetes on these tempting obscurities, but it is as well to remember perhaps that *Les Cydalises*, so Nerval told Arsène Houssaye, "est venue malgré moi sous forme de chant." Although later than the other *Odelettes*, and somewhat chimeric in content, it belongs to the early collection by style and language, and is a glance back from the terror of his present to the happier days of his past, again to be found in *La Cousine*.

In *Lyrisme et Vers d'Opéra* we have more poems written "par amour," with the same facility as the *Odelettes*. *La Sérénade*, an imitation of Uhland's *Ständchen*, is an excellent example of the sort of standard for which Nerval was always striving in work of this kind.

It is in *Les Chimères* and *Autres Chimères* that we reach the third period, the *"supernaturaliste"* poems which, Nerval wrote, "perdraient de leur charme à être expliqués, si la chose était possible." These poems are filled with just those mysterious references that beset the reader of *Aurélia*. The poetry is again formal and direct, if more rhetorical in style, with none of the syntactical obscurity to be found in French poetry later in the century. The language is lucid, but the message is, as even Béguin has to confess, "à la fois d'une essence religieuse, proprement ineffable, et de nature très subjective."

Of this group, *El Desdichado*—"ce blason de haute noblesse lyrique et de destin accablé," as Henri Strentz calls it—has always attracted most comment, and T. S. Eliot borrowed from it for *The Waste Land*. It presents typical complexities which have been studied in detail by specialist scholars like Paul Gautier, Jeanine Moulin, Pierre Audiat, André Rousseaux, and Fernand Verhesen. But it is not hard for the general reader to see at once that the poet himself is the "desdichado," the unfortunate one, the outcast. He it is who is "le ténébreux," "le veuf" (because of Jenny), and he is inconsolable because the image of Aurélia, the memory of whom saturates the poem, evades him. When "el desdichado" cries out, "Ma seule étoile est morte," it is Nerval himself mourning the loss of Jenny and his ideal of womanhood. In line 4, he makes one of his numerous references to Dürer's engraving *Melancolia I* which gradually came to personify the grief by which he was haunted, and which attracted criticism from both Baudelaire and Michelet. In line 9 we have another memory of his childhood, for in *Sylvie* we read how at the village festival he kissed, and was kissed by, the Queen of the Festival—Adrienne. Caught in the round dance, in the orbit of desire, the poet illides the laws of physics and those of the psyche.

Finally, in the last triplet, Nerval recalls his own tragedy. Twice he himself had made a "descente aux enfers," and twice he had recovered and returned to normal life, while "les soupirs de la sainte" refer to Adrienne, the childhood love who became a nun, according to his suppositions, and died in a convent. "Les cris de la fée" point to Jenny who, as we know from *Aurélia*, appeared several times to Nerval after her death in the guise of a fairy or goddess. Most of Nerval's femininity conceptions are in this poem, in fact, from "la reine de Saba" to the blonde English girl, Octavie, whom he usually associated with Pausilippus, or Posilipo, where he took her and where, possibly, he learnt of her crippled husband. Nearly all Nerval's poetry has this autobiographical level; in another "chimère," *Le Christ aux Oliviers*, he makes a Christ in his own image, an "insensé sublime," an "Icare oublié qui remontait les cieux," this Christ-identification polarizing the now frequently expressed dislike of Jehovah, "le dieu vainqueur" and force of inhibition, the super-ego.

The exhibitionist quality of the neurotic is indeed very evident in this transference of the Rousseauian "good life" of the instincts to Christ: the erotic pressure behind the poems, meanwhile, forces the rhetorical apostrophes on the poet. He knows he is guilty, damned, he challenges God, and attempts to dramatize the virginity of the instincts. He associates himself with heroic rebels, as in the poem *A Madame Ida Dumas*. There is nothing very new in another Manfred struggling to liberate his potentialities against the fabric of society—Nerval's *Pensée de Byron* recognizes this fellow spirit—but Nerval's attitude to his material in *Les Chimères* is extraordinary. Owing to his insanity he can push further than the romantic hero. He shatters the microcosm-macrocosm relationship in these poems, he *is* the universe, and at the end of *Aurélia* he rides beside Christ to the new Jerusalem and learns "le secret du monde des mondes."

The remainder of Nerval's poems fall more happily into place if we will concede his method in this period, epitomized in *El Desdichado*. Thus *Myrtho*, *Horus*, and the other poems of this group, are all experiences of different visions, while *Vers Dorés* recalls another central theme of *Aurélia*, the Pythagorean premise of the transmigration of souls. In this poem we see Nerval's longing for a synthesis of religions and that sense of the one behind the many which tends to categorize him as a mystic poet:

> Respecte dans la bête un esprit agissant:
> Chaque fleur est une âme à la Nature éclose;
> Un mystère d'amour dans le métal repose;
> 'Tout est sensible!' Et tout sur ton être est puissant.

The poems of *Autres Chimères* are in many cases merely rewritten versions of *Les Chimères*: *A J. Y. Colonna* is a repetition, with amendments, of the earlier *Delfica*. None of the poems of *Autres Chimères*, either new or rewritten, were published in Nerval's lifetime. But it was to these poems that he developed in technical ability; one can scarcely compare the youthful enthusiasm and intransigeance of *La Mort de l'Exilé*, which appeared in 1826, with the beautiful *Une Femme est l'Amour*, which came out just after his death in 1855, and in which the gratitude to woman is doubly impressive in the light of Nerval's own life. *Après Ma Journée Faite* is one of the old songs of the Valois which Nerval collected and put on paper for the first time. It is impossible to tell how much of what he recorded in these poems belonged to oral tradition and how much came from himself, but many of these songs had never been printed before. We owe a debt to

Nerval—for better or for worse—every time we hear Jean Sablon sing *Sur le Pont d'Avignon*.

Finally, we have the brave *Épitaphe*, found among the poet's papers after his death, but not published until 1897. In it we can once again, and for the last time, appreciate Nerval's courageous attitude to his own fate. Here is a man who lived in constant dread of madness overtaking him permanently, who had for the past fifteen years known nothing but misfortune, bidding farewell to life without a trace of bitterness. Throughout all this poetry, even the most obscure of it, Nerval takes us by his side and invites us to be his intimate. Devoid of the slightest pretentiousness he is a poet who will surely live as one of the most likeable figures in recent literature. And it was for this very kindness of nature that he paid so dearly. As Kléber Haedens has put it, "L'excès des vertus les plus estimables peut décider des faiblesses malheureuses, et l'être le plus simple et le plus généreux qui ait jamais paru ne fut pas épargné."

* * *

In conclusion, a word should be said as to Nerval's influence. If we may say that the Renaissance witnessed in Europe a change in phantasy, a shift in libido, from the invisible to the visible, so we may say that the Symbolist movement evinced a similar shift in libido, this time from the visible to the invisible, from the material to the spiritual world. So Baudelaire, who worked towards what for us is the matrix of modern letters, saw photography, in his celebrated *Salon de 1859*, as the spirit of progress revenging itself on the masses, and Daguerre its dreadful Messiah.

Baudelaire, in his art criticism which anticipated that of Worringer and T. E. Hulme, denied the external world validity as a source of art, it was only of significance in that it contained hidden analogies with the spiritual world. Hence, in his article "Morale du Joujou," [15] Baudelaire championed the child's approach to nature as a new method for the artist. The child used nature, Bau-

[15] *Le Monde Littéraire*, April 17th, 1853.

delaire presciently observed, as "pure excitation," as a point of departure for the presentation of an inner state, suppressing all detail and going to the essence of the thing—as when it destroyed a toy to reach its heart.

So Baudelaire realized that art had to recapture innocence, if it was to live, and to do this it was necessary to free the imagination. Nature unexplained, he wrote in "Le Gouvernement de l'Imagination," an article backed by his delightful letter on vegetables to Desnoyers in 1855, unsifted by the imagination, only presented a spectacle of general abasement. Art, as in a woman's make-up, refined and civilized the chaotic nature of her normal face. One need but add to this Samuel Cramer's comment in Baudelaire's novel, *La Fanfarlo*, that reproduction was the vice of love, and we are already in the climate of Wilde and Beardsley.

In another article, "Puisque Réalisme il ya a," Baudelaire defended what he called Poe's drunkenness as "une méthode de travail," and in this he theoretically approaches Nerval. Again and again Baudelaire attacked false nature, and upheld artists, like Delacroix, who worked, not from the detail outwards, like Meissonier, not from nature to spirit, but from inner spirit to a corresponding nature. Baudelaire, and the symbolists who succeeded him, saw in the photographic realism of their day only an indolence of spirit which deprived the exterior world of all significance. By leaning heavily on memory-sensation as a source of analogy, by using what De Quincey had called the "palimpsest" of the brain for the recording of images, and then inviting the imagination to arrange these at will, Baudelaire paved the way for Proust. Naturally, then, didacticism was for Baudelaire a prime heresy in art. Spiritual values alone were worth seeking, for all human systematologies, including those of ethics, were fallible.

Nerval takes his place in this literary movement which was, to some extent, the rationalization of an aesthetic dilemma, for it gave the artist, whose position in the social organism was being threatened, a new and privileged position in mankind. The poet became an intercessor and he carried priest-like qualities. Baude-

laire put the poet in heaven in his *Bénédiction*, a supreme accolade
to be conferred on the poet again by Stefan George in his lovely
poem, *Ich forschte bleichen eifers nach dem horte*. That this led to
art-for-art's sake and to the justification of the emotional state as
valid per se, was no fault of Baudelaire's, who had always argued
that any wealth of imagination should be met with a similar efflo-
ration of discipline.

For Nerval also, who more than anyone was responsible for the
phrase ' ivory tower," and who was equally born into a society
where the artist's position was undefined, the material world was
fallible and utility the negative of art. Like Baudelaire, and somewhat like Hart Crane in America, Nerval wrote in the teeth of the
utilitarian concept of the universe, and all these men died, like
Cyrano, fencing with their shadows, their invisible, yet deadly
enemy "la Sottise," and exclaiming "c'est bien plus beau lorsque
c'est inutile."

This frustration, that of the pure poet, reached a height perhaps
in the théâtre de l'Oeuvre of the eighteen nineties but, as Dada
was to show, to be positivized the movement had to be accompanied by that sublimation of desire which leads to letters. Axel,
the symbolist hero par excellence, has all the seeds of Dada in
his make-up. "Vivre?" he cries to Sara at the end of the play,
"les serviteurs feront cela pour nous ... J'ai trop pensé pour
daigner agir!" How close we are here to that monstrous carica-
ture of the modern intellectual given us in M. Teste!

Villiers' Baron Bathybius Bottom with his fantastic "machine
à gloire," his Edison longing to create a beautiful woman with
spare parts in *L'Eve Future* (like Apollinaire's hero creating children from old newspapers), we have here all the elements from
which Dada was to construct itself in its early demonstrations,
some of them, significantly, at the théâtre de l'Oeuvre. But Tzara's two monocles, the antics of Cocteau, Picabia, and others of
this time, are essentially based on the same antagonism to utili-
tarianism; so a typical Dada exhibit would be a flat-iron with
spikes in its base, a tea-cup lined with fur, an inverted urinal.

Now Nerval never envisaged his theories (or, rather, the way he wrote, for he never pretended to be a literary theoretician) being carried as far as this, but it is in his interest to mention briefly how he has been taken up by contemporary surrealists.

Guillaume Apollinaire's *Les Mamelles de Tirésias*, first put on in 1917, carried with it a preface, supposedly written in 1903, in which he claims to have forged the adjective surrealist to define a new tendency in art. Since then, it has been confessedly that the Twentieth-Century surrealists have looked to the spirit of *Aurélia*. Here, they seem to have felt, was a work that would set them free. So, in the *Premier Manifeste du Surréalisme* of 1924, André Breton writes:

> nous désignâmes sous le nom de SURRÉALISME le nouveau mode d'expression pure que nous tenions à notre disposition ... à plus juste titre encore, sans doute aurions-nous dû nous emparer du mot SUPERNA-TURALISME, employé par Gérard de Nerval dans la dédicace des *Filles du Feu.*

Both Breton and Eluard (the owner, while he lived, of the most important extant Nerval manuscripts) have confessed to their dialectical insistence on dreams and insanity in art; Breton and Aragon signed an essay terming hysteria a new means of expression. Desnos, Tzara, Soupault, all at one time moved with their painter colleagues in what has been called a belief in "hallucinatory intuition." It was, as Georges Lemaître has written, by a "voluntary recourse to simulated insanity," that the surrealists hoped to beat down the barriers of inhibition in the conscious and reap where Nerval had sowed. For them, madness was the rubric of our agony. Sensing what they felt to be the insanity or chaos of our material life, they craved the formalism of the wholly private world. "Le surréalisme vous introduira dans la mort," writes Breton, "qui est une société secrète." The idea of madness being vision is not something new, of course; the conjunction of seer and madman we meet in the ancient Hebrew mind, the ecstatic emoter, is eventually reproved by Hosea ("the spiritual man is mad" - IX, 7). Lautréamont's Maldoror was in some respects the "fol délicieux," which Nerval has been called, taken to desperate conclusion. The danger, however, is to read into Nerval a sponsoring, or tolerance, of surrealist doctrine which he did not own. Whereas the surrealists were to interpret the insane world as a prolongation of our experience in the sane, Nerval saw a clear line between his normal and abnormal lives. While, then, it is true that he suffered the madness of the "immediate" man, in Kierkegaard's sense in *Either/Or*, that of the artist or lover indifferent to life, the trauma, in other words, of adolescence introduced by an urban civilization, yet he himself always saw the two levels of experience as separate. The subtitle of *Aurélia* is *Le Rêve et la Vie*, not *ou la Vie*. Moreover, does he not begin with the sentence, "Le rêve est une seconde vie," meaning *another* life? [16]

Although Rimbaud's famous statement, "Je est un autre," has been variously explicated, in general critics have taken it to mean that the visionary is separate from his everyday self. Nerval would have found exactly this separation in Rousseau's *Dialogues*. And Anna Balakian, in her admirable study of the origins of surrealism, has pointed out how Nerval always introduces his dreams with some such comment as "je fis un rêve." Moreover, the idea of the double, or "sosie," occurs constantly throughout Nerval's whole work.

Miss Balakian has demonstrated what is virtually a misreading of Nerval for their own purposes by certain surrealist writers, not to mention an apparent mistranslation of Achim von Arnim's *Die Majorats-Herren* which Breton used in the same interests. The surrealists found an intellectual respectability in Nerval and they read the *Aurélia* as a narcissistic reverie, whereas in fact the moments of narcissism in the work are moments of horrified self-recognition—"O terreur! ô colère! c'était mon visage . . ." Nerval emerges from this re-reading as something he never posed as;

[16] The ivory or horned gates of dream with which Nerval opens the *Aurélia* are explained by Penelope in Book XIX of *The Odyssey*; Nerval is clearly aware of her distinction throughout.

Norman Cohn has called *Aurélia* "Dali in words" in *Horizon*, and
Dali writes, "I register without choice and with all possible exacti-
tude the dictates of my subconscious, my dreams," a statement
fortunately belied by the intricately careful conscious composition
of his pictures. It was the method of *Aurélia* which attracted the
surrealists, the hint in Nerval's work of that possession by a force
outside oneself which drove men like Jarry, Hart Crane, Modi-
gliani, and others, to stifle their conscious in alcohol in the belief
that they became more "free" if the psyche could ejaculate directly.
This attitude is debatable, but to say that Nerval advocated it is
not—he never did.

> A Surrealist writer is not supposed to make any effort to express and
> organize his sentiments or thoughts. He must be content to listen to
> the voice of his subconsciousness.

So writes Lemaître. How different this is from Nerval's terror—
"Je n'ai pu percer sans frémir ces portes d'ivoire ou de corne qui
nous séparent du monde visible."

The world of *Aurélia* is a world of lost happiness, of inharmo-
nious nature, and of conscious spiritual pilgrimage. An act of atonement and redemption, it was his *Vita Nuova*, to which he never
lived to add a *Commedia*. Nerval frequently refers to Dante's
autobiography of adolescence and the XXIII Canzone of the
Vita Nuova, structurally the highest, and the closest to Guido Gui-
nizelli, bears remarkable resemblance to *Aurélia* with its visions
which Dante said came to him when out of his mind. But the
Vita Nuova is a consciously shaped phantasy, as its strict archi-
tecture shows, and we should not valuably pursue this comparison.

The surrealists purposefully broke away from the tradition of
the artistic presentation of private emotions to synthesize with
the public emotions of an audience. Since the artist's private consciousness is molded willy-nilly by the public world, is it not,
they argued, important even in its total retreat? Further, is there
not a common "I" in any dream, a "collective unconscious" with
its store of "archetypes" or "primordial images?" It is hard not

to find theories like these more than excuses for spiritual fatigue. For, as has often been remarked, poetry may be a dream but a dream is not necessarily poetry. Coleridge allows us, for instance, to be his privileged dreamer for a while. Le douanier Rousseau's painting *Le Rêve* of 1910 is more permanent than the equally "sur-naturel" *Dans le Rêve*, say, of Odilon Redon not because there are more "archetypes" in it but because through conscious control it affects us communally more than does Redon's picture.

In this sense Nerval does comprise within his life and work the whole of the surrealist movement. Indeed many of his dreams are in danger, unlike *Kubla Khan*, of being non-affective for in many of them it is hard to share in either subject or object. At its worst, in the last leaves of *Aurélia* perhaps, his phantasy obeys only the laws of the dreamed object, to which his conscious talent becomes a slave, in the same way that his common-sense life be-came enslaved to the dream state and we find a multiplicity of examples of him obeying chance happenings as "fate." Here indeed is the secret society of the dead.

Fortunately, of course, Nerval controlled the majority of his writings by traditional techniques, which are what make them vital today, just as Dali's work may last not for its phantasy—there is little of this in a Dali painting—but for the more formal gifts demonstrated. Those of Nerval's contemporaries, for instance, who did not control their work by conscious technique are not known now. Borel will remain a lesser figure than Nerval. Charles Coligny is today forgotten, although his life and interests were similar to Nerval's. The Jungian theory of the "collective un-conscious," brought to us from the pre-Socratics (with the excep-tion of Heraclitus), endangered art for only a short while, how-ever; phantasy was poured into art by the surrealists and all too often poetry ceased to act, its life was atrophied to magic. For Nerval the dream was not something that should deprive the poet of artistic liberty; he knew too well, hence his dread, that the laws of the dream are ineluctable and coerce the dreamer. For him the dream, separate from common-sense life, was an aspect of behavior, one previously unexplored, and thus a part of humanity to be revealed to all.

It is, finally, possible to push this conception to Nerval's detriment. Antonin Artaud, writing of van Gogh, claimed that the authentic lunatic is a man strangled by society because he utters unbearable truths, a man who prefers to be incarcerated rather than forfeit a superior idea of human honor. Cyril Connolly tells us that Nerval's madness "contributed more to the community than many another's sanity." There is a grain of truth, a disturbing grain of truth, in these lively speculations, but Artaud's is on the whole a romantic conception. Competent studies of insanity remind us that the deranged try pathetically to conform, rather than exploit the chaos of their condition. It is one thing to think of Nerval as the first surrealist, it is quite another to hold him responsible for the vulgarizations of surrealism in our day. The whole erotic sensibility of the *Aurélia*, for example, is now reduced to the pornography of Breton and Eluard's *L'Immaculée Conception*.

The difficulty our society seems to find in accomodating genius turns it so often over the hairline—for the two are physiologically close—into madness. Genius is a kind of madnes in our midst, but madness is not genius. Aside, then, from this rather obvious relevance to our time, and aside from what is rapidly becoming a curio interest in connection with surrealism, Nerval's work is principally valuable to us today for its form, its harmony, and good taste, when such are at a discount. As Baudelaire accepted the challenge of Malherbe, Nerval won the artistic freedom he knew in *Sylvie* from a complete mastery of technique. "Chose étrange," writes Paul de Saint-Victor, "au milieu du désordre intellectuel qui l'envahissait, son talent resta net, intact, accompli." It must never be said that Nerval indulged in lunacy.

One cannot conclude on a harsh note to a man who saw his padded cell as an Oriental pavilion. Like us, Nerval was born "dans les jours de révolutions et d'orage, où toutes les croyances ont été brisées," but the first thing we sense in his work is a feeling of immediacy and friendliness, that kind of innate kindness which

starts out from the portrait of the poet by his friend (and enthu-
siastic balloonist), Nadar. Heine, who saw himself in Nerval,
wrote of him:

C'était vraiment plutôt une âme qu'un homme, je dis une âme d'an-
ge... Cette âme était essentiellement sympathique. Et c'était un grand
artiste... il était tout candeur enfantine; il était d'une délicatesse de
sensitive; il était bon...

Such was "le bon Gérard;" continually good-natured, he pre-
supposed in others the same felicitous freedom from all bitterness
inherent in himself, and he was rewarded by a circle of devoted
friends. His lovable sincerity, the perfect pellucidity of his language coupled with his unaffectedly limpid style, these qualities
have even been called banal—there could be no sadder commentary
on our century. Nerval's letter to the young Princesse de Solms,
on January 2nd, 1853, is a masterpiece of compassion that sums
up his character completely; he had just given his all, he writes,
to a poor family he had found by chance living in misery in the
rue Saint-Jacques. Go to them, he begs Mme de Solms, [17] and
help them, and—put on your best clothes, for I have promised
them that a Princess is coming.

The search into the mind for a new myth, and an historically
non-recognizable myth, which surrealism represents, seemed at

[17] Another extraordinary lady involved on the fringe of Nerval's life and aspirations, Marie Laetitia Studolmine Wyse, Princesse de Solms, and later Contessa Rattazzi, was the daughter of an English M.P., Sir Thomas Wyse. After her marriage
to Frédéric de Solms, she became a sort of Madame de Staël of the Second Empire.
Shortly after Nerval wrote her this appeal she was expelled from France by Napoleon III and led a checkered career in Italy. However, she obtained permission to
return to France and, her husband having died in America, married Count Rattazzi
who was involved in the Cavour-Castiglione affair and whom she obliged to fight
a number of duels on her behalf. She herself wrote several books, painted, dabbled
dangerously in politics, and edited a review. The Princess Caroline Murat pays a
long tribute to her in her memoirs. It is interesting, if not coincidental, that in the
inventory of her tastes given by Frederic Loliée her favorite book should appear
as *La Nouvelle Héloïse*. She died in Paris in 1902, having first published Nerval's
hitherto unknown poem *Épitaphe*.

first to offer a limitless potential. Yet now even Henry Miller, "the American Céline" as he has been called, admits that surrealism is "a confession of intellectual and spiritual bankruptcy." This is, however, not something to gloat over. When we hear Nerval cry from the asylum, we are aware of our own disaster, of which our art is an aspect.

In Canto 3 of *Childe Harold's Pilgrimage*, when he comes to mention the heroine of *La Nouvelle Héloïse* and Rousseau's unrequited love for the Comtesse d'Houdetot, Byron writes that Jean-Jacques knew "how to make madness beautiful." Nerval, too, was Lord Pilgrim in truth. Adrienne was the spirit who celebrated Christ the conqueror of hell. Aurélia was the divine intercessor for whom he was prepared to die. Such was the twist he gave to Hoffmann's vampire. Nerval's lot was to suffer human experience intensified to a personal purgatory, and we must see that his influence, however it may have been taken up and interpreted, yet evinces that painstaking evolution which is the progress of art. Like Kit Smart, like Hölderlin, van Gogh, and the rest of the "great abnormals" increasing in our midst, Nerval voiced a convulsion of humanity in advance. He was under the same accusation with his Savior, for they said He is beside Himself.

GEOFFREY WAGNER

SYLVIE

Recollections of Valois [1]

1 The text used for this translation, and for that of *Emilie*, is the one established by Nicolas I. Popa, and published in the first part of the sixth volume of the *Oeuvres Complètes de Gérard de Nerval* (Paris, Librairie Ancienne Honoré Champion, 1931), under the direction of Aristide Marie, Jules Marsan, and Edouard Champion. *Sylvie* was first published in the *Revue des Deux Mondes* for August 15th, 1853. *Emilie* first appeared in *Le Messager* for June 25th, 26th, and 28th, 1839, under the title *Le Fort de Bitche, Souvenir de la Révolution française*, and signed "G." The first edition of *Les Filles du Feu*, the volume in which these two stories were assembled, was published in Paris by D. Giraud on August 16th, 1854; on October 7th of this same year Nerval signed over his author's rights to this volume to Michel Lévy. Both stories are given here whole.

I. – A LOST NIGHT

I came out of a theater [2] where I used to spend every evening in the proscenium boxes in the role of an ardent wooer. The theater was sometimes full, sometimes empty. I myself cared little whether I saw stalls filled with thirty amateurs brought in under duress and boxes filled with out-of-date hats and dresses—or whether I were part of a house trembling with animation, crowned at every level with flowering silks, glittering jewels, and radiant faces. I was indifferent to what I saw in the house and the stage itself scarcely attracted my attention until, in the second or third scene of some dismal masterpiece of those days, a face I knew so well lit up the vacant boards and gave life to the empty apparitions around me with the breath of a single word.

In her I felt myself alive, and she seemed to live for me alone. Her smile filled me with infinite beatitude; her voice was so gentle and so vibrant, yet strong in pitch, that I thrilled with joy and love. For me she was perfection, she answered all my enthusiasms, every whim. She was as lovely as day itself in the foot-lights that lit her from below, and pale as night when their dimmed glare left her illumined from above by the rays of the chandelier and displayed her more naturally, shining in her own shadowed beauty, like the divine Hours which stand out so clearly, with stars on their foreheads, against the brown backgrounds of the frescoes at Herculaneum.

For a whole year I did not think of asking who she might be in real life. I was afraid to cloud the magic mirror which gave me her image—all I had heard was some gossip about the woman,

---

[2] The Variétés theater, where Jenny Colon sang between 1834 and 1835.

rather than the actress. I took as little notice of it as of the rumors about the Princesse d'Élide or the Queen of Trébizonde, for one of my uncles, who had lived through the end of the Eighteenth Century (and lived as one had to live, in those days), had early warned me that actresses were not women and that nature had denied them hearts. No doubt he spoke of the actresses of his own day, but he had told me so many stories of illusions and deceptions, shown me so many portraits on ivory (charming medallions which he subsequently used to decorate his snuff-boxes), exhibited so many yellowing letters, such a heap of faded favors, telling me their history and final outcome, that I became accustumed to think ill of all actresses without making any allowance for changes in time.

We were then living in a strange period, such as usually succeeds revolutions or the decline of great reigns. It was no longer the gallant heroism of the Fronde, the elegant, dressed-up vice of the Regency, or the scepticism and insane orgies of the Directoire. It was an age in which activity, hesitation, and indolence were mixed up, together with dazzling Utopias, philosophies, and religious aspirations, vague enthusiasms, mild ideas of a Renaissance, weariness with past struggles, insecure optimisms—somewhat like the period of Peregrinus and Apuleius. Material man longed for the bouquet of roses which would regenerate him from the hands of the divine Isis; the goddess in her eternal youth and purity appeared to us by night and made us ashamed of our wasted days. We had not reached the age of ambition, and the greedy scramble for honors and positions caused us to stay away from all possible spheres of activity. The only refuge left to us was the poet's ivory tower, which we climbed, ever higher, to isolate ourselves from the mob. [3] Led by our masters to those high places we breathed at last the pure air of solitude, we drank oblivion in the legendary golden cup, and we got drunk on poetry and love. Love, however,

---

[3] This sentence, more than any other, is the source of the expression "ivory tower." Thus it is interesting to find the phrase, often so loosely used, in the context Nerval gives it here, writing as he was in an era of rapidly increasing materialism.

of vague forms, of blue and rosy hues, of metaphysical phantoms!
Seen at close quarters, the real woman revolted our ingenuous souls.
She had to be a queen or goddess; above all, she had to be
unapproachable.

Yet some of us were not entirely taken with these Platonic paradoxes, and through our renewed reveries of Alexandria we occasionally waved the torch of the underground gods that lights the
darkness for a moment with its trail of sparks. So, coming out
of the theater in the bitter sadness of my vanished dream, I gladly
joined a group which used to dine together in some numbers, and
with whom every melancholy was dissipated by the inexhaustible
energy of a few brilliant minds. These lively, wild, frequently
sublime minds are invariably to be found at times of renaissance
or decadence, and our discussions achieved such heights that the
more fearful among us used to look out of the windows to see
whether the Huns, Tartars, or Cossacks were not on the way to
cut short these arguments of sophists and rhetoricians.

"Wine, woman—there you have wisdom!" Such was the sentiment of one of our younger members. Someone said to me: "For
some time now I've been meeting you in the same theater, every
time I go there. Which of them do you go for?"

Which! It seemed to me impossible to go there for any other.
However I let slip a name.

"Well," my friend said, indulgently, "over there sits the happy
man who has just taken her home and who, according to the rules
of our club, probably won't go to her again until the night is over."

Without much emotion I looked at the man indicated. He was
young, well dressed, with a pale, nervous face, good manners, and
eyes marked by melancholy and tenderness. He was throwing
money on a table of whist and losing it with indifference.

"What does it matter to me," I said. "He, or somebody else.
There had to be some man, and he seems to me worthy of her
choice."

"What about you then?"

"Me? I pursue an image, no more."

As I went out I passed through the reading room and looked mechanically at a newspaper to see, I think it was, the state of the stock market. Among the ruins of my fortune there was a fair amount in foreign bonds. There had been a rumor that after having been passed over for several years they were about to be recognized; this had resulted from a change of ministry. The bonds were already quoted high. I was rich again.

Only one thought came into my mind at this change in my circumstances—that the woman I had been in love with for so long was mine if I liked. My finger touched my ideal. But was it not just another illusion, a mocking printer's misprint? No. The other newspaper confirmed it. The sum I had gained reared itself before me like a golden Moloch. I thought: "What would that young man say if I were to go and take his place beside the lady he has left alone?" I shuddered at the idea. My pride revolted.

No! Not like this! A man cannot kill love with gold at my age! I will not be a corrupter. Besides, this is a notion from another age. Who can say that this woman is venal? My glance strayed vaguely through the newspaper in my hand and I read these two lines: *"Fête du Bouquet provincial.*—Tomorrow the archers of Senlis are to return the bouquet to the archers of Loisy." [4] These extremely simple words aroused in me a whole new set of impressions, a memory of country life I had long ago forgotten, a distant echo of the simple festivals of my childhood. Horn and drum resounded far off in the woods and hamlets, the girls were weaving garlands and arranging, as they sang, bouquets tied in ribbons. A heavy cart, drawn by oxen, took their gifts as it passed, and we, the children of the district, formed the escort with our bows

---

4 The more austere scholarship of recent years has disallowed the possibility of this tournament. Although *Sylvie* was once taken to be topographically accurate, it has now been shown that Nerval gave himself considerable licence with the facts of his beloved district. Place-names have been confused and dates rearranged. Flowers blossom out of season. Some of the walks Nerval takes in *Sylvie*, for instance, are of the order of forty kilometers over rough country, a sizeable feat for the young man to perform in the time allotted.

and arrows, dignifying ourselves with the title of knights—without realizing that we were simply repeating from age to age a Druid festival that had survived the new monarchies and the novel religions.

II. – ADRIENNE

I went to bed but could not rest. Lost in a kind of half-sleep, all my youth passed through my memory again. This state, when the spirit still resists the strange combinations of dreams, often allows us to compress into a few moments the most salient pictures of a long period of life. [5]

I fancied for myself a château of the time of Henry IV, [6] with its pointed roofs covered with slates, its ruddy façade and coigns of yellow stone, and a large green space framed in elms and lime trees, their leaves pierced by the fiery shafts of a setting sun. On the lawn some girls were doing a round dance and singing old airs handed down to them by their mothers in such a naturally pure French you felt that this was indeed that old country of Valois, where the heart of France has been beating for more than a thousand years.

I was the only boy in the round, and I had brought with me my young companion, Sylvie, a little girl from the next village, bright and fresh, with black eyes, a regular profile, and lightly tanned skin ... I loved her alone, she was the only one I had eyes for—until then! In the round we were dancing I had barely noticed a tall, lovely, fair-haired girl they called Adrienne. All at once, in accordance with the rules of the dance, Adrienne and I found ourselves alone in the center of the circle. We were of the same height. We were told to kiss and the dancing and the chorus whirled around us more quickly than ever. As I gave her this

[5] When Proust compared his "madeleine" episode with *Sylvie*, it is of suggestions like this that he must surely have been thinking.

[6] The château at Mortefontaine corresponds exactly to Nerval's description here; see also the beginning of Section XI, and the poem *Fantaisie*.

kiss I could not resist pressing her hand. The long tight curls of her golden hair brushed my cheeks and from that moment on an inexplicable confusion took hold of me.

The girl had to sing a song in order to regain her place in the dance. We sat around her and straight away, in a fresh, penetrating, slightly filmy voice, like a true daughter of that misty region, she sang one of those old ballads, full of melancholy and love, which always tell of the sufferings of a princess confined in a tower by her father as a punishment for having fallen in love. The melody ended at each stanza in those wavering trills which show off young voices so well, especially when, in a controlled tremor, they imitate the quavering tones of old women.

As she sang, the shadows came down from the great trees, and the first moonlight fell on her as she stood alone in our attentive circle. She stopped, and no one dared to break the silence. The lawn was covered with thin veils of vapor which trailed white tufts on the tips of the grasses. We imagined we were in paradise. Finally I got up and ran to the gardens of the château, where some laurels grew, planted in large faïence vases with monochrome bas-reliefs. I brought back two branches which were then woven into a crown and tied with a ribbon. This I put on Adrienne's head and glistening leaves shone on her fair hair in the pale moonlight. She was like Dante's Beatrice, smiling on the poet as he strayed on the verge of the blessed abodes.

Adrienne rose. Showing off her slender figure she made us a graceful bow and ran back to the château. They said she was the grandchild of one of the descendants of a family related to the ancient kings of France. The blood of the house of Valois flowed in her veins. For this one day of festival she had been allowed to mix in our games; but we were not to see her again, for the next morning she returned to the convent where she was a boarder.

When I got back to Sylvie I saw she was crying. Her tears were on account of the crown that my hands had given the fair singer. I offered to go and gather another for her, but she said she would not consider it, she was not worthy of one. I tried to excuse myself in vain, she did not speak a word to me the whole of the way home.

I myself was called back to Paris to continue my studies and I bore with me this double image—of a tender friendship sadly broken, and of a vague, impossible love, one that caused me painful thoughts impossible to assuage in college philosophy.

The figure of Adrienne alone remained triumphant, a mirage of fortune and beauty, sharing my hours of heavy study and making them sweeter. During my next year's vacation I learnt that this lovely creature, whom I had scarcely seen, was consecrated to a nun's life by her family.

III. – RESOLUTION

Everything was explained to me by this half-dreamed memory. That impalpable and hopeless love I had conceived for a woman of the theater, that love which seized me each evening when the curtain went up, and left me alone only in sleep, this had its seed in the memory of Adrienne, a flower of the night efflorescent in the moon's pale glimmer, flesh-colored and fair phantom gliding over the green grasses half-bathed in whitish vapors. The likeness of this long forgotten figure was now drawn before me with a curious clarity; it was a pencil drawing blurred by time that had been converted into a picture, like those old sketches of the masters you admire in some museum and then you find, somewhere else, the dazzling original.

To love a nun in the form of an actress! . . . but what if they were one and the same!—It was enough to drive you mad! That fascination is fatal in which the unknown leads you on like a will-o'-the-wisp hovering over the reeds in still water . . . But let us get back to reality.

Why have I for three years forgotten Sylvie, whom I loved so much? . . . She was a very pretty girl, the loveliest in Loisy.

She is still alive, good and pure-hearted, no doubt. Once more I can see her window with the grape-vines enlaced among the roses, and the cage of linnets hung up on the left. I hear the sound of her sonorous spindles and her favorite song:

> The fair lady is sitting
> Beside the swift stream...

She is waiting for me. Who would marry Sylvie? She is so poor. In her village, and those nearby, there are good peasants, dressed in smocks, with horny hands, lean faces, and sunburnt skins. She loved only me, the little Parisian, who went to Loisy to see his poor uncle, now dead. For three years I have frittered away in lordly fashion the little he left me, which would have been enough for my whole life. With Sylvie I would have kept it. Now good luck has given me back some of it. There is still time.

What is she doing at this moment? Is she asleep?... No, she is not asleep; today is the festival of the bow, the only celebration of the year when you dance all night. [7] She's there.

What time is it?

I had no watch.

In the midst of all the bric-a-brac splendors which it was then the custom to collect to give local color to an old-fashioned apartment, there shone the restored brilliance of a tortoiseshell Renaissance time-piece. Its gilded dome, surmounted by the figure of Time, was supported by caryatids in the Medici manner, resting in their turn on rearing horses. The historical figure of Diana, leaning on her stag, was in low relief under the face on which the enamelled figures of the hours were displayed on an inlaid background. The works, excellent ones, no doubt, had not been wound up for two centuries. I had not bought that clock in Touraine to tell the time.

I went down to the concierge. The cuckoo-clock there told me it was one in the morning.—In four hours, I said to myself, I can be at the ball at Loisy.

[7] August 24th, the night of Saint Bartholomew's.

There were still five or six cabs on the Place du Palais-Royal, waiting for the habitués of clubs and gambling houses.

"To Loisy," I said to the first.

"Where's that?"

"Near Senlis. Eight leagues."

"I'll take you to the coach-office," said the driver, who was less concerned than I was.

What a dreary track that Flanders road is at night. It only becomes beautiful when you reach the forest region. All the time those two lines of monotonous trees, grimacing in vague shapes; beyond them, square slabs of green, and of ploughed earth, bounded on the left by the bluish hills of Montmorency, Ecouen, and Luzarches. Here is Gonesse, a vulgar little town full of memories of the Ligue and the Fronde...

IV. – A VOYAGE TO CYTHERA [8]

Some years had gone by. The time when I had met Adrienne in front of the château was already only a memory of childhood. I was at Loisy once again, at the time of the annual festival. Once again I joined the knights of the bow and took my place in the company I had been part of before. The festival had been organized by young people from the old families who still own some of those old châteaux hidden in the forest there, and these mansions have suffered more from time than from revolutions. From Chantilly, Compiègne, and Senlis flocked happy cavalcades to take their places in the rustic procession of the companies of the bow. After the long walk through the villages and little towns, after Mass in the church, after the trials of skill and the prize-giving, the winners were invited to a banquet given on an island shaded by limes and poplars, in the middle of one of those pools fed by the Nonette and the Thève. Beflagged boats bore us to the island, which had been selected because of the existence on it of an oval

---

[8] This section is a studied embellishment of Watteau's famous picture *L'Embarquement pour Cythère*.

temple with columns that could serve as banquet-hall. There, as at Ermenonville, the countryside is dotted with those light, late Eighteenth-Century edifices that philosophical millionaires were inspired to plan after the dominant taste of their day. I think this temple must have originally been dedicated to Urania. Three columns had collapsed and carried down part of the architrave in their fall; but the interior of the hall had been swept, garlands had been hung between the columns, and a new youth had been given this modern ruin that belonged to the paganism of Boufflers and Chaulieu rather than to that of Horace.

Perhaps the crossing of the lake had been devised in order to recall Watteau's *Voyage à Cythère*. Only our modern clothes spoiled the illusion. The immense festival bouquet had been taken from the cart that carried it and placed in a large boat; the train of young girls dressed in white, who accompanied it according to custom, sat on the benches, and this graceful *theoria*, a revival from the days of antiquity, was reflected in the calm waters of the pool separating it from the banks of the island, so rose-colored in the evening sun with its thorn thickets, its colonnade, and clear foliage. All the boats soon reached land. The flower-basket, ceremoniously carried, occupied the center of the table and everyone sat down, the most favored men next to the girls. For this you only had to know their parents. That was why I found myself next to Sylvie. Her brother had met me during the festival and made fun of my not having visited their family for so long. I pleaded my studies in Paris as excuse and assured him that I had come for that very reason.

"No," said Sylvie, "he's forgotten me. We are village folk, and Paris is far above us."

I tried to close her mouth with a kiss, but she went on pouting at me, and her brother had to intervene to get her even to hold out her cheek to me in an indifferent way. I had no pleasure in this kiss, a favor that many others obtained, for in such a patriarchal district, where every passer-by is greeted, a kiss is no more than a mark of politeness among honest folk.

A surprise had been arranged by those who had organized the festival. At the end of the meal we saw a wild swan, which had been held captive under the flowers until then, fly up from the depths of the huge basket. With its strong wings it lifted up a tangle of garlands and crowns of flowers, finally dispersing them on all sides. While the bird flew joyfully into the last gleams of the sun, we caught the flower-crowns at random and each man instantly decorated the brow of the girl beside him. I was lucky enough to get one of the finest and, smiling, Sylvie this time allowed me to kiss her more tenderly than before. I understood that I had thus erased the memory of another occasion. My admiration for her at this moment was undivided, she had become so beautiful! She was no longer the little village girl I had scorned for someone older and more schooled in the graces of society. Everything about her had improved. The charm of her black eyes, so seductive in childhood, had become irresistible; under the arched orbit of her eyebrows her smile had something Athenian about it as it suddenly illumined her regular and placid features. I admired this countenance, worthy of antique art in the midst of the irregular baby-faces of her companions. Her delicately tapering hands, her arms which had grown whiter as they rounded, her lithe figure, all made her quite another creature from the girl I had seen before. I could not resist telling her how different from her old self I now found her, hoping in this way to cover over my former, rapid infidelity.

Everything else, too, was in my favor, her brother's friendship for me, the enchanting impression of the festival, the evening hour and even the place, where, by a phantasy in happy taste, had been reproduced an image of the stately gallantry of old times. As often as we could we escaped from the dancing to talk about our recollections of childhood and to dream together admiring the sky's reflection on the dark leaves and still waters. Sylvie's brother had to tear us away from this meditation by telling us it was time to return to the somewhat distant village where their parents lived.

V. – THE VILLAGE

They lived in the old keeper's lodge at Loisy. I went back with them and then returned to Montagny, where I was staying with my uncle. I left the road to cross a small wood separating Loisy from Saint-S- and soon plunged into a sunken path that skirts the forest of Ermenonville; I then expected to strike the walls of a convent which one has to follow for a quarter of a league. From time to time the moon was hidden by clouds and scarcely showed up the dark sandstone rocks and the heather that became more abundant as I advanced. To right and left were fringes of woods with no marked paths, and always ahead of me rose the Druidical rocks of the district, which still guarded the memory of the sons of Armen whom the Romans put to death. From the top of these sublime masses I saw the distant pools stand out like mirrors on the misty plain, but I could not tell which one it was where the festival had been held.

The air was warm and perfumed; I decided to go no further, but to lie down on the heather and wait for morning. When I woke up, I gradually recognized the points near the spot where I had lost my way in the night. To my left I saw the long line of the walls of the convent of Saint-S-, 9 the Gens d'Armes hills, with the shattered ruins of the old Carolingian palace. Near it, above the tops of the trees, the tall ruins of the Abbey of Thiers outlined against the horizon its broken walls pierced with trefoils and ogives. Further on, the manor-house of Pontarmé, still sur-rounded by its moat, began to reflect the first light of day, while to the south the tall keep of La Tournelle and the four towers of Bertrand-Fosse rose up on the first slopes of Montméliant.

The night had been dear to me and I thought only of Sylvie. Still, the sight of the convent gave me the idea for a moment that possibly it was the one where Adrienne was. The chimes of the

9 Saint-Sulpice-du-Désert, pleasantly resuscitated and romanticized by Nerval, the grounds being in the ownership of Mme de Feuchères (Adrienne).

matin bell were still in my ears, and had no doubt awakened me. For an instant I had the notion of climbing the highest point of the rocks and peering over its walls; but on reflection I stopped myself—it would have been a profanation. The dawning day banished this vain memory from my mind and left only the fresh features of Sylvie.

"I'll go and wake her up," I said to myself, and continued on my way to Loisy.

There stood the village at the end of the path round the wood—twenty thatched cottages, their walls covered with climbing roses and vines. Some early women wool spinners, red handkerchiefs around their heads, were already working together in front of a farm. Sylvie was not among them. Since she has learnt to make fine lace she has become quite a lady, while her parents remain simple villagers. Without causing any surprise I went up to her room; she had already been up for some time and was moving her lace bobbins which made a gentle clicking on the green cushion resting on her knees.

"So there you are, lazybones," she said, with her divine smile, "I'm certain you've only just got out of bed."

I told her of the sleepless night I had spent and of my wanderings among the woods and rocks when I had lost my way. She sympathized with me for a moment.

"If you don't feel too tired, I'll take you on some more wanderings. We'll go and see my great-aunt at Othys."

I had scarcely replied when she jumped up joyously, arranged her hair in front of a mirror, and put on a country straw hat. Innocence and joy leapt from her eyes. We started out, following the Thève, across meadows sown with buttercups and daisies, then along the Saint-Laurent woods, from time to time crossing streams and hedges to shorten the way. Blackbirds sang in the trees and when we brushed the bushes blue tits flew gaily away.

Now and again we came across those periwinkle trailers so beloved of Rousseau, their blue corollas open in the long tendrils of coupled leaves, humble creepers that hindered my companion's nimble feet. Indifferent to memories of the philosopher of Geneva, she looked here and there for scented strawberries while I talked to her of *la Nouvelle Héloïse*, several passages of which I recited by heart.

"Is it pretty?" she asked.

"Sublime."

"Is it better than Auguste Lafontaine?" [10]

"More tender."

"Oh well," she said, "I must read it. I shall tell my brother to bring it me the next time he goes in to Senlis."

And I continued to quote fragments of *Héloïse* while Sylvie gathered strawberries.

VI. – OTHYS

As we came out of the wood, we found large clumps of purple foxglove; she picked a big bunch and said, "For my aunt. She'll be so happy to have these lovely flowers in her room."

We had only a short stretch of level ground to cross before reaching Othys. The village steeple soared above the bluish hills which run from Montméliant to Dammartin. The Thève once again rippled over rocks and pebbles, narrowing as it neared its source, where it slumbers in the meadows, spreading into a little lake surrounded by gladioli and irises. Soon we reached the first houses. Sylvie's aunt lived in a little thatched cottage built of irregular pieces of sandstone trellised with hops and virgin vines. She lived alone on a few acres of land which the village folk had farmed for her since her husband's death. A visit from her niece always put the house in a turmoil.

"Good morning, Aunt," exclaimed Sylvie. "Here are your children. And very hungry." She kissed her aunt tenderly, placed the bunch of flowers in her arms, then, remembering to introduce me, said, "This is my sweetheart!"

[10] Auguste Lafontaine (1758-1831), a popular sentimental novelist of the time.

I, in turn, kissed her aunt who said, "He's nice . . . So he's fair-haired!"

"He's got nice fine hair," Sylvie said.

"That won't last long," her aunt replied, "but you have plenty of time in front of you, and you're dark, you'll go together very well."

"We must get him something to eat, Aunt," said Sylvie. And she began looking in the cupboards and pantry, where she found milk, bread and sugar, and laid the table, without too much order, with plates and dishes of earthenware decorated with large flowers and cocks of brilliant plumage. A bowl of Creil porcelain, in which strawberries were swimming in milk, was made the centerpiece, and, after she had stolen a few fistfuls of cherries and gooseberries from the garden, she put two vases of flowers at either end of the cloth. But her aunt made the excellent remark: "That can do for dessert. Now you let me get to work."

She unhooked the frying-pan and flung a bundle of wood into the high fire-place. "I don't want you to touch it," she told Sylvie who was anxious to help her. "Think of spoiling those pretty fingers which can make finer lace than they do at Chantilly! You gave me some and I know what lace is."

"Oh, yes, Aunt . . . If you have any old pieces, I could use them as patterns."

"Well, go and look upstairs," she answered. "There may be some in my chest-of-drawers."

"Can I have the keys then?" Silvie asked.

"Bah!" replied her aunt. "All the drawers are open."

"That's not true, there's one that's always kept locked." And while the good lady was cleaning the frying-pan after having warmed it over the fire, Sylvie took off her aunt's belt a little key of chased steel and held it up to me triumphantly.

I followed her quickly up the wooden stairs that led to the bedroom. O sacred youth, O holy old age! Who could ever have thought of sullying the purity of a first love in such a sanctuary of faithful memories? In an oval gilt frame, hung at the head of the rustic bed, the portrait of a young man of the good old times smiled from dark eyes and fresh lips. He wore the uniform of a gamekeeper of the House of Condé; his semi-military bearing, his rosy, kindly, face, his candid forehead under the powdered hair, enhanced this probably mediocre pastel with the graces of youth and simplicity. Some unknown artist, invited to join the hunting parties of the prince, had done his best to portray the keeper and his young bride, who could be seen in another medallion, attractive and mischievous-looking, lissom in her open corset laced with ribbons, and teasing, with her pert profile, a bird perched on her finger. It was the same good old lady, however, who was at that moment bent over the hearth cooking. I could not help thinking of the Funambules fairies [11] who put wrinkled masks over their own charming faces, which they uncover at the end of the piece when the Temple of Love appears with its whirling sun shining with magic fires.

"Oh, dear aunt," I cried out, "how lovely you used to be."

"And what about me?" asked Sylvie, who had succeeded in opening the famous drawer. In it she had found a great dress of flame-colored taffeta, whose folds rustled loudly. "I must see if it fits," she said. "I shall look like an old fairy."

The ever-young fairy of myth, was what I said to myself. Sylvie had already undone her own muslin dress and let it slip to her feet. Her old aunt's dress, rich in material, fitted Sylvie's slender figure perfectly and she told me to hook it up for her.

"Oh! These straight sleeves look quite ridiculous," she said. Yet the lace-edged sleeves showed off her bare arms splendidly, her breasts being framed in the corsage of yellow tulle and faded ribbons which had so little held in her aunt's vanished charms.

[11] The théâtre des Funambules was, as its name suggests, originally a vaudeville theater. It lasted from 1816 until 1862, and in 1830 began encouraging pantomime productions, especially fairy pantomimes such *Le Songe d'Or, l'Oeuf rouge et l'Oeuf blanc*, for which Deburau was chiefly responsible. Nodier, the author of *Le Songe d'Or*, Viard, and Champfleury wrote mimes for this theater, as did Nerval himself, for he would obviously delight in something of this sort. In 1862 the beautiful boulevard du Temple, where the theater was situated, was pulled down by Haussmann.

"Come on, hurry up! Don't you know how to hook up a girl's dress yet?" Sylvie said to me. She looked like Greuze's *Village Bride*.

"You need powder," I said. "We must find some."

She rummaged again through the drawers. What riches were there! How good it all smelled, how it shone and glittered with brilliant colors and humble tinsel! Two mother-of-pearl fans, slightly broken, pots with Chinese subjects on them, an amber necklace and a thousand trifles among which shone two little white wool slippers, their buckles encrusted with paste diamonds!

"Oh, I must put them on," Sylvie cried, "if only I can find the embroidered stockings."

A moment later we unrolled some silk stockings of a delicate rose color with green clocks; but her aunt's voice, accompanied by a sizzling from the pan, suddenly brought us back to reality.

"Quick," said Sylvie, "you go on down." And in spite of all I could say she would not let me help her on with her shoes and stockings. Meanwhile her aunt was turning out the contents of the pan on to a dish—a slice of bacon and some eggs. Sylvie's call soon brought me back to her.

"Get dressed quickly!" she said. She herself was fully dressed and she showed me the keeper's wedding costume all put out on the chest-of-drawers. In a moment I had turned myself into the bridegroom of the previous century. Sylvie was waiting for me on the stairs and we went down together, hand in hand.

Her aunt turned and saw us and gave a start. "Oh, my children!" she said and began to cry, soon smiling through her tears. It was the image of her own youth, a vision at once cruel and charming. We sat down beside her, touched and almost grave. But soon our gay spirits came back to us as, the first shock over, the dear old soul could think of nothing else but recounting the stately ceremonies of her own wedding. She even discovered in her memory those alternating songs, then customary, which went from one end of the nuptial table to the other, and the simple epithalamion which accompanied the young couple as they went home after the dance. We repeated the artless rhythms of these verses, with the pauses and assonances of their time, flowery and passionate like the Song of Songs. We were the bride and bridegroom for a whole summer morning.

VII. — CHÂALIS

It is four in the morning; the road plunges into a dip of land and then rises again. The carriage is going by Orry, then on to La Chapelle. To the left there is a road that runs along the wood of Hallate. It was along there that Sylvie's brother drove me one evening in his little cart to a country ceremony. It was, I believe, Saint Bartholomew's Eve. His little horse flew through the woods and unfrequented roads as if to some witches' Sabbath. We reached the paved road again at Mont l'Évêque and a few minutes later stopped at the keeper's lodge at the ancient Abbey of Châalis—Châalis, yet another memory!

This former retreat of emperors now merely offers for our admiration the ruins of its cloisters with their Byzantine arcades, the last of which still stands out reflected in the pools—a forgotten fragment of those pious foundations included in the properties that used to be called "the forms of Charlemagne." In this district, cut off from the movement of roads and cities, religion has preserved especial traces of the long stay made there by the Cardinals of the House of Este in the times of the Medici; its customs and emblems still retain something gallant and poetic, you breathe a perfume of the Renaissance beneath the chapel arches with their slender moldings, decorated by Italian artists. The figures of saints and angels are silhouetted in rose on vaults of a delicate blue and carry an air of pagan allegory that reminds one of the sentimentalities of Petrarch and of the fabulous mysticism of Francesco Colonna. [12]

[12] In another story, *Angélique*, which precedes *Sylvie* in the collection, the reader has already learnt how Nerval's eye was seduced by this painter's rather glamorous frescoes for Hippolyte d'Este, who was Cardinal of Ferrara and from 1541 to 1572 Abbé of Châalis.

We were intruders, Sylvie's brother and I, in the private festival that took place that night. A personage of very noble birth, who at that time owned the estate, had had the idea of inviting several families of the district to a sort of allegorical representation, in which some of the pupils of the neighboring convent were to take part. It was no imitation of the tragedies of Saint-Cyr but went back to the first lyric attempt introduced into France at the time of the Valois. What I saw performed was like a mystery play of ancient times. The costumes were long robes, varied only in their colors, of azure, hyacinth, and of the color of dawn. The action took place among angels, on the ruins of the shattered world. Each voice sang one of the splendors of this vanished world, and the angel of death declared the causes of its destruction. A spirit arose from the abyss, holding in its hand a flaming sword, and summoned the others to come and adore the glory of Christ, the conqueror of hell. This spirit was Adrienne, transfigured by her costume as she already was by her vocation. The halo of gilt cardboard around her angelic head seemed to us, quite naturally, a circle of light; her voice had gained in strength and range, and the endless *fioriture* of Italian singing embroidered the severe phrases of stately recitative with their bird-like trills.

As I retrace these details I have to ask myself if they were real or if I dreamed them. Sylvie's brother was a little drunk that evening. For a while we stopped at the keeper's house—where I was greatly struck to see a swan with spread wings displayed above the door, and inside some tall cupboards of carved walnut, a large clock in its case, and trophies of bows and arrows of honor over a red and green target. An odd dwarf, wearing a Chinese cap, and holding a bottle in one hand and a ring in the other, seemed to be inviting the marksmen to aim true. The dwarf, I am sure, was cut out of sheet-iron. But is the apparition of Adrienne as real as these details, as real as the indisputable existence of the Abbey of Châalis? Yet I am certain it was the keeper's son who took us into the hall where the play took place; we were near the door, behind a large audience, who were seated and seemed deeply

moved. It was Saint Bartholomew's Day—a day singularly connected with memories of the Medici, whose arms, impaled with
those of the House of Este, decorated those old walls ... Perhaps
this memory is an obsession! Luckily the carriage stops here on
the road to Plessis; I escape from the realm of reverie and have only
a quarter of an hour's walk over little-used paths to reach Loisy.

VIII. – THE BALL AT LOISY

I entered the ball at Loisy at that melancholy yet still gentle
hour when the lights grow pale and tremble at the approach of
day. The lime-trees, in deep shadow at their roots, took on a
bluish tint at the top. The bucolic flute no longer struggled so
keenly with the song of the nightingale. Everyone looked pale
and in the dishevelled groups I had difficulty in finding faces I
knew. At last I saw Lise, a friend of Sylvie. She kissed me.

"It's been a long time since we've seen you, Parisian!" she said.

"Yes, a long time."

"And you arrive at an hour like this?"

"I came by the coach."

"None too quickly."

"I wanted to see Sylvie. Is she still at the ball?"

"She never leaves until dawn. She likes dancing so much."

In an instant I was at her side. Her face seemed tired, but her
black eyes still shone with the Athenian smile of old. A young
man stood near her. She made a sign to him that she would not
take the next dance. He bowed and went away.

Day was breaking. We left the ball, hand in hand. The flowers
hung in Sylvie's undone hair; the bunch at her breast drooped
also on her rumpled lace, the skillful work of her own fingers.
I offered to take her home. It was now broad daylight, but the
sky was overcast. The Thève murmured on our left, leaving pools
of still water at each winding in its course, and here white and
yellow water-lilies bloomed and the frail embroidery of the water-
flowers spread out like daisies. The fields were covered with stooks

and hayricks, whose odor went to my head without inebriation, as had at other times the fresh scent of the woods and thorn thickets.

We had no intention of crossing these again.

"Sylvie," I said, "you don't love me any more."

She sighed. "My friend," she said, "one has to find some reason. Things don't go as we want them to in life. Once you spoke to me of *la Nouvelle Héloïse*; I read it, and shivered as I came straight away on the sentence—'Every young girl who reads this book is lost.' [13] Yet I read on, relying on my judgment. Do you remember the day we put on my aunt's wedding clothes? ... The illustrations in the book also showed lovers in the old costumes of past days, so that for me you were Saint-Preux, and I saw myself in Julie. Ah! Why didn't you come back to me then? But they said you were in Italy. [14] You must have seen far prettier girls than me there!"

"Not one, Sylvie, with a look like yours, not one with the pure outline of your face. You are an antique nymph without knowing it. Besides, the woods of this district are as beautiful as those of the Roman Campagna. There are masses of granite no less sublime here, and a waterfall that cascades over the rocks like the one at Terni. I saw nothing there that I can regret here."

"And in Paris?" she said.

"In Paris..."

I shook my head without answering. Then suddenly I thought of the empty image which had led me astray for so long.

"Sylvie," I cried, "may we stop here?"

I threw myself at her feet. Weeping warm tears I confessed my irresolutions, my caprices. I described the fatal specter who had crossed my life.

"Save me," I concluded, "I am coming back to you for ever."

---

[13] Nerval misquotes. The passage runs as follows: "No pure girl has read novels... She who, despite the title of this book, shall dare to read a single page of it, is lost..." ("Jamais fille chaste n'a lu de romans... Celle qui, malgré ce titre, en osera lire une seule page, est une fille perdue...")

[14] This would have been about 1834.

She looked at me tenderly ... At that moment our conversation was interrupted by violent shouts of laughter. Sylvie's brother rejoined us. He was bubbling over with that good country fun which always follows a night of festival and which copious refreshments had developed beyond measure. He called up the young gallant of the ball, who was hiding in the thorn bushes a little way away but who lost no time in joining us. This lad was scarcely any firmer on his feet than his friend, and seemed still more embarrassed by the presence of a Parisian than by Sylvie's. His open face, his deference mingled with embarrassment, prevented me from any annoyance with him I might have felt for his role of dancer on whose account they had stayed so long at the ball. I did not consider him very dangerous.

"We must go home," Sylvie said to her brother. "We'll meet soon," she said to me, offering her cheek.

The lover was not offended.

IX. – ERMENONVILLE

I had no wish to sleep. I went to Montagny to revisit my uncle's house. A great sadness came over me when I caught sight of its yellow front and green shutters. Everything seemed to be in the same state as of old; only, I had to go to the farmer's to get the key of the front-door. When the shutters had been opened I looked affectionately at the old furniture preserved in the same state and rubbed up from time to time, the tall walnut-wood cupboard, two Flemish paintings said to be the work of an ancient painter, an ancestor of ours, large engravings after Boucher, and a whole series of framed illustrations from *Emile* and *la Nouvelle Héloïse* by Moreau; on the table was a stuffed dog which I had known alive as the old friend of my wanderings through the woods, the last King Charles perhaps, for it belonged to that lost breed.

"The parrot is still living," the farmer informed me. "I've taken him home with me."

The garden presented a wonderful picture of wild vegetation. In one corner I recognized the child's garden I had laid out in the past. With a shudder I entered the study where there was still a small library of choice books, old friends of the man who was now dead. On the desk there lay some ancient relics discovered in his garden, vases, and Roman medals, a local collection that had given him happiness.

"Let's go and see the parrot," I said to the farmer. The parrot asked for food as it had done in its happiest days, and looked at me with its round eye, bordered by wrinkled skin, which reminds you of the experienced look of an old man.

Filled with the sad ideas recalled by this late visit to such beloved spots, I felt I had to see Sylvie again, the only living and still youthful face that linked me to the district. I took the road to Loisy again. It was noon; everyone was asleep, tired from the festival. Ermenonville is about a league away by the forest road and I suddenly had the idea that it would distract me to walk there. It was fine summer weather. At first I delighted in the coolness of this road which seemed like the avenue of a park. The great oaks of a uniform green were only varied by the white trunks of the birches with their quivering leaves. The birds were silent and the only sound I heard was that of the woodpecker tapping the trees to hollow out its nest. For a moment I was nearly lost, for the signposts marking the different roads in various places had lost their lettering. Finally, leaving the "Desert" to my left, I arrived at the dancing-ring where the old men's bench still remains. All the memories of philosophical antiquity, revived by the former owner of the estate, crowded back on me at the sight of this picturesque illustration of *Anacharsis* and *Emile*.

When I saw the waters of the lake glittering through the branches of the hazels and willows, I completely recognized a spot to which my uncle had often taken me on our walks: it was the "Temple of Philosophy" which its originator had not been fortunate enough to finish. It is shaped like the temple of the Sybil and, still erect under the shelter of a clump of pines, displays the names of all great thinkers from Montaigne and Descartes to Rousseau. [15] This unfinished building is already no more than a ruin, with ivy gracefully festooning it, and the brambles invading its broken steps. As a child I had seen there those festivals at which girls dressed in white came to receive prizes for study and good conduct. Where are the rose-bushes which surrounded the hill? The eglantine and wild raspberry hide the last of them, reverting to their wild state. As for the laurels, have they been cut down— as we learn from the song of the girls who do not want to return to the woods? No, those shrubs from gentle Italy have died under our misty skies. Fortunately the privet of Virgil still flourishes, as if to support the master's words inscribed above the door—*Rerum cognoscere causas.* Yes, this temple is falling like so many others, and man, tired or forgetful, has turned away from its threshold, while indifferent nature will reconquer the soil that art took from her; but the thirst for knowledge will live on for ever, the source of all strength and activity.

Here are the island poplars and the tomb of Rousseau, empty of his ashes. O wise man! You gave us the milk of the strong and we were too feeble to profit from it. We have forgotten your lessons, which our fathers knew, and we have lost the meaning of your words, the last echo of ancient wisdom. But do not let us despair and, as you did at your last moment, let us turn our eyes to the sun!

I saw the château again, the peaceful waters surrounding it, the waterfall murmuring among the rocks, and that raised walk connecting the two parts of the village, marked with four dove-cotes at its corners, and the lawn that stretches out beyond like a savanna overlooked by shady slopes; Gabrielle's tower is reflected from afar in the waters of an artificial lake, starry with ephemeral flowers; the water foams, the insects hum . . . You must shun the treacherous air it exhales and gain the dusty rocks of the "Desert" and then the moors where the purple broom relieves the

[15] This building was indeed dedicated to Montaigne and it bore the names of Newton, Descartes, Voltaire, W. Penn, Montesquieu, and Rousseau.

green of the ferns. How solitary it all is and how sad! Sylvie's
enchanting gaze, her wild running, her happy cries, once gave
such charm to the places I have just been through. She was still
a wild child, her feet were bare, her skin sun-burnt in spite of the
straw hat whose long ribbon streamed out carelessly with the
tresses of her black hair. We used to go and drink milk at the
Swiss farm, and they told me: "What a pretty sweetheart you have
there, little Parisian!" Oh! No peasant boy would have danced
with her then! She only danced with me, once a year, at the Festival of the Bow.

X. – BIG CURLY

Again I took the road to Loisy; everyone was up. Sylvie was
dressed like a fine lady, practically in the city fashion. She took
me up to her room with all her old ingenuousness. Her eye still
sparkled with a charming smile, but the marked arch of her eyebrows gave her from time to time a serious look. The room was
simply decorated, though the furniture was modern; a gilt-edged
mirror had replaced the old wall-glass where an idyllic shepherd
offered a nest to a blue and pink shepherdess. The four-poster
bed, chastely draped with old flowered chintz, had been succeeded
by a walnut-wood bed hung with a net curtain; in the cage by
the window there were canaries where there had once been linnets.
I was anxious to leave the room, for it contained nothing of the past.

"You're not working at your lace today?" I asked Sylvie.

"Oh, I don't make lace any more, there's no demand for it in
the country; even at Chantilly the factory is closed."

"What do you do, then?"

She went to a corner of the room and produced an iron instru-
ment that looked like a long pair of pliers.

"What's that?"

"They call it the 'mechanic;' it's for holding the leather of
gloves while they're being sewn."

"Ah! So you are a glove-maker, Sylvie?"

"Yes. We work for Dammartin here, it's paying well at present; but I'm not doing anything today; let's go where you like."

I turned my eyes in the direction of the road to Othys; she shook her head; I realized that her old aunt was no longer alive. Sylvie called up a little boy and made him saddle a donkey.

"I'm still tired from yesterday," she said, "but the ride will do me good; let's go to Châalis."

And so there we were crossing the forest, followed by the little boy carrying a switch. Sylvie soon wanted to rest and I kissed her as I urged her to sit down. Our conversation could no longer be very intimate. I had to tell her of my life in Paris, of my travels . . .

"How can anyone travel so far?" she said

"I am surprised myself when I see you again."

"Oh, you just say that!"

"You must admit you weren't so pretty in those days."

"That I don't know."

"Do you remember the time when we were children, and you the bigger?"

"And you the cleverer!"

"Oh, Sylvie!"

"They put us in the donkey's panniers, one each side."

"And we called each other 'thou' . . . Do you remember teaching me to catch fresh-water shrimps under the bridges over the Thève and the Nonette?"

"And do you remember your foster-brother one day pulling you out of the 'waater,' as he called it?"

"Big Curly! It was he who told me I could get across the 'waater.' "

I quickly changed the conversation. This recollection had vividly recalled the time when I visited the district, wearing a little English jacket that made the peasants laugh. Sylvie alone thought me well-dressed, but I did not dare to remind her of this opinion of so distant a time. I do not know why, but my mind went back

to the wedding costumes we had put on at her aunt's cottage at
Othys. I asked what had become of them.

"Ah! Dear aunt," Sylvie said, "she lent me the dress for the
dance at Dammartin carnival two years ago. Poor aunt, the next
year she died."

She sighed and wept so that I could not ask her how she happened to go to a fancy-dress ball; but I know that, thanks to her
skill as a working woman, Sylvie was no longer a peasant girl.
Her relations alone had remained in their original status, and she
lived among them like an industrious fairy, shedding abundance
about her.

XI. – THE RETURN

The view widened as we left the wood. We had come to the
bank of the Châalis lakes. The cloister galleries, the chapel with
its pointed ogives, the feudal tower, and the little château that
had sheltered the loves of Henry IV and Gabrielle were tinged
with the evening glow against the dark green of the forest.

"It's a Walter Scott landscape," said Sylvie.

"And who has been telling you about Walter Scott?" I asked
her. "You must have read a lot in the last three years! ... Per-
sonally, I am trying to forget books, and what delights me is to
see this old Abbey with you again, the ruins we used to hide in
as little children. Do you remember, Sylvie, how frightened
you were when the guardian told us the story of the red
monks?"

"Oh, don't talk about it!"

"Well then, sing me the song of the fair maiden carried off
from her father's garden, under the white rose-tree."

"It's not sung any more."

"Have you become a musician?"

"A little."

"Sylvie, Sylvie, I am certain you sing opera arias!"

"And what's wrong with that?"

"Because I liked the old songs, and you won't know how to sing them any more."

Sylvie warbled a few notes from a grand aria out of a modern opera . . . She *phrased!*

We had strolled past the neighboring ponds and reached the green lawn, surrounded with limes and elms, where we had so often danced. I was conceited enough to point out the old Carolingian walls and to decipher the coats-of-arms of the House of Este.

"What about you?" Sylvie said. "How much more you've read than me! You're quite a savant, it seems."

I was irritated by her tone of reproach. Up to now I had been looking for a suitable place to renew our morning's moment of expansion; but what could I say to her, accompanied by a donkey and a very wide-awake small boy, who took a delight in coming up close to hear how a Parisian talked? Then I was unlucky enough to tell her about the apparition at Châalis, which had remained in my memory. I took Sylvie to the very hall of the château where I had heard Adrienne sing.

"Oh, do let me hear you!" I said to her. "Let your dear voice echo beneath these roofs and drive away the spirit that torments me, whether it be from heaven or from hell!"

She repeated the words and the song after me:

> Angels of Heaven, descend without delay
> To the pit of purgatory! . . .

"It's very sad," she said.

"It's sublime . . . I think it's by Porpora, [16] with words translated in the Sixteenth Century."

"I don't know," Sylvie answered.

We went back by way of the valley, following the road to Charlepont, which the peasants, not very exact etymologists, called "Châllepont." Sylvie, tired of riding, leaned on my arm. The

---

[16] Nicolas Porpora (1686-1766), an Italian composer of church music.

road was deserted; I tried to speak of what was in my heart, but somehow I could only find commonplace expressions, or else suddenly some pompous phrase from a novel—which Sylvie might have read. When we reached the walls of Saint-S- we had to watch our steps. We went through marshy meadows with little winding streams.

"What has become of the nun?" I suddenly asked.

"You and your nun ... Well, you see, that had an unhappy ending."

Sylvie would not tell me another word. Do women truly feel that such and such words come from the lips and not from the heart? One would scarcely think so, seeing that they are so easily deceived, and noticing the choice they most often make: there are some men who play the comedy of love so well! I could never do so, although I knew that some women knowingly allow themselves to be deceived. Besides, there is something sacred about a love that goes back to childhood ... Sylvie, whom I had seen grow up, was as a sister to me. The thought of seducing her was impossible ... Quite another idea came into my head. At this moment, I said to myself, I should be at the theater. What part is Aurélia (for that was the actress's name) playing this evening? Of course, the part of the princess in the new play. Ah, how moving she is in the third act ... and in the love scene of the second! And with that wrinkled *jeune premier* ...

"Thinking again?" asked Sylvie, and she began singing:

> At Dammartin are three fair maids,
> And one's as pretty as the day ...

"You little rogue," I cried, "you know perfectly well that you remember the old songs."

"If you came here more often, I would pick them up again," she said, "but we must be practical. You have your life in Paris, I have my work here; we mustn't be too late getting home: tomorrow morning I have to be up with the sun."

XII. – PÈRE DODU

I was about to answer, I was about to fall at her feet, I was about to offer her my uncle's house, which I could still buy (there were several co-heirs and the property had remained intact), [17] when at that moment we arrived at Loisy. Supper was waiting for us. The patriarchal smell of the onion soup was noticeable from a distance. Some neighbors had been invited for this day following the festival. I immediately recognized an old wood-cutter, Père Dodu, who had told us such comic or terrible evening yarns in in the past. By turns shepherd, messenger, gamekeeper, fisherman, poacher even, Père Dodu made cuckoo-clocks and turnspits in his spare time. For some time now he had been consecrated as Ermenonville guide for English tourists, and he took them to Rousseau's places of meditation, relating the philosopher's last moments. He was the little boy whom Rousseau had employed to classify his plants for him and whom he had ordered to gather the stalks of hemlock from which he used to press the juice into his cup of coffee. The landlord of the Golden Cross disputed this detail with him—whence a prolonged feud. Père Dodu had for some time been in the possession of several entirely innocent secrets, such as how to cure a cow by saying a verse of the Bible backwards and making the sign of the cross with the left foot, but he had given up these superstitions in good time—thanks, he used to say, to his talks with Jean-Jacques.

"So there you are, little Parisian!" Père Dodu said to me. "Have you come to seduce our girls?"

"Me, Père Dodu?"

"You take them off into the woods while the wolf's away, don't you?"

"Père Dodu, you know you're the wolf."

"I used to be, as long as I could find sheep; at the moment I only meet goats, and they know how to defend themselves all right! But you Parisians, you're artful. Jean-Jacques was so right

---

[17] This was the Clos de Nerval, from which the poet took his name.

when he said, 'Man is corrupted in the poisoned atmosphere of cities.' "

"Père Dodu, you know very well that man is becoming corrupt everywhere."

Père Dodu began to sing a drinking song; it was in vain that they tried to stop him at a certain risky couplet (which everyone knew by heart). Sylvie refused to sing, in spite of our entreaties, saying that people no longer sang at table. I had already observed that the lover of the night before was seated at her left. There was something familiar in his round face and ruffled hair. He got up and came behind my chair, saying: "You don't remember me, Parisian?"

A good woman, who had just come in for dessert after having waited on us, said in my ear, "Don't you remember your foster-brother?"

Without her warning I would have made a fool of myself.

"So it's you, Big Curly!" I said, "the fellow who pulled me out of the 'waater.' "

Sylvie burst out laughing at this recognition.

"Not to mention," he said, as he embraced me, "that you had a fine silver watch, and on the way back you were far more concerned about the watch than yourself, because it had stopped. You said, 'The brute's drownded, it won't go tic-tac, whatever will Uncle say?' . . ."

"A brute in a watch!" said Père Dodu. "So that's what they bring up children to believe in Paris!"

Sylvie was sleepy and I fancied I was completely lost in her esteem. She went upstairs to her room and as I kissed her, she said, "Come and see us tomorrow."

Père Dodu had remained at table with Sylvain [18] and my foster-brother; we chatted for a long time over a flask of Louvres ratafia.

"All men are equal," declared Père Dodu in between two couplets. "I drink with a pastry-cook as I would with a prince."

Where's the pastry-cook?" I asked.

[18] Sylvain appears in *Les Faux Saulniers* (1850), as the brother of Sylvie.

"Look beside you—a young man ambitious to set himself up."

My foster-brother seemed embarrassed.   I understood it all.
The fatality had been reserved for me to have a foster-brother in
a district made illustrious by Rousseau—who wanted to suppress
wet-nurses!   Père Dodu informed me that there was much talk
of a marriage between Sylvie and Big Curly, who wanted to set
up a pastry business in Dammartin.   I asked no more.   Next day
the coach from Nanteuil-le-Haudoin took me back to Paris.

XIII. – AURÉLIA

To Paris!   The coach took five hours.   I was in no hurry to get
there before the evening.   Around eight o'clock I was in my usual
stall; Aurélia lent her charm and inspiration to some verses feebly
inspired by Schiller for which we were indebted to a talent of
the time. [19]   In the garden scene she was sublime.   During the
fourth act, when she did not come on, I went and bought a bouquet
of flowers at Madame Prévost's.   In it I placed a most tender letter
signed "An Unknown."   I said to myself, That's something of the
future settled.   And the next day I was travelling to Germany.

What was I going to do there?   Try and get my feelings into
order.   If I were writing a novel, I should never get anyone to
believe in the story of a heart simultaneously smitten by two loves.
Sylvie slipped from me through my own mistake; but the sight
of her for a single day had sufficed to elevate my soul; henceforth
I placed her like a smiling statue in the Temple of Wisdom.   Her
gaze had held me back on the brink of an abyss.   Still more vigor-
ously I rejected the idea of presenting myself to Aurélia, to struggle
with so many common lovers who scintillated for an instant by
her side and then fell back broken.   I said to myself: Some day
we shall see if the woman has a heart.

One morning I read in a newspaper that Aurélia was ill.   I wrote

[19] Apparently Pierre Lebrun's tragedy *Marie Stuart*, also attacked in 1840 by
both Dumas and Gautier.

to her from the mountains of Salzburg. My letter was so full of German mysticism that I could not expect much success from it, but then I did not ask for an answer. I counted somewhat on chance and on—*the unknown*.

Months passed. While I was travelling and idling, I had undertaken to put into poetic action the love of the painter Colonna for the fair Laura, whom her parents made a nun, and whom he loved until death. Something in the subject touched on my own constant preoccupation, and, the last line of the play written, I thought only of returning to France. [20]

What can I say now that is not the story of so many others? I passed through all the circles of those places of purgatory called theaters. "I ate the drum and drank the cymbal," to use the apparently meaningless phrase of the initiates of Eleusis. It doubtless means that when necessary we have to pass beyond the limits of nonsense and absurdity: for me, reason was conquering and holding my ideal.

Aurélia had accepted the principal part in the drama I brought back from Germany. [21] I shall never forget the day she allowed me to read the piece to her. The love scenes were written expressly for her. I believe I read them with spirit, but above all enthusiastically. In the conversation that followed I revealed myself as the *Unknown* of the two letters. She said to me, "You're quite crazy, but come and see me again . . . I have never met anyone who knew how to love me."

O woman! You are looking for love . . . what am I doing?

During the following days I wrote her what were doubtless the most tender and beautiful letters she had ever received. Her replies were full of good sense. One moment she was touched, called me to her, and admitted to me that it was very difficult for her to break off an earlier attachment.

[20] Nerval's projected drama of which he speaks here, *Francesco Colonna*, never reached the stage, but its worksheets have come down to us.

[21] This drama again seem to have been abortive. Nerval also planned a drama on the death of Rousseau.

"If it is really for me myself that you love me," she said, "you will understand that I can only belong to one man."

Two months later I received a gushing letter. I hurried to her. Meanwhile someone had given me a precious piece of information. The handsome young man I had met one night at the club had just joined the Spahis.

Next summer there were races at Chantilly and the company to which Aurélia belonged gave a performance. Once in the country the players were for three days at the order of the manager. I had become friendly with this fellow, a former Dorante in the comedies of Marivaux, for a long time a *jeune premier* in drama, his last success having been the lover's part in the play imitated from Schiller in which my opera-glasses had revealed him to me as so wrinkled. Off the stage he seemed younger, and as he was still slim he could still produce an effect in the provinces. He had fire. I went with the company in the capacity of "gentleman poet" and I persuaded the manager to give some performances at Senlis and Dammartin. He inclined at first to Compiègne, but Aurélia sided with me. Next day, while negotiations were going on with the owners of the halls and the local authorities, I hired some horses and we took the road to the ponds of Commelle to lunch at the castle of Queen Blanche. Aurélia, in riding habit and her fair hair loose, rode through the forest like a queen of old time, and the peasants stopped in amazement. Madame de F- [22] was the only lady they had ever seen so imposing and so graceful in her manner of greeting. After lunch we went down into the Swiss-like villages, where the waters of the Nonette work the saw-mills. These scenes, so dear to my memory, interested Aurélia without arresting her. I had planned to take her to the château near Orry to the same square of green where for the first time I had seen Adrienne. She showed no emotion. Then I told her everything; I told her the origin of that love half-seen in my nights, then dreamed of, then realized in her. She listened to me seriously and told me: "It's not me you are

[22] This is the Baronne de Feuchères, referred to in detail in the Introduction.

in love with. You expect me to say, 'The actress is the same person as the nun.' You are simply seeking for drama, that's all, and the end eludes you. Go on, I don't believe in you any more."

These words were a flash of light. The strange enthusiasms I had felt for so long, the dreams, tears, despairs, and tenderness . . . weren't they then love? Then where is love?

That evening Aurélia played at Senlis. I thought I detected a weakness in her for the manager—the wrinkled *jeune premier*. The man had an excellent character and had done a great deal for her.

One day Aurélia told me: "There's the man who really loves me!"

XIV. – LAST LEAVES

Such are the delusions which charm and beguile us in the morning of life. I have tried to set them down without too much order but many hearts will understand mine. Illusions fall, like the husks of a fruit, one after another, and what is left is experience. It has a bitter taste, but there is something tonic in its sharpness— forgive me this old-fashioned manner. Rousseau claims that the contemplation of nature is a balm for everything. Sometimes I try to find my woods of Clarens lost in the mists somewhere to the north of Paris. All that has altered.

O Ermenonville, land where the old idylls lived, retranslated from Gessner, you have lost your lone star which shone for me with a double light. Now blue, now rose-colored, like the deceptive star of Aldebaran, it was Adrienne or Sylvie—two halves of a single love. One was the sublime ideal, the other the sweet reality. What are your lakes and shades to me now, what is your "Desert?" Othys, Montagny, Loisy, poor neighboring villages, Châalis (oh, that they would restore it), you have retained nothing of this past! Sometimes I need to revisit these scenes of solitude and reverie. In my own sad heart I find fugitive traces of a time when the natural was affected; sometimes I smile when I read on the side of granite memorials some verses of Roucher [23] which I once thought sublime—or benevolent maxims over a fountain or a grotto dedicated to Pan. The ponds, dug at such expense, are expanses of stagnant water disdained by the swans. No longer does the hunt of the Condé pass by with their noble women riders, no more do the horns answer each other from afar, multiplied by their echoes!... Today there is no direct road to Ermenonville. Sometimes I go there by Creil and Senlis, sometimes by Dammartin.

It is only in the evening that you reach Dammartin. I put up at an inn called the Image of Saint John. As a rule they give me quite a clean room, hung with old tapestry and a pier-glass on the wall. This room is a last return to that bric-a-brac I long ago gave up. I sleep snugly under the eiderdown, customary in those parts. In the morning I open my window, framed in vines and roses, and discover with delight ten leagues of green horizon on which the poplars are aligned like armies. Here and there a few villages nestle under their steep spires, built, as they put it here, like pointed bones. First there is Othys—then Ève, then Ver; Ermenonville would be visible through the woods if only it had a spire, but in that philosophic spot the church has been neglected. I fill my lungs with the pure air from the plain and go down in good spirits to pay a visit to the pastry-shop.

"So there you are, Big Curly!"

"Hallo, little Parisian!"

We exchange a few affectionate punches of childhood, then I climb a certain staircase where my arrival is greeted by the happy cries of two children. Sylvie's Athenian smile lights her lovely features. I say to myself, Perhaps this is happiness; and yet...

Sometimes I call her Lolotte and she finds a certain resemblance in me to Werther, less the pistols, which are out of fashion these days. While Big Curly prepares breakfast, we take the children for a walk in the avenues of lime-trees which encircle the ruins

[23] Jean-Antoine Roucher (1745-1794), a minor poet of the Eighteenth Century and a victim of the Revolution.

of the old brick towers of the château. While the little ones amuse themselves by shooting a few arrows from their father's bow into the target on the shooting-ground of the Companions of the Bow, we read a little poetry or a few pages from those short books that are scarcely ever written now.

I forgot to say that on the day when Aurélia's company gave a performance at Dammartin, I took Sylvie to see it and asked her if she did not think the actress like someone she knew.

"Who do you mean?"

"Do you remember Adrienne?"

She burst out laughing and said, "What an idea!" Then, as if reproving herself, she sighed and added, "Poor Adrienne! She died in the convent of Saint-S-... about 1832."

EMILIE

"No one really knows the story of Lieutenant Desroches who got himself killed last year at the battle of Hambergen, two months after his marriage. If it really was suicide, may God forgive him! But a man who dies in defense of his country does not deserve to have his actions given that name, in my opinion, whatever may have been his intentions."

"Here we are back again," said the Doctor, "to the question of capitulation of conscience. Desroches was a philosopher who decided to give up life: he wanted his death to be of some service, so he threw himself gallantly into the battle and killed as many Germans as he could, saying—This is the best I can do, I am now content to die. And as he received the fatal saber thrust, he cried out, 'Long live the Emperor.' Ten men from his Company will tell you the same thing."

"And that doesn't make it any less of a suicide," Arthur answered. "All the same, I don't agree that it would have been right to have refused him church burial ..."

"If you argue in that way, you disgrace the self-sacrifice of Curtius. [1] That young Roman knight may have been ruined by gambling, unhappy in love, and tired of life, who knows? But surely it is noble, when you have made up your mind to leave this world, to make your death useful to others, and that it why you cannot call Desroches a suicide, because suicide is simply the supreme act of egoism, which is why it is despised by men ... What do you say, Arthur?"

"I was thinking of what you were saying just now, I mean that Desroches, before dying, killed as many Germans as he could."

[1] Lacus Curtius rode to his death in a chasm in the Roman forum in 362 B.C. in order, as he thought it from the soothsayers, to save the city.

"Well?"

"Well then, those good fellows are going to give rather an unhappy testimony of the death of our Lieutenant before God. You must allow me to say that this suicide strikes me as extremely like homicide."

"What nonsense! The Germans are our enemies."

"But are there any enemies for the man who has made up his mind to die? At that moment every instinct of nationality is wiped out, and I doubt if one thinks of any other country than the other world, or of any other emperor than God. But here is the Abbé, listening to us without a word, and I trust I am not talking against his ideas. Come now, Abbé, give us your opinion. Try and make us agree. It's a very complicated question, and the story of Desroches, or rather what the Doctor and I imagine we know about it, sounds every bit as involved as these deep discussions it has brought up between us."

"Yes," said the Doctor, "one hears that Desroches was greatly distressed by his last wound, the one that disfigured him so terribly. It may be that he caught a look of scorn or ridicule on the face of his young bride. Philosophers are sensititive people. In any case, he died and at his own wish."

"At his own wish, since you insist; only don't call death in battle suicide. You're making a contradiction in terms, exactly like what's going on in your mind; you die in battle because you come across something that happens to kill you; you don't die as you wish."

"So you'd like to call it fate?"

"One moment," interrupted the Abbé, who had been collecting his thoughts during this discussion, "you are going to think it strange of me to contradict your paradoxes and suppositions ..."

"No, go ahead, by all means; you undoubtedly know more about the case than we do. You've been living at Bitche [2] for some time now; they say Desroches knew you, perhaps he even confessed to you ..."

[2] A town in the Moselle region, close to the Franco-German border at that time.

"In which case I should have to keep silent; unfortunately Desroches did not, and yet his death was a Christian death, believe me; and I am going to tell you what caused it, and how it occurred, so that you may see that he was an upright man as well as a good soldier, who died for humanity, for himself, and according to the wishes of God at one and the same time.

"Desroches joined his regiment when he was fourteen years old, at a moment when most of our men were being slaughtered on the frontier and the Republican Army was calling up children. He was weak, pale, and slender as a girl, and his comrades hated to see his young shoulder sink under the weight of his gun. You must have heard the story of how permission was obtained from his Captain to have it cut down six inches. With his rifle thus suited to his strength, Desroches did splendidly in the campaigns in Flanders; later on, he was posted to Haguenau, to the part where we, or rather you, were fighting for so long.

"At the time of which I am going to speak, Desroches was in in the prime of life and as ensign gave his regiment service far in advance of this rank, for he was almost the only man to survive two reinforcements. Two years and three months ago he had just been promoted to full Lieutenant when, leading a bayonet charge, he received a Prussian saber cut across the face at Bergheim. The wound was ghastly; the field-surgeons, who had often joked with him over having gone through thirty engagements without a scratch, shook their heads when they saw him. 'If he recovers,' they said, 'the poor chap will either be weak-minded or mad.'

"The Lieutenant was sent back to Metz to recover. A good many miles of the journey went by without his being aware of it; once in a decent bed, however, and well cared-for, he was able to sit up after five or six months. Three more, and he could open one eye and see things. He was prescribed tonics, sunlight, movement, and then short walks. One morning, supported by two companions, he set out trembling, his head spinning, towards the quai Saint-Vincent, which is close by the military hospital, and there they sat him down in the promenade, in the midday sun, under the lime-trees of the park: the poor fellow thought he was seeing the light of day for the first time.

"By continuing in this way he was soon able to walk on his own, and every morning he went and sat on the same bench in the promenade, his head a mass of black bandages which almost entirely covered his face. As he went, he could always count on a friendly greeting from the men who passed by, and on a gesture of deep sympathy from the women. This, however, gave him little comfort.

"But once seated on his bench the very thought of his good luck in being alive, and in these pleasant surroundings, after such a shock, made him forget his misfortunes. The old fortress, ruined since the time of Louis XVI, spread its delapidated ramparts in front of him. The lime-trees, now in flower, cast thick shadows on his head, while at his feet, in the valley that dipped away from the promenade, the Moselle, overflowing its banks and flooding the fields, gave the meadows of Saint-Symphorien fresh life and verdure between its two arms; then there was the little island of Saulcy, where the powder-magazine was isolated, strewn with shady trees and cottages; finally the white, foamy falls of the Moselle, the twists in its course sparkling in the sunlight, and in the distance—the last of the landscape he could see—the Vosges mountains bluish and misty in full daylight: such was the sight which he grew to love, thinking that there lay his own country, not conquered territory, but true French soil, whereas these rich new provinces, for which he had fought, were fugitive and fickle in their beauty, like the woman we have won yesterday and will lose tomorrow.

"Around the early days of June the heat was intense, and Desroches had chosen a bench well in the shade. One day two ladies came and sat down beside him. He greeted them quietly and went on looking at the countryside, but his appearance was so unusual that the two ladies could not resist plying him with sympathetic questions.

"One of them, reasonably elderly, turned out to be the aunt of the other, whose name was Emilie and who earned her living by doing gilt embroidery on silk or velvet. Desroches had followed their example and in answer to his own questions the aunt informed him that the young girl had left Haguenau to keep her company, that she embroidered for churches, and that she had been an orphan for some time.

"The next day the bench was taken in the same way and by the end of the week its three occupants were firm friends. In spite of his weakness and his humiliation at the attentions the young girl lavished on him as if he were the most harmless old man, Desroches felt light-hearted, full of jokes, and more inclined to rejoice over his unexpected good fortune than to distress himself about it.

"Then, on his way back to the hospital, he remembered his frightful wound, his scarecrow appearance over which he had so often despaired, but which habit and convalescence had made him consider much more leniently.

"Desroches had certainly never dared take off the already unnecessary dressing over his wound, nor look at himself in the mirror. From now on the thought of doing so was more frightening than ever. However, he ventured to lift up one corner of the protective bandage, and he found underneath a scar, still slightly pink, but not at all too repulsive. He continued the examination and discovered that the various parts of his face had been sewn together reasonably well, and that his eyes were as clear and healthy as ever. He was missing some of the hairs in his eyebrows, true, but that was a small matter! The oblique weal across his face from forehead to ear, well . . . it was a saber cut, received in an attack on the lines at Bergheim, and nothing could be nobler—there were enough songs to prove that.

"So Desroches was astonished to find himself so presentable after all the time he had spent as a stranger to himself. Cleverly he concealed the hair that had gone grey on his wounded side, combing it under the thick brown hair on his left. He drew his mustache out as far as possible over the line of the scar and, putting on his new uniform, he went next day to the promenade in reasonable triumph.

"In fact, he was so well set-up and turned out, his sword slapped his thigh so gracefully, his shako had such a martial tilt forward, that no one recognized him on his way to the gardens; he got to the bench under the lime-trees first and sat down, outwardly in his customary calm, but inwardly profoundly agitated and far paler than usual, in spite of the approbation of his mirror.

"The two ladies were not long in arriving, but at the sight of a smart officer occupying their usual place they immediately turned and walked away.

'What!' he called out after them. 'You don't recognize me?'

"You must not imagine that this is the prelude to one of those stories of pity converted into passion, as in contemporary opera. From now on the Lieutenant had serious intentions. Happy to be taken for an eligible young bachelor again, he quickly put the ladies at ease and discovered that they seemed quite disposed to continue their friendship with him, transformed as he was. Their reserve yielded before his frank declaration. Besides, the match was suitable from every point of view: Desroches had a little family property near Epinal; Emilie had inherited from her parents a small house at Haguenau which she let as a restaurant and which brought in five or six hundred francs. Of this, it is true, she gave half to her brother Wilhelm, chief clerk to the notary public at Schennberg.

"The arrangements completed, it was decided to hold the wedding at Haguenau, for this was really the young girl's home: the only reason she had been in Metz for so long was in order to be with her aunt. In any case it was agreed that they should return to Metz after the marriage. Emilie was delighted to be seeing her brother again. More than once 'Desroches felt surprised that this young man was not in uniform like everyone else these days; they told him he had been excused service on account of his poor health. Desroches was full of sympathy for him.

"So the betrothed pair and Emilie's aunt set out for Haguenau; they had places in the public vehicle that stages at Bitche, then a simple coach of leather and wickerwork. The road, as you know, is a beautiful one. Desroches, who had only gone along it in uniform with a sword in his hand, and in company with three or four thousand other men, admired now the solitude, the queerly-shaped rocks, and the view edged with a lacy line of dark green hills traversed far off by long valleys. The fertile plains of Saint-Avold, the Sarreguemines factories, the compact little copses of Limblingue, where poplars, ashes, and pines extended their various banks of foliage, ranging from grey to dark green— but you know well what a magnificent and charming view it is. [3]

"The travellers arrived at Bitche and at once went to the inn called the Dragon. Desroches sent to the fortress for me. I went immediately and saw his new family. I complimented the young girl who was exceptionally beautiful, with a gentle manner, and seemed greatly in love with her future husband. All three lunched with me here, where we are now sitting. Several officers, friends of Desroches, had heard of his arrival and came to the inn to get him to have dinner with them at the fortress restaurant where the garrison-staff ate. So it was agreed that the ladies would retire early and the Lieutenant give his last evening as a bachelor to his comrades.

"It was a lively dinner-party; everyone felt something of that happiness and gaiety Desroches had brought with him. They spoke enviously of Egypt, and Italy, complaining bitterly of the bad luck which kept so many good fellows cooped up in frontier fortresses.

'Yes,' grumbled some of the officers, 'we're suffocating here. This life's so wearing and monotonous, you might as well be at sea, living here like this without any fighting or distraction, not even the chance of promotion. "That fort is impregnable." That's what Napoleon said when he passed through here on his way to

---

[3] Nerval is likely to have posted along this route on one of his trips to Germany.

the Army in Germany.   About all we have is the opportunity to die of boredom.'

'No, my friends,' replied Desroches, 'I'm afraid it wasn't much more amusing in my time; for I was stationed here, and I complained just as loudly as you.   I had obtained my commission by virtue of wearing out government-issue boots on every road imaginable and I only knew three things: drill, the direction of the wind, and as much grammar as one gets from a village schoolmaster.   So, when I was made Second Lieutenant and sent to Bitche with the Second Battalion of the Cher, I looked on my tour of duty here as an excellent chance for some real uninterrupted study. With this idea in mind I assembled a collection of books, maps, and charts.   I had studied tactics and I learnt German without any trouble, since scarcely any other language is spoken in this good old French district.   In this way my time here, so much more tedious for you who have far less to learn, seemed to pass quickly.   It didn't seem long enough.   And, when night came, I escaped to a stone room under the main spiral staircase.   I hermetically stoppered the loopholes and lit my lamp and worked.   It was a night like that . . .'

"Here Desroches paused a moment.   He drew his hand over his eyes, emptied his glass, and went on without finishing the sentence.

'You all know,' he said, 'the little path leading up here from the plain—the one they've blocked by blowing a huge rock out of the ground and leaving a pit.   Well, that path was always deadly for enemy troops trying to attack the fort; no sooner had the poor devils begun to climb up than they were raked with four twenty-fours that swept the path the whole length of its ascent. I suppose those guns are still there . . .'

'You must have done pretty well,' said a Colonel to Desroches. 'Was it then you won your promotion?'

'Yes, Colonel, and it was there I killed my first man, the one and only human being I have ever fought hand to hand and killed directly.   That's why I shall never like the sight of this fort.'

'What's that you say?' they exclaimed. 'Twenty years of military service, fifteen pitched battles, perhaps fifty engagements in all, and you pretend you've only killed one man?'

'I didn't say that, gentlemen: of the ten thousand cartridges I've rammed into my rifle, who can say how many found their mark? But I assert that at Bitche my hand was stained with the blood of an enemy soldier for the first time, and my arm first felt that shock of thrusting a sword into a human breast to the kill— until the hilt quivered.'

'That's right,' one of the officers interrupted, 'the foot-soldier does a lot of killing without thinking about it. To tell the truth, gunfire is more intention to kill than execution. As for the bayonet, it only plays a small part, even in the most disastrous charges; ground is held or lost without too much close fighting. The rifles of both sides engage, then let up when resistance gives way. Now the cavalry, for instance, they really do have to fight hand to hand . . .'

'And so,' went on Desroches, 'just as you never forget the last look of a man you kill in a duel, his death-rattle, the sound of his fall, so I carry with me, almost in remorse—yes, laugh if you will—the pale, dreadful sight of that Prussian Sergeant I killed in the little powder-magazine of this fort.'

"Everyone was silent and Desroches began to tell them about it:
'It was night and, as I have just explained to you, I was working. At two o'clock the sentries were the only ones awake. They patrolled in complete silence so that any sound was suspicious. However, I kept on hearing movement in the gallery underneath my room; someone bumped against a door which gave a creak. I ran out into the corridor and listened. I called to the sentry in a low voice—no reply. In a second I had summoned the gunners, buckled on my uniform, and with my unsheathed sword in my hand was leading the way to where the noises were. About thirty of us arrived all at once at the circular central spot where the galleries converge and, in the lantern light, we recognized the Prussians who had been let in through the postern gate by a traitor.

They dashed forward in confusion, firing as they saw us, the shots making terrific detonations under the low, shadowy ceilings.

'So there we were, face to face; men came running up all the time, the defenders pouring down into the gallery until you could scarcely move. There was a space of about six to eight feet between the opposing forces, a field of battle left vacant for a few seconds, so surprised were we French, so disappointed the Prussians.

'However, this hesitation did not last long. Torches and lanterns, hung by gunners on the walls, lit the scene and a kind of old-fashioned fighting took place. I was in the front rank, opposite a huge Prussian Sergeant covered with stripes and decorations. He carried a rifle but there was such a crush he could scarcely manipulate it. I remember every one of these details vividly. I don't know if he even intended to resist me; I threw myself on him and plunged my sword into his noble breast; his eyes widened in a horrible way, his fists clenched, and he toppled into the arms of his comrades.

'I don't remember what happened then; I found myself in the first courtyard, covered with blood; the Prussians had retreated through the postern gate, and our gunfire accompanied them back to their encampment.' 4

"When Desroches had finished, there was a long silence, and then they discussed other matters. The look of sadness that fell over the faces of those soldiers after the story of this somewhat ordinary misfortune was very strange and sad, when you come to think of it ... and you could tell just how much a man's life was worth, even a German's life, Doctor, if you looked into the uneasy faces of those professional killers."

"I agree," answered the Doctor, slightly taken aback, "the shedding of blood is a terrible thing, however it happens; still, Desroches did nothing wrong; he simply defended himself."

"Who knows?" muttered Arthur.

"You were talking about capitulation of conscience, Doctor,

4 This incident, which Nerval has considerably embroidered, took place at Bitche in 1793.

you tell us if the death of that Sergeant wasn't a bit like murder. Is it certain that the Prussian would have killed Desroches?"

"War's war. What do you want next?"

"All right, war's war. You kill a man who neither knows you nor sees you at three hundred yards in the darkness. Face to face and with a furious look you slaughter men for whom you have no hatred. And for this we pat ourselves on the back and feel very proud. It's considered quite an honorable business among Christian people!

"Desroches's adventure, however, caused different reactions in the minds of his listeners. Bedtime came and Desroches himself was one of the first to forget his dismal story for, from the little room he had been given, he could see through the heavy trees a certain window in the hôtel du Dragon, where a night-light was shining. There lay his future. When, in the middle of that night, the challenges of the patrolling guards woke him up, he told himself that in another emergency his courage could never again electrify his being as it had before, and this thought oppressed and alarmed him. The next day, before the morning gun was fired, the Captain of the Guard opened a door for him and he found the two ladies, strolling by the outer fortifications, waiting. I went with them as far as Neunhoffen, for they were to be married at the Haguenau registry office, after which they were returning to Metz for the religious ceremony.

"Emilie's brother, Wilhelm, welcomed Desroches cordially enough, and the two brothers-in-law measured each other up now and again. Wilhelm was of medium height, but well-knit. His fair hair was already receding, as if long study or great grief had weakened him, and he wore dark glasses because, he said, his eyes were so poor that the least light pained him. Desroches had brought a bundle of papers with him, which the young law student examined carefully. Then Wilhelm produced the title-deeds to his family property, insisting that Desroches should inspect them, but he was dealing with a man who was trusting, unselfish, and in love, and the investigation did not last long. This attitude seemed to flatter Wilhelm somewhat; he began taking Desroches's arm as they walked, he began offering him the use of his best pipes, and he introduced him to his friends at Haguenau.

"All this entailed much smoking and beer-drinking and after ten introductions Desroches begged for mercy and from then on was allowed to spend his evenings alone with his fiancée.

"A few days later the two lovers of the promenade bench were married by the Mayor of Haguenau, a worthy functionary who must have been Burgomaster before the French Revolution; he had often held Emilie in his arms when she was a little child and possibly he had even registered her birth; thus the day before her marriage he had whispered to her, 'Why aren't you marrying a good German?'

"Emilie did not seem to give much thought to matters of nationality. Meanwhile, the Lieutenant's mustache no longer offended Wilhelm for, to tell the truth, there had been some coolness between the two men at first. Desroches, however, had made great concessions, Wilhelm a few for his sister's sake, and with Emilie's aunt tactfully guiding every interview, there was perfect agreement between them. After the signing of the marriage settlements Wilhelm embraced his brother-in-law most cordially. By nine in the morning all was in order and the four of them set out for Metz that day. At six in the evening the coach stopped at the hôtel du Dragon at Bitche.

"Travel is none too easy in this district of streams and woods; there are ten hills to every mile you go, and the coach shakes up its passengers pretty badly. This was probably the main reason for the young bride's feeling slightly unwell when they reached the inn. Her aunt and Desroches stayed with her, and Wilhelm, who was feeling famished, went down to the little dining-room where the officers dined at eight o'clock.

"This time no one knew of Desroches's arrival. The soldiers of the garrison had spent a field-day in the Huspoletden woods. Desroches was determined not to be taken from his wife's side and told the landlady not to mention his name to a soul. The three of them stood at the window and watched the troops re-enter the fort, and then later, as the evening darkened, they saw the canteens fill up with soldiers in undress uniform coming for their Army bread and goat's-milk cheese.

"Wilhelm, meanwhile, trying to pass the time and assuage his hunger, had lit a pipe and was lounging near the doorway, breathing in both tobacco smoke and the smell of cooking, twin pleasures for an unoccupied and hungry man. Seeing this middle-class traveller with his cap over his ears and his dark glasses fixed on the kitchen, the officers took it that he was going to dine with them and looked forward to meeting him; perhaps he had come from a distance, could tell a good joke, had some news—this would be a stroke of luck. Alternatively, if he came from the district and maintained a stupid silence, they could poke fun at the simpleton.

"A Second Lieutenant from the military school approached Wilhelm with simulated politeness.

'Good evening, sir. Do you have any news from Paris?'

'No, sir, do you?' Wilhelm replied quietly.

'Good Lord, we never leave Bitche, how on earth would we know anything?'

'And I never leave my office.'

'Are you in the Engineers?'

"This quip, aimed at Wilhelm's spectacles, delighted the other officers.

'I am clerk to a notary, sir.'

'Really? That's odd, at your age.'

'Do you wish to see my passport, sir?' said Wilhelm.

'Of course not.'

'All right. If you assure me you are not simply making a fool of me, I will answer all your questions.'

"The officers became more serious.

'I asked you, without any ill intention, if you were in the Engineers, since you have glasses on. Perhaps you don't know it, but the officers of that corps are the only ones allowed to wear them.'

'Does that mean I am necessarily in the Army, then . . .'

'But everyone's in the Army today. You aren't twenty-five yet, you must be in the Army; or perhaps you're rich, perhaps you have an income of fifteen or twenty thousand francs, your parents have made certain sacrifices for you . . . in which case you wouldn't be eating at this inn table.'

"Wilhelm shook out his pipe. 'I suppose, sir, you have the right to subject me to this inquisition; let me, however, answer you categorically. I have no income, I am simply a clerk to a notary, as I informed you. I have been excused service on account of my eyes. In a word, I am short-sighted.'

"This declaration was greeted with roars of laughter.

'My dear chap, my dear chap,' Captain Vallier cried out, slapping him on the shoulder, 'you're perfectly right, you know the proverb—Be a coward and keep on living!'

"Wilhelm flushed crimson. 'I am not a coward, Captain, as I will prove to you whenever you like. What's more, my papers are in order and, if you are a recruiting officer, I will show them to you.'

'That's enough,' several of the officers exclaimed, 'let the fellow alone, Vallier. He's a perfectly peaceful chap with every right to dine here.'

'Yes, of course,' said the Captain, 'let's sit down and eat. No harm meant, young man. You're quite safe, I'm not the recruiting doctor and this isn't the recruiting room. To show there's no ill feeling, what about a wing of this tough old animal they try to pass off as a chicken?'

'Thank you,' said Wilhelm, whose appetite had vanished, 'one of those trout at the end of the table will be enough for me.' And he signed to the waitress to bring him the plate.

'Are they trout, really?' The Captain watched Wilhelm as he took off his spectacles to eat. 'Well, well, you've got better eyesight than I have; look here, frankly, you could handle a gun as well as the next man . . . but somebody used influence, you've made good use of it, all right. You prefer a peaceful existence, eh? Like everyone else. But if I were in your shoes I wouldn't be able to read about young men of my age being killed in Germany in the Army Bulletins without my blood boiling. Perhaps you aren't French?'

'No,' said Wilhelm, in a tone of strained satisfaction. 'I was born at Haguenau. I am not French, I am German.'

'German? But Haguenau is on this side of the Rhine frontier, it's one of the finest villages in the French Empire. Province of the Lower Rhine. Look at the map.'

'I come from Haguenau, I tell you, which was ten years ago a German village, today French. ⁵ And I shall always be German, just as you would always be French, if your country ever belonged to Germany.'

'These are dangerous things you're saying, young man. Be careful.'

'Perhaps I am wrong,' Wilhelm continued impetuously. 'Since I cannot change my feelings, perhaps I should keep them to myself. But you yourselves led the matter on and forced me either to justify myself at any price, or be considered a coward. Yes, now you know the motive which, to my mind, justifies my making such use of a very real infirmity, but one which, I suppose, would not stand in the way of someone who wanted to defend his country. Yes, I must admit the truth, I have no hatred for the people you are fighting today. If it had been my misfortune to have had to march against them, I imagine I too would have had to lay waste German territory, burn German villages, kill my fellow-countrymen or, if you prefer, my former fellow-countrymen, and—who knows?—kill, yes, kill my own flesh and blood, some friends of my father's, in some group of pretended enemies ... Come now, surely you can see that it's better for me to be busying myself with documents in the office of the notary of Haguenau ... Besides, there has been enough blood shed in my family. My father gave his, to the last drop, you see, and so I ...'

'Your father was a soldier?' interrupted Captain Vallier.

'My father was a Sergeant in the Prussian Army and he defended

⁵ Actually both Haguenau and Bitche have been French since 1648.

this territory you are occupying today for a long time. Finally he was killed in the last assault on the fort at Bitche.'

"Everyone became extremely interested at Wilhelm's last words which had put an end to their previous desire to refute his nonsense about his nationality.

'So it was in '93?'

'In '93, on November 17th. My father had left Pirmasen the day before to rejoin his Company. I know he told my mother that by means of a bold plan the fort was going to be taken without a shot fired. Twenty-four hours later he was brought back to us dying; he passed away on our doorstep, after he had made me swear to stay with my mother. She survived him by only fifteen days.

'I later learnt that in the night's attack a young soldier's sword had pierced his chest, thus killing one of the finest grenadiers in the Army of Prince Hohenlohe.'

'But this is the story we've just heard,' said a Major.

'Yes,' agreed Captain Vallier, 'that's exactly the same story as Desroches killing the Prussian Sergeant.'

'Desroches!' Wilhelm exclaimed. 'Do you mean Lieutenant Desroches?'

'Oh no, no,' one of the officers went on hastily, realizing that they were on the brink of a terrible revelation. 'The Desroches we're talking about was a light infantryman of the garrison who was killed four years ago, the first time he went into action.'

'So he's dead, is he,' said Wilhelm, mopping his brow from which the perspiration was streaming.

"A few minutes later the officers took their leave of him and withdrew. Desroches, from his window, saw them go, and went down into the dining-room where he found his brother-in-law leaning over the long table with his head in his hands.

'Well, well, asleep already?... I'm going to have something to eat. My wife's finally got to sleep and I'm famished... Let's have a glass of wine, it'll wake us up and you'll keep me company here, won't you?'

'No, I have a headache,' said Wilhelm, 'I'm going up to bed. By the way, those gentlemen told me some interesting things about the fort. Can you show me over it tomorrow?'

'But of course I can, old man.'

'Right. I'll wake you up in the morning.'

"Having eaten, [6] Desroches went up and fell asleep in the other bed in Wilhelm's room—he was not sleeping with his wife until after the religious ceremony had taken place. Wilhelm lay awake all night, at times silently weeping, at times staring furiously at Desroches, who smiled in his dreams.

"What we call presentiment is very like the pilot-fish which warns an enormous, semi-blind marine mammal of some sharp rock sticking out here, or of a sandbank there. We go through life so mechanically that some of the more careless of us would bang or even kill themselves without having a moment to think of God, if nothing ever troubled the surface of their happiness. Some grow gloomy over the way a raven is flying, others for no apparent reason, and yet others wake up extremely anxious if they have had some sinister dream. Such is presentiment. You are going to be in danger, says the dream; look out, cries the raven; be sad, murmurs the depressed mind.

"Towards the end of the night Desroches had a strange dream. He was in some passage under the earth; behind him stalked a white shape whose garments kept brushing Desroches's heels; when he turned round, the shadow sank back; eventually it withdrew so far away that Desroches could only see a white speck; this speck grew bigger and brighter until it filled the whole underground place with its radiance. Then it went out. He heard a slight noise. It was Wilhelm coming into the room with his hat on and wearing a long blue cloak.

"Desroches woke up with a start.

[6] The Champion text, which I have used, gives "soupira." Nicolas Popa, however, amends this to "soupa," which is far more likely in the circumstances. In the same way I have adopted Popa's correction of the Champion "Sirmasen"—some lines up—to "Pirmasen."

'Good Lord!' he exclaimed. 'Have you been out already this morning?'

'You must get up,' Wilhelm replied.

'But will they let us in at the fort?'

'I'm sure they will. All except the guards are out drilling.'

'Already! All right, I'll be with you ... Just give me a moment to say good-morning to my wife.'

'She's quite all right, I've seen her. Don't worry about her.'

"Desroches was somewhat surprised by this reply, but he put it down to impatience and gave in once again to this fraternal authority which he would soon be able to shake off.

"As they crossed the square on their way to the fort, Desroches looked up at one of the windows of the inn. Emilie is asleep, he thought. But the curtain moved, closing slightly, and Desroches thought he saw someone step back from the windowpane as if to avoid being seen by him.

"They were admitted to the fort without difficulty. A disabled Captain, who had not been at the Dragon the previous evening, was officer in charge of the outer guard. Desroches asked for a lantern and began taking his silent companion over room after room.

"Desroches spent some time showing various points of interest to Wilhelm, who paid little attention and then said: 'Aren't you going to show me the underground passages?'

'Of course, if you wish, but I assure you it won't be very pleasant. The damp down there is terrible. The gunpowder is kept under the left wing and that we can't visit without a special permit. To the right are the water-mains and the saltpeter. Down the center, the countermines and galleries ... Do you know what one of those vaults is like?'

'It doesn't matter, I'm curious to see the place where so many sinister encounters have taken place ... where you yourself, so they say, were once in danger of your life.'

"Desroches thought, I'm to be spared nothing. But he said, 'This way then, brother, this gallery leads to the iron postern gate.'

"The lantern-light flickered dismally on the mildewed walls, its reflection shivering here and there on saber blades and gun barrels corroded by rust.

'What weapons are these?' inquired Wilhelm.

'Taken off the Prussians killed during the last attack on the fort. My comrades hung them up here as trophies.'

'So several Prussians were killed here, then?'

'A great many were killed at this central meeting-place...'

'Did you not kill a Sergeant here, a tall, elderly man with a red mustache?'

'Yes, I did. Did I tell you the story?'

'No, you did not. But at dinner last night I heard about that exploit... which you so modestly kept from us.'

'What's the matter, brother? Why have you turned so pale?'

"In a loud voice Wilhelm answered:

'Don't call me brother, call me enemy!... Look, I'm a Prussian! I am the son of that Sergeant you murdered.'

'Murdered!'

'Or killed, what's the difference! Look, here's where your sword went in.'

"Wilhelm had thrown off his cloack and he now pointed to a tear in a green uniform he had on, his father's uniform which he had reverently kept.

'You—the son of that Sergeant! For God's sake, say you're joking!'

'Joking! Does one joke about such a frightful deed as that?... My father was killed here, his noble blood reddened these stones; perhaps this was his saber! Go on, take another one down and let me have my revenge... Come on, it isn't a duel, it's German against Frenchman. *En garde!*'

'My dear Wilhelm, you're mad. Put that rusty sword down. Do you want to kill me... was it my fault?'

'So now you have a chance to kill me as well, double or quits. Come on, defend yourself.'

'Wilhelm! Kill me, then, unarmed; I'm going crazy, my head's spinning... Wilhelm! I did what every soldier has to do. Think

about it for a moment . . . What's more, I'm your sister's husband;
she loves me. Oh no, this is impossible.'

'My sister! . . . and that's exactly why we can't both of us remain
alive! My sister! She knows all about it and she's never going to
set eyes on the man who made her an orphan again. Yesterday
you said your last goodby to Emilie.'

"Desroches gave a dreadful cry and threw himself on Wilhelm
to disarm him; it was a lengthy fight, for the younger man answered
Desroches's shaking with a strength born of fury and desperation.

'Give me that saber, you idiot!' Desroches cried out. 'Give
it me! No, you shan't kill me, you infernal madman . . . dreamer! . . .'

'That's it,' Wilhelm shouted out in a stifled tone, 'kill the son
in the same gallery . . . the son's a German, too . . . yes, German! . . .'

"At that moment footsteps were heard and Desroches let go.
Wilhelm was overcome and did not stir . . .

"Those footsteps were mine, gentlemen," said the Abbé. "Emilie had come to the presbytery and told me everything. The poor
child wished to put herself under the protection of the Church.
I restrained the pity welling up from my heart, and when she asked
if she could still love her father's murderer, I said nothing. She
understood, shook my hand, and left in tears. Then I had a presentiment. I followed her to the inn and when I heard them tell
her that her brother and her husband had gone together to the
fort, I suspected what might be happening. Luckily I arrived in
time to stop those two men, out of their minds, one with anger,
the other with grief, from committing a further atrocity.

"Although now disarmed, Wilhelm still resisted Desroches's
pleading; he was overcome, but his eyes still flashed with fury.

"I reproached him for his obstinacy. 'It is you,' I said, 'who
are resurrecting the dead and bringing up these dreadful happenings
again. Aren't you a Christian? Do you want to trespass on God's
justice? Do you want to become the real criminal, the real murderer in this affair? Atonement will be made, be sure of that;
but it's not for us to anticipate it or force it.'

"Desroches shook my hand and said to me: 'Emilie knows everything. I shall never see her again. But I know what I have to do, to give her back her freedom.'

'What are you saying?' I cried. 'Suicide?'

"At this word Wilhelm got up and took Desroches's hand. 'No,' he said, 'I have been wrong. I've been the really guilty one. I should have kept this secret suffering to myself.'

"I will not describe the anguish we all went through on that fateful morning; I used every religious and philosophic argument I knew without finding a satisfactory way out of that cruel situation; a separation was, in any case, inevitable, but how state the grounds in court? It would not only have been a painful ordeal for all of them, but there would also be political danger in bringing the dreadful affair to light.

"First and foremost, I devoted myself to defeating Desroches's dark intentions and to trying to induce in him religious sentiments which would make suicide seem like a crime. You know that the poor fellow had been fed Eighteenth-Century materialism at school. Since his wound, however, his ideas had changed considerably. He had become one of those somewhat sceptical Christians—of whom we have so many—who have concluded that, after all, a little religion never did anyone any harm, and who resign themselves to consulting even a priest just in case there might be a God! It was because of this vague sympathy with religion that he accepted my commiserations. Some days went by. Wilhelm and his sister were still at the inn; for Emilie had fallen ill after the shock. Desroches stayed at the presbytery with me and spent his days reading pious books that I lent him. One day he went to the fort by himself, stayed there for some hours, and, on his return, showed me a sheet of paper with his name on it; it was an appointment as Captain to a Regiment just leaving to join the Partouneaux division.

"After about a month we heard the news of his glorious, and yet singular, death. Whatever may have been the sort of frenzy that drove Desroches into the thick of the battle, his example was apparently a splendid encouragement to the whole Battalion which had sustained heavy losses in the first charge . . ."

All three men were silent as the Abbé finished his story. Each was thinking how strange had been this life and this death. Rising to his feet, the Abbé said: "If you like, gentlemen, we can alter our usual walk this evening and, by following that avenue of poplars going yellow in the sunset, I will take you to the Butte-aux-Lierres. From there we shall be able to see the cross of the convent where Madame Desroches withdrew."

AURELIA

Life and the Dream [1]

[1] The text used for this translation is the one established by Mlle Diane de Rossi, and published as Nerval, *Aurélia*, Genève, Éditions d'Art Albert Skira, 1944. It was collated with the text published in Nerval, *Oeuvres*, texte établi, annoté et présenté par Albert Béguin et Jean Richer, Paris, Gallimard, "Bibliothèque de la Pléiade," 1952, which appeared during the course of this translation. Part I, comprising ten chapters and covering a period of approximately ten years, was published in *La Revue de Paris* for January 1st, 1855; Part II, covering only about two years, appeared in the same review for February 15th, 1855. Substantially it is this original text translated here. Excellent English translations, of the emended Gautier/Houssaye text which Béguin/Richer do not accept, have been made by Richard Aldington (London, Chatto and Windus, 1932), and Vyvyan Holland (London, First Edition Club, 1933). I might perhaps add that the Béguin/Richer *Oeuvres* reprints the edition of *Les Filles du Feu* which I have utilized, namely that established by Nicolas Popa "dont l'édition commentée est impeccable." However, this recent selection of the *Oeuvres* does not include *Emilie*.

PART ONE

I.

Our dreams are a second life. I have never been able to penetrate without a shudder those ivory or horned gates which separate us from the invisible world. The first moments of sleep are an image of death; a hazy torpor grips our thoughts and it becomes impossible for us to determine the exact instant when the "I", under another form, continues the task of existence. Little by little a vague underground cavern grows lighter and the pale gravely immobile shapes that live in limbo detach themselves from the shadows and the night. Then the picture takes form, a new brightness illumines these strange apparitions and gives them movement. The spirit world opens before us.

Swedenborg called these visions *Memorabilia*; he owed them more often to musing than to sleep; *The Golden Ass* of Apuleius, Dante's *Divine Comedy*, are two poetic models of such studies of the human soul. Following their example I am going to try to describe the impressions of a long illness which took place entirely within the mysteries of my soul; I do not know why I use the word "illness," for as far as my physical self was concerned, I never felt better. Sometimes I thought my strength and energy were doubled, I seemed to know everything, understand everything. My imagination gave me infinite delight. In recovering what men call reason, do I have to regret the loss of those joys? . . .

This *Vita Nuova* had two phases for me. Here are the notes belonging to the first. A woman whom I had loved for a long while, and whom I shall call Aurélia, was lost to me. The circumstances of this event, which was to have such a great effect on my life, are of little importance. Each one of us can search his

memory for the most heart-rending emotion he has known, the
most terrible blow that fate has inflicted on his soul. It is a question
of deciding whether to go on living, or die. I will later explain
why I did not choose death. Condemned by the woman I loved,
guilty of a fault for which I could no longer hope for forgiveness,
nothing was left to me but to throw myself into vulgar distractions.
I affected gaiety and lack of concern. I travelled about the world,
and was foolishly fascinated by variety and caprice. I fell in love
with the costumes and curious habits of distant peoples, for it
seemed to me that in this way I was changing the conditions of
good and evil, the terms—so to speak—of what for us Frenchmen
are the "feelings."

"What madness," I told myself, "to go on platonically loving
a woman who no longer loves you. This is the evil result of your
reading. You have taken the conceits of poets quite seriously
and fashioned for yourself a Laura or a Beatrice out of an ordinary
person of the present century . . . You'll forget her directly you
start a new affair."

The dizzy whirl of a merry carnival in an Italian town dispelled
all my melancholy ideas. I was so happy at the relief I felt that
I informed all my friends of my joy and, in my letters, gave them
as the permanent state of my spirit what was but a feverish over-
excitement.

One day a very well-known woman arrived in the town. She
made friends with me and, accustomed as she was to giving an
effect of both pleasure and brilliance, drew me without difficulty
into the circle of her admirers. At the end of an evening during
which she had been both simple and yet full of a charm that everyone had felt, I imagined myself so smitten by her that I wrote
to her without waiting a moment. I was so happy to feel my heart
capable of a new love! . . . In this artificial enthusiasm I borrowed
the same forms of expression which, so short a while ago, I had
used to declare a true and long-felt love. As soon as the letter
had gone, I wanted to take it back, and in my solitude I dreamed
over what seemed to me a profanation of my memories.

The next evening lent my new love the glamor of the night before. The lady showed herself affected by what I had written, being at the same time astonished by my sudden ardor. I had, in one day, gone through many stages of those feelings that a man can experience for a woman with sincerity. She confessed that my letter had surprised her and yet made her proud.

I tried to be convincing, but despite all I endeavored to say I could no longer attain the same high style of my letter in our talks, with the result that I was reduced to avowing—with tears in my eyes—that I had deceived myself and abused her. Perhaps my maudlin confidence had charm, however, for my vain protestations of affection were replaced by a friendship far stronger in its gentleness.

II.

Later I met her in another town, where there was also the lady with whom I was hopelessly in love. [2] By chance they met each other, and there is no doubt that my new friend took the opportunity of softening towards me the one from whose heart I had been exiled. The result was that one day I found myself at the same party as her, and she came up to me, holding out her hand. How was I to interpret this action and the sad long look which accompanied her greeting? I imagined it meant forgiveness for the past. The divine accent of pity gave the simple words she addressed to me an indescribable value as though something re-

---

[2] The two women are Marie Pleyel and Jenny Colon. The meeting between them, though, is thought to be apocryphal. Nerval met Marie Pleyel in his 1839-40 stay in Vienna (probably on December 22nd, 1839) after his liaison with Jenny of 1837-38, and it is Vienna that, at the end of *Aurélia*, provides the sinner with the key word *pardon*. Pierre Audiat shows that, if the meeting did take place, it is likely to have been in Brussels—"dans une froide capitale du Nord," as the *Pandora* puts it—which city Jenny visited at the time Nerval and Marie Pleyel were there, in order to perform in *Piquillo* at the théâtre de la Monnaie. By a quirk of circumstance, "Adrienne" (Sophie de Feuchères) died in London on the very day of this première of *Piquillo* at Brussels.

ligious had mingled with the sweetness of a love until then profane,
and impressed upon it the quality of eternity.

An imperative duty compelled me to return to Paris, but I was
firmly resolved not to stay there more than a few days and then
to come back to my two friends. Joy and impatience induced in
me a kind of giddiness which was aggravated by the business of
having to settle my affairs. One evening, at about midnight, I was
returning to the quarter where I lived, when I happened to raise
my eyes and notice the number on a house, lit by a street-lamp.
The number was that of my own age. As I looked down I saw
in front of me a woman with hollow eyes, whose features seemed
to me like Aurélia's. I said to myself: "I am being warned of
either her death or mine." For some reason I decided on the latter
of the two ideas, and had the impression that it would come about
at the same time on the following day.

That night I had a dream which confirmed me in my belief.

I was wandering about a vast building composed of several
rooms, some of which were given up to study, others to conversation or philosophical discussion. Rather interested I remained
in one of the first of these, and thought I recognized my old in-
structors and fellow-students. The lessons on Greek and Latin
authors went on in that steady hum which sounds like a prayer
to the goddess Mnemosyne. I passed on into another room where
the philosophical discussions were taking place. I took part in one
for a while, then went to look for my own room in a sort of inn
with gigantic staircases crowded with hurrying travellers.

I got lost several times in the long corridors and then, as I was
going through one of the central galleries, I was struck by a strange
sight. A creature of enormous proportions—man or woman I do
not know—was fluttering painfully through the air and seemed
to be struggling with heavy clouds. At last, out of breath and at
the end of its strength, it collapsed into the middle of the dark
courtyard, catching and crumpling its wings on the roofs and bal-
ustrades. For a moment I was able to observe it closely. It was
colored with ruddy hues and its wings glittered with a myriad

changing reflections. Clad in a long gown of antique folds, it looked like Dürer's *Angel of Melancholy*. I could not keep myself from crying out in terror and this woke me up with a start.

The next day I hurried to see all my friends. Mentally I said farewell to them and, telling them nothing of what was in my mind, I talked warmly on mystical matters. I surprised them by being particularly eloquent. It seemed to me as if I knew everything and that in those last moments of mine the mysteries of the world were being revealed to me.

That evening, as the fatal hour approached, I was seated with two of my friends round a table discussing painting and music, defining my idea of the generation of colors and the meaning of numbers. One of them, Paul, wanted to take me home, but I told him I was not going back.

"Where are you going?" he asked me.

"*To the East*." [3]

And, as he walked with me, I began searching the sky for a star I thought I knew as having some influence on my fate. When I had found it, I went on walking, following the streets from which it was visible, walking, as it were, towards my destiny, anxious to see the star up to the moment when death would strike me down.

When we had reached a junction of three streets, however, I refused to go any further. It seemed that my friend was employing superhuman strength to make me move. He grew larger in my eyes and took on the aspect of an Apostle. The spot on which we stood seemed to rise up and lose its urban appearance: on a

---

[3] Jules Janin gives a contemporary account of Nerval's hallucinated behavior here. Indeed Audiat, one of the most assiduous, and severe, critics of Nerval's work believes that Nerval actually used Janin's account when composing this episode of *Aurélia*. It should be said that there are several critics who feel that Nerval had little, if any, original imaginative ability, and they support their views by discoveries of this kind. The newcomer to Nerval, meanwhile, is advised to approach these questions of literary detection through the following general volume: Aristide Marie, *Gérard de Nerval. Le Poète—L'Homme*, Paris, Librairie Hachette, 1914, a new edition of which is being prepared as I write.

hill, surrounded by enormous solitudes, that scene became a struggle
between two spirits, like a Biblical temptation.

"No," I cried, "I don't belong to your Heaven. Those in that
star are waiting for me. They went before the revelation you have
announced to me. Let me go to them, for the one I love belongs
to them, and it is there we are to meet again."

III.

Here began what I shall call the overflowing of the dream into
real life. From that moment on, everything took on at times a
double aspect—and did so, too, without my powers of reasoning
ever losing their logic or my memory blurring the least details
of what happened to me. Only my actions were apparently in-
sensate, subject to what is called hallucination, according to human
reason . . .

Many times the idea has occurred to me that in certain ·serious
moments in life some Spirit of the outer world becomes suddenly
embodied in the form of an ordinary person, and influences or
tries to influence us without the individual in question having
any knowledge of it or remembering anything about it.

Seeing that his efforts were useless, my friend had left me, no
doubt imagining that I was prey to some obsession which the
walk would calm away. When I found myself alone, I pulled
myself together with an effort and set off again in the direction
of the star, from which I had never removed my eyes. As I walked
along I sang a mysterious hymn which I seemed to remember
having heard in a previous existence, and which filled me with
ineffable joy. At the same time I took off my terrestrial garments
and scattered them about me. The roadway seemed to lead continually upwards and the star to grow bigger. Then I stood still,
my arms outstretched, waiting for the moment when my soul
should break free from my body, attracted magnetically by the
rays of the star. A shudder went through me. Regret for the earth

and for those I loved there gripped my heart, and so ardently within myself did I beseech the Spirit drawing me up towards it that it seemed as if I went down again among men. A night patrol surrounded me. I had the idea that I had grown very big and that since I was possessed of electrical forces I would overthrow all who approached me. There was something comic in the care I took to spare the strength and lives of the soldiers who had picked me up.

If I did not think that a writer's duty is to analyze with sincerity what he feels in grave moments of life, and if I had not in view to be useful, I would stop here, and make no attempt to describe my later experiences in a series of visions which were either insane or, vulgarly, diseased.

Stretched out on a camp bed, I thought I saw the sky unveil itself to me as if to make me full of remorse for having wished, with all the strength of my spirit, to step down again on the earth I was leaving ... Immense circles took shape in infinity, like the orbs formed by water when something falls in and disturbs it. Each region was peopled with radiant faces and took on color, moved and melted in turn, and a Divinity, always the same, tossed away smiling the furtive masks of its various incarnations and at last imperceptibly took refuge in the mystic splendors of the Asiatic skies.

By one of those phenomena that everyone must have experienced in certain dreams, this celestial vision did not make me oblivious of what was going on around me. Lying on the camp bed, I heard the soldiers talking about some unknown person, who had been arrested like me, and whose voice had rung out in the same room. By a strange effect of vibration it felt as though his voice was echoing in my own chest, and that my soul was, so to speak, assuming a dual existence—distinctly divided between vision and reality. For a second I thought of making an effort to turn towards the person in question; then I shivered as I remembered a well-known German superstition which says that everyone has a *double* and that when you see him death is close at hand. I shut my eyes and went into a confused state of mind where the fantastic or real figures around me broke up into a thousand fugitive shapes. Once I saw by me two of my friends who were there reclaiming me: the soldiers pointed me out: then the door opened and someone of my build, whose face I could not see, went out with my friends to whom I called out vainly.

"But there's some mistake!" I cried. "They came for me and someone else has gone out."

I made so much noise that they put me in a cell.

For some hours I remained there in a sort of stupor: finally the two friends whom I imagined I had seen already came to fetch me in a carriage. I told them everything that had happened, but they denied having come during the night. I dined with them quite calmly. But as night approached, it seemed that I had to dread the same hour which, the day before, had nearly proved fatal to me. I asked one of them for an Oriental ring he wore on his finger, which I looked on as an ancient talisman. I took a scarf and knotted the ring around my neck, taking care to turn the stone, which was a turquoise, on to a place on the nape of my neck where I felt a pain. 4 I was convinced that it was through this spot that my soul would try to leave my body, at the moment when a certain ray from the star I had seen the night before coincided, in relation to myself, with its zenith. Either by chance, or as a result of my profound preoccupation, I fell down as though struck by a thunderbolt at the same time as on the evening before. I was put on a bed, and for a long time I lost the meaning and connection of images that came to me. This state lasted for several days. I was taken away to an asylum. Many of my friends and relations came to see me there without my being aware of it. The only difference as far as I was concerned between waking and sleeping was that in the former everything was transfigured in my eyes. Everyone who came near me seemed changed, material objects appeared in a dim penumbra that softened their shapes; shafts of light and the combinations of colors were dis-

4 Nerval placed the ring on the "Brahma's hole" of Vedic literature.

torted in such a way as to keep me in a constant series of inter-
linked impressions, whose credibility was continued in the dream
state, more abstracted as it was from exterior elements.

IV.

One evening I was positive I had been removed to the banks
of the Rhine. In front of me were sinister rocks, their silhouettes
dimly outlined in the gloom. I went into a cheerful house, where
a ray from the setting sun cut through the green shutters which
were festooned with vines. It appeared to me that I was entering
a house I knew well, belonging to one of my mother's uncles,
a Flemish painter who had been dead for more than a century.
Half-finished pictures hung here and there: one was of the famous
water-spirit of these parts. An old woman servant, whom I called
Marguerite and whom I seemed to have known from infancy,
said to me:

"Why don't you lie down on your bed? You've come a long
way and your uncle won't be in until late. We'll wake you up
for supper."

I lay down on a four-poster bed whose drapes were decorated
with large red flowers. In front of me, hung on the wall, was a
rustic clock and on this clock was a bird which began to talk like
a human being. I had the idea that my grandfather's soul was in
that bird, but I was no more astonished by his new shape and
speech than I was to find myself transported a century back. The
bird talked to me about living members of my family and of those
who had died at various times or other as if they were all contemporaries, and said to me:

"You see your uncle took care to paint *her* portrait in
advance ... Now *she* is with us."

I turned to a canvas of a woman dressed in an old German
costume: she was leaning over a river bank, her eyes fixed on a
cluster of forget-me-nots. Then little by little the darkness thick-
ened and the shapes, sounds and the feeling of places became con-

fused in my sleepy spirit; I thought I was falling into a chasm that crossed the world. I felt myself carried painlessly along on a current of molten metal, and a thousand similar streams, the colors of which indicated different chemicals, criss-crossed the breast of the world like those blood-vessels and veins that writhe in the lobes of the brain. They all flowed, circulated and throbbed just like that, and I had a feeling that their currents were composed of living souls in a molecular condition, and that the speed of my own movement alone prevented me from distinguishing them. A whitish light filtered bit by bit into these channels, and at last I saw spread out before me a new horizon like an enormous cupola in which were scattered islands surrounded by luminous waves. I found myself on a bright shore, in this sunless day, and I saw an old man tilling the earth. I recognized him as the man who had spoken to me through the bird's voice, and, either because he told me directly or because I understood it innately, it became clear to me that our ancestors take the forms of certain animals in order to visit us on earth, and that thus they are present as silent observers of the various phases of our existence.

The old man left his work and came with me to a house that stood nearby. The surrounding countryside reminded me of a part of Flanders where my parents lived and have their graves today. The hedged field skirting the wood, the neighboring lake, the river where the laundry is done, the village itself with its steep street, the hills of dark rock and their tufts of broom and heather— it was a rejuvenated image of the places I had loved. Only the house I went into was unknown to me. I understood it had existed in some former period, and that in this world I was now visiting the ghosts of material things accompanied those of human bodies.

I entered a large room where a crowd of people had gathered. On all sides I found faces I knew. The features of dead relations, whom I had mourned, were there reproduced in others who, clad in more ancient costumes, gave me the same paternal greeting.

They appeared to have collected for a family banquet. One of these relations came up and embraced me tenderly. He wore ancient clothes, the colors of which seemed to have faded, and his smiling face beneath his powdered hair somewhat resembled my own. He seemed to me to be more definitely alive than the others and, as it were, in closer contact with my own spirit. He was my uncle. He made me sit next to him and a kind of communication was established between us. I cannot say I heard his voice; only, as my thoughts settled on some question, the explanation immediately became clear to me, and images took distinct shape before my eyes like animated pictures.

"Then it's true," I exclaimed delightedly, "that we are immortal and retain here the replicas of the world we once inhabited. What happiness to think that everything we've loved will always exist around us!... I was very tired of life."

"Don't be too quick to rejoice," he said, "for you still belong to the world above and you have still to undergo hard years of trial. The abode that so delights you has itself its sorrows, its struggles, and its dangers. The earth on which we lived is still the theater where our destinies are woven and unravelled. We are the gleams of that central fire which gives it life and which is already growing weak..."

"What!" I cried. "Do you mean the earth could die and we be hurled into oblivion?"

"Oblivion," he answered, "does not exist in the sense it is understood, but the earth itself is a material body whose soul is the sum of the souls it contains. Matter can no more perish than mind, but it can be modified according to good and evil. Our past and future are intimately connected. We live in our race and our race lives in us."

This idea immediately became clear to me. The walls of the room seemed to open onto infinite perspectives and I saw an uninterrupted chain of men and women, in whom I was and who were myself: the costumes of every nation, visions of every country, all appeared to me distinctly at the same time, as if my faculties of observation had been multiplied—and yet not muddled—by a phenomenon of space comparable to that of time, whereby a century of action is concentrated in a minute of dream. My amazement grew as I saw that this vast assembly was composed only of those people who were in the room, and whose shapes I had seen separating and combining in a thousand fugitive aspects.

"There are seven of us," I said to my uncle.

"That is, in fact," he replied, "the emblematic number of every human family and, by extension, seven times seven, and so on." Seven was the number of Noah's family; but one of the seven was mysteriously related to the previous generations of the Elohim! 5 ... Imagination, in a lightning-flash, showed me the multiple gods of India like symbols of families as it were primitively concentrated. I fear to go further for there is also in the Trinity a terrible mystery... We are born under Biblical laws...

This answer, which I cannot hope to make comprehensible, remains very obscure even to me. No metaphysical terms exist in which to express the perception which came to me then of the relationship between this conglomeration of people and universal harmony. In father and mother we can see the analogy of the electric forces of nature; but how can we establish the individual forces that emanate from them, and from which they themselves emanate, like the *face* of a collective cosmogony whose component elements are simultaneously multiple and limited? You might as well enquire of the flower why it has that number of petals or that number of divisions in its corolla ... or the earth of the shapes it assumes, the sun of the colors it creates.

V.

Everything around me changed its form. The spirit with whom I was talking no longer looked the same. He was now a youth who received ideas from me rather than vice versa... Had I trav-

5 The Elohim, the Hebrew God or Gods, are often mentioned by Nerval. An excess of intellectual curiosity, the longing to understand the divine mysteries, Faust's fault, means for Nerval not only an infidelity to the Christian religion, but also, by association, to Aurélia.

elled too far in these vertiginous heights? I seemed to understand
that these questions were obscure and dangerous, even for the
spirits of that world I now saw ... Perhaps, too, some superior
power forbade me those enquiries. I saw myself wandering through
the streets of a busy, unknown city. I noticed that it was composed of many little hills and dominated by a mountain which
was covered with houses. Among the inhabitants of this metrop-
olis I distinguished certain men who appeared to belong to a
special nation; their keen, determined air and energetic cast of
countenance made me think of some independent warrior race
from the mountains, or from some seldom-visited islands; and
yet these men had managed to maintain their fierce individuality
in the center of a large city and surrounded by a mixed population
of ordinary people. Who were they? My guide made me climb
up steep and noisy streets where the various sounds of industry
could be heard. We went higher still by means of long flights
of steps, beyond which the view opened out. Here and there were
terraces clad in trellises, small gardens laid out on a few level spaces,
roofs, lightly-built summer-houses painted and carved with fantastic patience: vistas linked together by long trains of climbing
verdure seduced the eye and delighted the mind like a delicious
oasis, a neglected solitude above the tumult and the noise below,
which was here no more than a murmur. People often talk of
outlawed races living in the shadows of some necropolis or cat-
acomb; but here, there could be no doubt, was the opposite.
A blessed race had made for itself this retreat beloved of birds,
flowers, of pure air and sunlight.

"These," my guide informed me, "are the ancient inhabitants
of the mountain dominating the city and upon which we now
stand. They have lived here for a long time, with their simple
customs, kindly and just, preserving the natural virtues of the
world's earliest days. The people round about honored them and
modelled themselves upon them."

Following my guide I descended from the point where I was
to one of those tall dwellings, the joined roofs of which presented

such a strange appearance. It seemed to me as though my feet were sinking into successive layers of buildings of various ages. These ghostly edifices continually kept on uncovering others in which the style of each individual century was visible. To me they looked like the excavations of old cities, except that they were airy, animated, and crossed with thousands of rays of light. Finally I found myself in a vast hall where I saw an old man working at a table at something I could not recognize. The moment I crossed the threshold a man, dressed in white, whose face I was not able to see clearly, threatened me with a weapon he held in his hand: but my guide signed to him to go away. It appeared as though they had wished to stop me from penetrating the mysteries of these retreats. Without asking my guide anything, I intuitively understood that these heights—and depths also—were the sanctuary of the primitive inhabitants of the mountain. Continually stemming the advancing waves of new races, they lived there, with their simple customs, loving and just, clever, brave, and inventive, quietly conquering the blind masses who had so many times encroached on their heritage. They were, in fact, neither corrupted, nor destroyed, nor enslaved! They were pure although they had conquered ignorance, and they had preserved in prosperity the virtues of poverty! A child was on the floor playing with crystals, shells and engraved stones, no doubt turning its lesson into a game. An elderly, but still beautiful, woman was busying herself with her household duties. Then several young people came in noisily, as though returning from work. I was amazed to see them all dressed in white; but it seemed that this was an optical illusion on my part; to make this clear to me my guide began to draw their costumes for me and give them bright colors, making me understand what they were like in reality. The whiteness that surprised me came, perhaps, from some especial brilliancy, from a trick of light in which the ordinary hues of the prism became confused.

I left the room and found myself on a terrace laid out as a garden. Here young girls and little children were walking about and playing.

Their clothes seemed to me to be white like the others, but they were trimmed with pink embroidery. These young people were so beautiful, their features so graceful, and the light of their souls shone so vividly from their delicate forms, that they all inspired a sort of love without preference and devoid of all desire, an epitome of all the intoxications of the vague passions of youth.

I cannot communicate the feelings I had among these charming creatures who, although strangers, were very dear to me. They were like a primitive, heavenly family whose smiling eyes sought mine in soft compassion. I began to shed scalding tears as if at the memory of some lost paradise. I felt bitterly that I was only a wayfarer in this strange land that I loved, and I trembled at the thought that I had to return to life. In vain the girls and children pressed round me to try to detain me. Already their enchanting forms were melting in a misty confusion; their lovely faces faded, their clear-cut features and sparkling eyes vanished into a shadow where still shone the last gleam of a smile...

Such was that vision, or such at least the main details I can remember. The cataleptic state in which I had been for some days was explained away to me in scientific terms, and the remarks of those who had seen me then irritated me when I realized that they attributed to mental aberration my actions and words which coincided with the various phases of what were for me a series of logical events. But I felt a greater affection than ever for those of my friends who, from kindness or patience, or because of a set of ideas similar to mine, made me give long accounts of the things I had seen in my mind. With tears in his eyes, one of them said to me:

"Is it not true there is a God?"

"Yes!" I answered enthusiastically.

And we embraced each other, like two brothers of that mystic country I had half-seen. What happiness I found at first in that belief! For thus the eternal doubt about the immortality of the soul, which troubles the greatest minds, had been solved for me. No more death, no more sadness, no more cares. My loved ones, relatives, and friends, had given convincing proof of their eternal existence, and I was only separated from them by the hours of the day. I waited for the hours of the night with a gentle melancholy.

VI.

Another dream of mine confirmed me in this belief. I suddenly found myself in a room which formed part of my grandfather's house, only it seemed to have grown larger. The old furniture glowed with a miraculous polish, the carpets and curtains were as if new again, daylight three times more brilliant than natural day came in through the windows and the door, and in the air there was a freshness and perfume like the first warm morning of spring. Three women were working in the room and, without exactly resembling them, they stood for relatives and friends of my youth. Each seemed to have the features of several of them. Their facial contours changed like the flames of a lamp, and all the time something of one was passing to the other. Their smiles, the color of their eyes and hair, their figures and familiar gestures, all these were exchanged as if they had lived the same life, and each was made up of all three, like those figures painters take from a number of models in order to achieve a perfect beauty.

The eldest spoke to me in a vibrant, melodious voice which I recognized as having heard in my childhood, and whatever it was she said struck me as being profoundly true. But she drew my attention to myself and I saw I was wearing a little old-fashioned brown suit, entirely made of needlework threads as fine as a spider's web. It was elegant, graceful, and gently perfumed. I felt quite rejuvenated and most spruce in this garment which their fairy fingers had made, and I blushingly thanked them as if I had been a small boy in the presence of beautiful grown-up ladies. At that moment one of them got up and went towards the garden.

It is a well-known fact that no one ever sees the sun in a dream, although one is often aware of some far brighter light. Material objects and human bodies are illumined through their own agencies. Now I was in a little park through which ran long vine arbors, loaded with heavy clusters of black and white grapes; and as the lady, guiding me, passed beneath these arbors, the shadows of the intertwined trellis-work changed her figure and her clothes. At last we came out from these bowers of grapes to an open space. Traces of the old paths which had once divided it cross-wise were just visible. For some years the plants had been neglected and the sparse patches of clematis, hops and honeysuckle, of jasmine, ivy, and creepers, had stretched their long clinging tendrils between the sturdy growths of the trees. Branches of fruit were bowed to the ground and a few garden flowers, in a state of wildness now, bloomed among the weeds.

At distant intervals were clumps of poplars, acacias and pine-trees, and in the midst of these were glimpses of statues blackened by time. I saw before me a heap of rocks covered with ivy, from which gushed a spring of fresh water whose splashes echoed melodiously over a pool of still water, half-hidden by huge water-lilies.

The lady I was following stretched her slender figure in a movement that made the folds of her dress of shot taffeta shimmer, and gracefully she slid her bare arm about the long stem of a hollyhock. Then, in a clear shaft of light, she began to grow in such a way that gradually the whole garden blended with her own form, and the flowerbeds and trees became the patterns and flounces of her clothes, while her face and arms imprinted their contours on the rosy clouds in the sky. I lost her thus as she became transfigured, for she seemed to vanish in her own immensity.

"Don't leave me!" I cried. "For with you Nature itself dies."

With these words I struggled painfully through the brambles trying to grasp the vast shadow that eluded me. I threw myself on a fragment of ruined wall, at the foot of which lay the marble bust of a woman. I lifted it up and felt convinced it was of *her* . . . I recognized the beloved features and as I stared around me I saw that the garden had become a graveyard, and I heard voices crying: "The universe is in darkness."

VII.

This dream, which began so happily, perplexed me deeply, for I did not discover what it meant until much later. Aurélia was dead.

At first I only heard that she was ill. Owing to my state of mind I only felt a vague unhappiness mixed with hope. I believed that I myself had only a short while longer to live, and I was now assured of the existence of a world in which hearts in love meet again. Besides, she belonged to me much more in her death than in her life ... A selfish enough thought for which my reason later paid with bitter remorse.

I did not like abusing a presentiment, however. Chance does strange things. But at that time I was still obsessed by a memory of our too rapid union. I had given her a ring of antique workmanship whose stone was a heart-shaped opal. As this ring was too big for her finger, I had conceived the fatal idea of having it cut down; I only realized my mistake when I heard the noise of the saw. I seemed to see blood flowing ... [6]

Medical treatment had restored me to health without having yet brought my mind back to the regular functioning of human reason. The house I was in was on a hill and had a large garden full of valuable trees. The pure air of the slopes on which it stood, the first breath of spring, the pleasure of a sympathetic society, all brought me long days of calm.

I was enchanted by the vivid colors of the early sycamore leaves, like the crests of cock pheasants. From morning to evening one could gaze over the plain to charming horizons, the graduated hues of which delighted my imagination. I peopled the hills and clouds with heavenly figures whose shapes I seemed to see distinctly. I wanted to fix my favorite thoughts more clearly, and with some

[6] An incident probably borrowed from Hoffmann, whose cabalist Dapfühl files down a ring belonging to his daughter Annette, thereby producing thick black blood. Jenny's death, to which Nerval refers in the lines before this, was on June 5th, 1842.

charcoal and a few bits of brick that I collected I had soon covered the walls with a set of frescoes recording my impressions.
One face dominated the rest—that of Aurélia, painted in the shape
of a divinity, as she had appeared to me in my dream. Beneath
her feet a wheel was turning and the gods processed behind her.
I succeeded in coloring this group by crushing out the juice from
plants and flowers. How many times have I dreamed in front
of that dear idol! I did more, I tried to shape the body of my
beloved in clay. Every morning I had to begin again, for the
lunatics, jealous of my happiness, took pleasure in destroying its
image.

I was given paper, and for a long time I set about producing, by
means of verses and inscriptions in every known language and a
thousand forms and stories, a sort of world history mingled with
memories of my studies and fragments of dreams made more
plausible by my obsession (which was itself prolonged by them).
I did not confine myself to the modern traditions of creation. My
thoughts went further. As if in memory I caught a glimpse of
the first covenant made, by means of talismans, by the genii of
old. I tried to put together again the stones of the *sacred table* and
to represent around it the first seven *Elohim* who shared the
world.

This system of history, borrowed from Oriental tradition, began
with the peaceful agreement of the powers of nature who formed
and organized the universe. The night before I worked, I imagined myself transported to a dark planet where the first germs
of creation were struggling. From the bosom of the still soft clay
gigantic palm-trees towered high, poisonous spurge and acanthus
writhed around cactus plants: the arid shapes of rocks stuck out
like skeletons from this rough sketch of creation, and hideous
reptiles snaked, stretched, and coiled in the middle of the inextri-
cable network of wild vegetation. Only the pale light of the stars
lit the bluing perspectives of this strange horizon; yet, as the work
of creation proceeded, a brighter star began to draw from it the
germs of its own future brilliance.

VIII.

Then the monsters changed shape. They cast off their first skins and raised themselves up more powerfully on their ernomous paws. The great mass of their bodies crushed the branches and vegetation, and in this chaos of nature they engaged in struggles in which I myself was part, for I had a body as strange as theirs. Suddenly a singular harmony echoed through our solitudes and it seemed as if the confused cries, roarings and hissings of these primitive beings now took on this celestial melody. Infinite variations followed, the planet grew gradually lighter, heavenly shapes appeared among the shrubs and in the depths of the groves and, thus mastered, all the monsters I had seen shed their weird shapes and became men and women; others, in their reincarnations, assumed the bodies of wild animals, fishes and birds.

Who had performed this miracle? A radiant goddess guided the speedy evolution of man through these new *metamorphoses.* [7] A distinct race was established. Beginning with the birds, it comprised also animals, fishes and reptiles. There were Divas, Peris, undines and salamanders. Whenever one of the creatures died, it was immediately born again in a more beautiful form and sang the glory of the gods. But one of the Elohim conceived the idea of creating a fifth race composed of earthly elements and to be called *Afrites.* This was the signal for a complete revolution among the Spirits who did not wish to recognize these new lords of the world. I do not know for how many thousands of years these battles raged drenching the earth in blood. Finally, three of the Elohim, together with the spirits of their race, were relegated to the south of the world where they founded vast kingdoms. They had taken with them the secrets of the heavenly *Cabala* which link the worlds, and they had gathered strength from the adoration of certain stars with which they were always in correspondence. These necromancers, exiled to the ends of the earth, had

[7] Cf. Dante, *Paradiso*, Canto X, ll. 37-39.

agreed to transmit their power to one another. Surrounded by women and slaves, each of their sovereigns was assured of being born again in the form of one of his children. Their life lasted a thousand years. When they were about to die, powerful Cabalists shut them up in well-guarded tombs where they were fed elixirs and life-giving substances. They preserved the semblance of life for a long time. Then, as the chrysalis spins its cocoon, they fell asleep for forty days to be born again as a little child which was later called to the kingdom.

The vivifying forces of the world, however, were exhausted in feeding these families, whose blood went continually to fertilize fresh offsprings. In vast subterranean chambers, hollowed in hypogea and pyramids, they had collected all the treasures of past races and certain talismans which protected them against the anger of the gods.

These strange mysteries took place in central Africa, beyond the Mountains of the Moon and ancient Ethiopa: for a long time I groaned there in captivity together with a whole section of the human race. The groves I had once seen so green bore only pale flowers now and faded foliage: an inexorable sun consumed these regions, and the weak children of the eternal dynasties seemed crushed beneath the weight of life. This impressive and monotonous grandeur, ruled by custom and priestly ritual, was a burden on all, yet no one dared escape it. The old men languished under the weight of their crowns and imperial ornaments, among the doctors and priests whose knowledge guaranteed their immortality. As for the masses, they were fixed for ever in a caste system, and could be certain of neither life nor liberty. At the feet of trees smitten with death or sterility, at the mouths of dried-up springs, children withered and pale girls weakened away on the scorched grasses. The splendor of the royal rooms, the majesty of the porticos, the brilliance of robes and ornaments, all these were poor consolations for the eternal dreariness of these solitudes.

Soon illness ravaged the people, plants and animals died, and the immortals themselves wasted away under their pompous cos-

tumes. A scourge, more terrible than any before, came suddenly
to rejuvenate and save the world. Orion let loose cataracts of
water in the heavens. Earth, overweighted by ice at its opposite
pole, half-turned on its axis, and the oceans overflowed their banks
and poured over the plains of Africa and Asia. The flood saturated the sands, filled the tombs and pyramids, while for forty
days a mysterious ark floated on the waters, bearing the hope of
a new creation.

Three of the Elohim had taken refuge on the peak of the highest
mountain in Africa. They began fighting. Here my memory
grows vague, and I do not know the result of their battle. But
I can still see a woman standing on a peak lapped by the waters
they abandoned, crying out with disheveled hair and struggling
against death. Her pitiful cries rose above the noise of the waters . . .
Was she saved? I do not know. Her brothers, the gods, had
condemned her; but over her shone the Evening Star throwing
its flaming rays upon her forehead.

The interrupted hymn of heaven and earth resounded again
in harmony to hallow the agreement of the new races. Noah and
his sons toiled painfully under the rays of a new sun and the sor-
cerers, crouched in their underworld, still kept their treasures
there and revelled in the silence and the darkness. Sometimes they
issued timidly out of their fastnesses and came to frighten the living
or spread the disastrous lessons of their knowledges among the
wicked.

Such were the memories I retraced by a sort of vague intuition
of the past: I shuddered as I reproduced the hideous character-
istics of those accursed races. Everywhere the suffering image
of the eternal Mother was dying, weeping, or languishing. All
through remote Asiatic and African civilizations a bloody scene
of orgy and carnage was constantly renewed, reproduced by the
same spirits under different forms.

The last one took place at Granada, where the sacred talisman
fell before the hostile blows of Christians and Moors. How many
more years yet has the world still to suffer, for the vengeance of

those eternal enemies must inevitably be renewed under other skies! They are the severed sections of the serpent that encircles the Earth ... separated by steel, they join together again in a hideous embrace cemented by human blood.

IX.

Such were the visions which filed, one by one, before my eyes. Gradually calm came back to me and I left the house which had been a paradise for me. A long while later fateful circumstances brought about a relapse which renewed this interrupted series of strange dreams.

I was walking in the country, preoccupied with some work connected with religious ideas. I passed in front of a house and heard a bird repeating some words it had been taught. Yet this muddled prattling seemed to me to have some sense. It reminded me of the bird in the vision I have recounted above, and I shuddered with a foreboding of evil.

A few steps further on I met a friend whom I had not seen for a long time, and who lived in a house nearby. He wanted to show me his estate and in the course of doing so he made me climb a raised terrace with him, from which could be seen a wide view. It was sunset. As we descended the steps of a rustic stair I stumbled and struck my chest against the angle of a piece of garden furniture. I had just enough strength left to get up and dash into the middle of the garden, thinking I had received a death blow and wanting, before I died, to cast a last glance at the setting sun. Through all the regrets that such a moment brings, I felt happy to be dying this way, at this hour, surrounded by the trees, trellises and autumn flowers. It was, however, no more than a swoon and I soon recovered sufficiently to return home and go to bed. I had an attack of fever. When I thought of the spot where I had fallen, I remembered that the view I had so admired overlooked a cemetery, the very one that housed Aurélia's grave. I had not really thought of it until then; otherwise I might have attributed my fall to the impression which the sight of it had made on me. That very circumstance gave me the idea of a more certain fatality and I regretted the more that death had not reunited me to her. Then, as I thought it over, I told myself that I was unworthy of it. I reviewed with bitterness the life I had led since her death and reproached myself, not with having forgotten her, which had not been the case, but with having outraged her memory in facile love affairs. Then I thought I would appeal to sleep; but *her* image, which had so often appeared to me, no longer returned to my dreams. At first my impressions were confused, and mixed with scenes of bloodshed. It seemed to me that a whole fatal race had been let loose in that ideal world I had previously seen, and of which she was the queen. The same Spirit who had threatened me when I entered the dwelling of those pure families who lived in the *Mysterious City* passed before me, no longer in the white robes he had worn then, together with the rest of his race, but dressed like an Oriental prince. I rushed towards him, threateningly, but he turned calmly and—to my terror and fury—it was my own face, my whole form magnified and idealized ... Then I remembered the man who had been arrested on the same night as myself and whom, as I thought, the guard had released under my name when my two friends came to fetch me. In his hand he held some weapon the shape of which I could not properly see, and one of those with him said: "That was what he struck him with."

I find it impossible to explain how in my own mind earthly events could coincide with those of the supernatural world; it is easier to *feel* than to express clearly. To me this referred to the blow I received in my fall. But what was this Spirit who was me and yet outside me? Was it the *Double* of the old legends, or that mystical brother Oriental people call *ar-rūh*? [8] Had I not once been struck by the story of the knight who had fought a whole night long in a forest against an unknown enemy who was

[8] The word Nerval uses here is "Ferouër," localizing his reference to the ancient Persians.

himself? However that may be, I do not think that human imagination has invented anything which is not true either in this world or in others, and I could not doubt what I had so clearly *seen* myself.

I had a terrible idea. Every man has a double, I said to myself. "I feel two men in myself," [9] a Father of the Church once wrote. The concurrence of two souls has infused this double seed in man's body, which shows similar halves in every organ of its structure. In everyone is a spectator and an actor, one who speaks and one who answers. The Orientals have seen two enemies in that, the good and evil genius of a man.

Am I the good or the evil? I asked myself. In any case my *other* is hostile to me . . . Who knows if there is not under certain circumstances or at a certain age in life a separation of these two spirits? They are both attached to the same body by material affinity, perhaps one is destined to honor and happiness, the other to annihilation and eternal suffering?

Suddenly a terrible flash of light pierced these obscurities . . . Aurélia was no longer mine . . . I thought I heard talk of a ceremony that was taking place somewhere else, and the preparations for a mystical marriage—my own—in which the *other* was to profit by the mistakes of my friends and of Aurélia herself. The dearest friends who came to see me and console me appeared uncertain, that is, the two halves of their souls were separated in relation to me, one side affectionate and confiding, the other full of death as far as I was concerned. In everything that these people said to me there was a double meaning even though they themselves were not aware of it since they were not living *in the spirit*, as I was. For an instant even this idea seemed comic when I thought of Amphitryon and Sosia. But what if this grotesque symbol were something else, what if it were, as in other old fables, the fatal truth under the mask of folly? Well, I told myself, I must fight

9 Nerval's "Père de l'Église" echoes Faust's famous remark:

Zwei Seelen wohnen, ach! in meiner Brust,
Die eine will sich von der andern trennen; (I, II, 305-306)

against this spirit of destiny, fight even against God himself with the weapons of tradition and science. Whatever he may do in the shadow and the night, I exist—and to conquer him I have all the time left me for life on this earth.

X.

How can I describe the strange despair to which these ideas gradually reduced me? An evil genius had my place in the soul world. Aurélia would take him for me, and the wretched spirit that animated my body, weakened, disdained, and unrecognized by her, saw itself eternally destined to despair or annihilation. I used all my willpower to penetrate further that mystery whose veils I had partly lifted. At times my dreams mocked my efforts and only brought me grimacing and fugitive faces. Here I can give only a rather odd idea of the result of this strife in my spirit. I felt I was sliding on a tightrope of infinite length. Earth, streaked with colored veins of molten metals, as I had already seen it, gradually grew brighter with the expansion of its central fire, whose whiteness was tinged with the pink glow that colored the walls of the inner globe. From time to time I was amazed to find large pools of water hanging in the air like clouds, and yet of such density that one could pick flakes off them. But it was clear that this was a different kind of liquid from earthly water, and that it was no doubt the evaporation of what constituted oceans and rivers in the spirit world.

I came to a huge, hilly shore, covered with a kind of reed, of a greenish color but yellowed at the tips as if partially shrivelled by the heat of the sun—yet I did not see the sun any more than on any other occasion. A castle dominated the hillside which I now began to climb. On the further slope of this an immense city lay stretched out. While I was crossing the hill, night had fallen and I saw lights in the houses and streets. On my way down I found myself in a market where they were selling fruit and vegetables like those in the South of France.

I went down by a dark flight of steps and found myself in the streets. The opening of a casino was being advertised and the details of its arrangements were being announced in posters. The typographical borders of these posters were composed of garlands of flowers so well drawn and colored they seemed real. Part of the building was still under construction. I went into a workshop where I saw workmen modelling in clay an enormous animal, the shape of a llama but apparently to be armed with great wings. This beast was as though impregnated with a jet of fire which gradually gave it life and made it writhe, pierced by a myriad purple threads forming veins and arteries, and fertilizing, so to speak, the inert matter which became covered instantaneously with a vegetation of fibrous appendages, fins, and tufts of wool. I stopped to look at this masterpiece in which, it seemed, the secrets of divine creation had been surprised.

"We have here," I was told, "the primitive fire which animated the first living creatures ... At one time it used to reach the earth's surface, but the springs have dried up now,"

I saw also jewellers' work in which two metals, unknown on earth, were used: one was red, and seemed to correspond to cinnabar, and the other was azure blue. The ornaments were neither hammered nor cut, but they took their shape and color and began to spread out like metallic plants produced by certain chemical reactions.

"Do you not create men, too?" I asked one of the workmen.

But he answered: "Men come from above and not from below. How could we possibly create ourselves? All we do here is to formulate, through successive advances of our industries, a more subtle matter than the one that forms the earth's crust. These flowers which seem natural to you, this animal which will appear to live, these will be merely the products of art, raised to the highest point of our knowledge, and everyone will look on them as such."

These were approximately the words which were either spoken to me or whose meaning I thought I could feel. I began to wander through the rooms of the casino where I saw a dense crowd, among whom I recognized several people I knew, some of them alive and some who had died at various times in the past. The former seemed not to see me, while the others answered me without appearing to know me. I now came to the largest room. It was completely hung with flame-colored velvet richly decorated with gold braid. In the center of this room was a couch in the shape of a throne. Some of the people passing by sat down on it to test its springiness; but as the preparations were not yet completed, they went into other rooms. There was some talk of a marriage and of the bridegroom who, they said, was to come and announce the beginnings of the festivities. Immediately a mad rage seized me. I imagined that the man they were waiting for was my *double*, and that he was going to marry Aurélia. I made a row, the gathering was thrown into consternation, and I began to speak violently, explaining my wrongs and calling on those who knew me for help. One old man said to me: "But you can't behave like this, you're frightening everyone."

I shouted out: "I know he has struck me once with his weapon, but I am not afraid and await him, knowing the sign with which to defeat him."

At that moment there appeared one of the workmen from the workshop I had visited. He was holding a long bar at the tip of which was a red-hot ball. I wanted to fling myself upon him, but the ball which he held out before him seemed to be continually threatening my head. Everyone around me seemed to be jeering at my impotence ... I stepped back to the throne then, my soul filled with unutterable pride, and raised my arm to make a sign which to me appeared to have magical power. A woman's cry, vibrant and clear, and filled with excruciating agony, woke me with a start. The syllables of the unknown word I had been about to utter died on my lips ... I threw myself on the floor and began praying fervently, weeping warm tears. But whose was the voice which had rung with such suffering through the night?

It was not part of my dream; it was the voice of a living person, and yet for me it was the voice and tone of Aurélia ...

I opened my window. All was quiet and the cry was not repeated. I enquired outside. No one had heard anything. Yet I was still positive that the cry had been real and that the air of the real world had rung with it ... Doubtless they would tell me that through a coincidence a woman in pain had cried out somewhere near the house at just that second. But in my belief terrestrial events were linked up with those of the invisible world. It is one of those strange relationships which I do not understand myself, and which it is easier to hint at than define ...

What had I done? I had disturbed the harmony of the magic universe, from which my soul drew the certainty of immortal existence. Perhaps I was cursed for having offended divine law by wishing to penetrate a terrible mystery. I could only expect anger and scorn! The furious shadows fled shrieking, describing fatal circles in the air, like birds before the approach of a storm.

PART TWO

Eurydice! Eurydice! 10

10 This invocation by Nerval-Orpheus prepares us for the more chaotic world of the Second Part. Separated now from the society of mankind the poet enters the deepest regions of hell itself. The last words of *Aurélia* thus echo this invocation, which the severed head of Orpheus still uttered as it floated on the river Hebrus.

I.

Lost once more!

All is finished, it is all over. Now I must die and die without hope. What then is death? Nothingness?... Would to God it were! But God Himself cannot make death a nothingness.

Why do I think of Him for the first time for so long? The system of destiny created in my mind admitted no such single sovereignty... or rather that royalty was merged in the sum of all beings... it was the god of Lucretius, powerless and forlorn in his own immensity.

She, however, believed in God and one day I surprised the name of Jesus on her lips. It slipped from them so softly that I wept. Dear God, those tears, those tears... they have been dry for so long. Give back those tears to me, O God.

When the soul drifts uncertainly between life and the dream, between the mind's disorder and the return to cool reflection, it is in religious thought that we should seek consolation; such I have never found in a philosophy which only gives us egotistical maxims or, at most, those twin tenets, empty experience and bitter doubt: it struggles against moral anguish by annihilating sensibility; like surgery, it can only cut out the suffering organ. But for us, born in days of revolutions and storms, when every belief was broken, brought up at best in a vague tradition satisfied by a few external observances, the indifferent adhesion to which is perhaps worse than impiety and heresy—for us it is very difficult, when we feel the need of it, to resurrect that mystic edifice already built in their ready hearts by the innocent and the simple. "The tree of knowledge is not the tree of life!" And yet, can we cast out of our spirits all the good or evil poured into them by so many learned generations? Ignorance cannot be learned.

I hope better of the goodness of God. Perhaps we are approaching the predicted time when science, having completed its cycle of analysis and synthesis, of belief and negation, will be able to purify itself and raise up the marvellous city of the future out of the confused ruins ... We must not hold human reason so cheap as to believe it gains by complete self-humiliation, for that would be to impeach its divine origin ... God will no doubt appreciate purity of intention; and what father would like to see his son give up all reason and pride in front of him? The apostle who had to touch to believe was not cursed for his doubt!

* * *

What have I been writing? Blasphemies. Christian humility does not speak in that way. Such thoughts are far from softening the soul. On their foreheads they bear the proud glitter of Satan's crown ... A pact with God Himself? ... O science! O vanity!

* * *

I had got together several books on the Cabala. I sank myself in study of these and succeeded in persuading myself that everything accumulated there by the human spirit over the centuries was true. The conviction I had formed of the existence of the exterior world coincided so well with my reading that I could no longer doubt the revelations of the past. The dogmas and rituals of various religions seemed to tally with it to such a degree that each one had in it a certain portion of those secrets, which constituted its means of expansion and defence. These powers could weaken, lessen, and disappear altogether, and this led to the invasion of certain races by others—none, however, could conquer or be conquered except by the Spirit.

"Yet," I told myself, "it is certain that human errors are intermingled in these sciences. The magic alphabet, the mysterious hieroglyphs have only come down to us incomplete and falsified, either by time or by men who have an interest in our remaining ignorant. Let us rediscover the lost letter, the effaced sign, let us recompose the dissonant scale, and we shall gain power in the world of the spirits."

Thus I thought I saw correspondences between the real world and the spirit world. The earth, its inhabitants and their history, were the theater in which we carried out the physical actions which prepared the existence and position of the immortal beings attached to its destiny. Without discussing the impenetrable mystery of the eternity of worlds, my thoughts went back to that time when the sun, like the flower that represents it and follows with bowed head its course in the skies, sowed on earth the fruitful seeds of plants and animals. It was nothing but this very ball of fire which, being a composite of souls, instinctively formed the common dwelling-place. The spirit of the Godhead, reproduced and, so to speak, reflected on earth, became the common type of human soul of which each was at once both God and man. Such were the Elohim.

* * *

When we feel unhappy we think of the unhappiness of others. I had neglected to call on one of my best friends who I had heard was ill. [11] As I went to the place where he was being treated, I reproached myself sharply for this omission. I was all the more miserable when my friend told me that he had been worse the night before. I went into a white-washed hospital ward. The sun traced cheerful triangular patterns on the walls and played on a vase of flowers which a nun had just arranged on the sick man's table. It was almost the cell of an Italian anchorite. His wasted face, the ivory-yellow of his skin, accentuated by the blackness of his beard and his hair, his eyes glittering with the last of the fever, perhaps also something in the arrangement of the hooded cloak flung over his shoulders, all this made him a somewhat

[11] Probably the poet and translator of Dante, Antony Deschamps de Saint-Amand (1800-1869) who was also treated by Dr. Blanche.

different person from the man I had known. He was no longer
the happy comrade of my work and play. There was something
of the apostle about him. He described to me how, at the worst
stage in his sufferings, he had been seized by a final delirium that
had seemed to him the supreme moment. Immediately his pain
had ceased as if by a miracle. It is impossible to convey what he
then told me—a blissful dream in the vaguest spaces of infinity,
a conversation with a being at once different from, and bound to,
himself, whom he asked where God was, as he imagined himself
dead. "But God is everywhere," his spirit answered. "He is in
you yourself and in us all. He judges you, listens to you, advises
you: you and *I* think and dream together, we have never left one
another, and we are eternal!"

I cannot quote any more of this conversation which I perhaps
heard or understood badly. I only know that the impression it
left on me was a deep one. I dare not attribute to my friend con-
clusions that perhaps I myself drew falsely from his words. I do
not even know if the resultant feeling is compatible with Christianity or not.

"God is with him!" I exclaimed to myself. "But He is no longer with me. Oh, misery, I have driven Him from me, I have
threatened Him, I have cursed Him! It was indeed He, the mystic
brother, Who drifted further and further from my soul and warned
me in vain. The Beloved Bridegroom, King of Glory, it is He
who has judged and condemned me, and taken to His own Heaven
the woman He gave me and of whom I am now unworthy for
ever!"

II.

I cannot describe the dejection into which these ideas threw me.
"I understand," I said to myself, "I have preferred creature to
Creator; I have deified my love and adored with pagan ritual her
whose last sigh was consecrated to Christ. But if His religion is
sincere, God may yet forgive me. He may give me her back if I

humble myself before Him; perhaps His spirit will return to me."

Thinking this, I wandered aimlessly through the streets. A funeral procession crossed my path, going to the cemetery where she was buried. I felt impelled to join the procession and go there.

"I do not know," I said to myself, "who this dead person is they are taking to burial; but I know now that the dead see and hear us; perhaps this person will be glad of a brother in sorrow, sadder than any of those following now."

This idea made me shed tears and no doubt they thought I was one of the deceased's best friends. O blessed tears! Your sweetness had been denied to me for so long! . . . My head grew clearer and a ray of hope led me on. I felt the power of prayer and took a delirious enjoyment in it.

I did not find out the name of the person whose coffin I had followed. The cemetery I went into was sacred to me for several reasons. Three of my mother's family had been buried there; but I could not go and pray on their graves for they had been taken away years ago to that distant country, their original home. For some time I looked for Aurélia's tomb but could not find it. The cemetery had been rearranged—perhaps also my memory had strayed . . . It seemed to me that this accident, this forgetfulness, added more to my damnation. I dared not mention to the officials the name of a dead woman over whom I had no religious rights . . . Then I remembered that in my room I had the exact plan of where her tomb was, and I ran back there, my heart pounding, my head distracted. I have already admitted how I surrounded my love with weird superstitions. In a little casket that had once belonged to *her* I kept her last letter. Dare I confess that I had made out of this casket a kind of reliquary which had brought back to me long travels in which the thought of her had followed me—a rose gathered in the gardens of Schoubrah, a strip of mummy-cloth brought back from Egypt, some laurel leaves from the river at Beirut, two little gilded crystals, mosaics from Saint Sophia, a rosary bead, and other things I have forgotten . . . finally the paper given me the day her grave was dug to enable me to find it again . . .

I blushed. My hands shook as I went through this crazy collection. I took the two pieces of paper and just as I was about to set off once more for the cemetery, I changed my mind.

"No," I told myself, "I am unworthy to kneel at a Christian woman's tomb; let us not add another profanation to so many others."

Then, to pacify the storm raging through my brain, I went out some distance from Paris to a little town where I had once spent happy times in my youth with some old relatives, since dead. I had often loved to go there to see the sunset near their house. There was a walk shaded with lime-trees which brought back to me the memory of girls, relations, with whom I had grown up. One of them . . . [12]

But could I ever have dreamed of comparing that vague childish love to the one which consumed my youth? I saw the sun sinking over the valley full of misty shadows; it vanished from sight, bathing the tips of the trees on the edges of the little hills with a rosy glow. My heart filled with the deepest sadness. I went and slept at an inn where I was known. The innkeeper spoke to me of one of my old friends who lived in the town and who had blown his brains out after some unlucky speculation . . . Sleep brought me dreadful dreams. I have only a nebulous memory of them. I was in a room I did not know and talking to someone from the outside world, perhaps the very friend I have just mentioned. There was an extremely tall mirror behind us. Happening to glance in it I thought I saw Aurélia. She seemed sad and pensive, and suddenly, whether she came out of the mirror, or whether, passing through the room, her reflection had appeared there for an instant, that sweet beloved face was with me. She held out her hand, let a sad glance fall on me, and said: "We shall meet again later . . . at your friend's house."

At once I thought of her marriage, the curse that kept us apart . . . and I said to myself: "Is it possible? Will she come back to me?" And I asked with tears in my eyes: "Have you forgiven me?"

[12] Sylvie.

But everything had disappeared. I was in a deserted spot, a rough acclivity strewn with rocks, in the midst of forests. A house I seemed to know dominated this desolate landscape. I walked to and fro along tortuous paths. Tired of walking among rocks and briars I sometimes tried to find an easier way through openings of the wood.

"They are waiting for me over there!" I thought.

I heard a clock strike a certain hour . . . I said to myself: *"It's too late!"*

Voices answered me: *"She is lost!"*

Deep night surrounded me. The distant house glittered as though lit for a feast and as if full of guests who had arrived in good time.

"She is lost!" I cried out to myself. "And why? . . . I understand. She has made a last effort to save me; I missed the supreme moment when pardon was still possible. From highest Heaven she could intercede for me with the Divine Spouse . . . and what does even my salvation matter? The abyss has claimed its prey! She is lost to me and lost to us all! . . ."

I seemed to see her in a flash of lightning, pale and dying, being borne away by dark horsemen . . .

The cry of pain and anger I uttered at that moment woke me up, panting.

"Oh God! Oh God! For her and her alone! Dear God, forgive me!" I cried, throwing myself on my knees.

It was day. As a result of an emotion it is difficult for me to explain, I immediately decided to destroy the two pieces of paper I had taken from the casket the night before—that last letter, alas, which, as I read it again, I wet with my tears, and the burial paper which bore the seal of the cemetery. "Find her tomb now!" I said to myself. "But I ought to have gone back there yesterday—and my fatal dream is but the reflection of a fatal day!"

III.

The flames devoured these last relics of love and death which were attached to the most sensitive fibers of my heart. I went out into the country with my sorrows and belated remorse trying, by tiring myself out with walking, to deaden my thoughts and perhaps ensure a less distressing sleep for the following night. With my idea that dreams opened up to man intercourse with the spirit world, I hoped, I still had hope! Perhaps God would be content with this sacrifice. Here I paused; it is too presumptuous to pretend that my state of mind was brought about only by a memory of love. Let us say rather that I dressed up with this idea the keenest remorse at a life spent in foolish dissipation, a life in which evil had often triumped, and whose errors I did not recognize until I felt the blows of misfortune. I no longer considered myself worthy to think of her, whom I had tormented in death having distressed her in life, and to whose sweet and sacred pity alone I owed a last glance of forgiveness.

The next night I only slept a few moments. A woman who had looked after me in my youth appeared to me in a dream and reproached me for a very serious fault I had once committed. I recognized her although she seemed much older than the last time I had seen her. This made me bitterly recall that I had neglected to visit her during her last moments. She seemed to say to me: "You did not weep for your old parents as much as you have for this woman. How then can you hope for forgiveness?" The dream grew confused. The faces of people I had known at various times passed rapidly in front of me. They filed past, becoming brighter, then fading, and falling back into the darkness like the beads of a broken rosary. Then I saw plastic images of antiquity vaguely take form before me, at first only in outline, and then more solidly; they seemed to represent symbols, whose meaning I grasped only with difficulty. Yet I think what it meant was: "All this was to teach you the secret of life and you have not understood it. Religions and legends, saints and poets, all concurred in explaining the fatal enigma, and you have interpreted it wrongly.... Now it is too late!"

I rose, terror-stricken, saying to myself: "This is my last day!" Ten years later the same idea that I have described in the first part of this narrative returned to me more definite and menacing. God had given me that time in which to repent, and I had not made use of it. After the apparition of the *Stone Guest*, I had sat down again to the feast!

IV.

The emotion resulting from these visions and the reflections they brought during my solitude was so sad that I felt lost. Everything I had ever done in my life appeared under its most unfavorable aspect, and in the kind of scrutiny of conscience to which I subjected myself my memory served up to me the oldest facts with singular clarity. Some sense of false shame prevented me from going to confess, perhaps the fear of involving myself in the dogmas and practices of a redoubtable religion, against certain points of which I had preserved philosophic prejudices. My early years were too impregnated with revolutionary ideas, my education had been too free, my life too rambling, for me to be able to accept easily a yoke which still, on many points, would offend my reason. I shuddered to think what kind of a Christian I should make, were it not that certain principles, borrowed from the free-thinking of the past two centuries, combined with the study of comparative religion, had halted me on this declivity.

I never knew my mother, who had insisted on following my father on his campaigns, like the wives of the ancient Goths; she died of fever and exhaustion in a cold province of Germany, and my father himself had never been able to direct my early ideas that way. The part of the country where I was brought up was full of strange myths and odd superstitions. One of my uncles, who was the chief influence on my early education, occupied himself

with Roman and Celtic antiques as a hobby. Sometimes he discovered, either on his land or nearby, effigies of gods and emperors, and his scholarly admiration made me regard these with
deep respect, while I learnt their history from his lips. A certain
statue of Mars in gilded bronze, an armed Pallas or Venus, a Nep-
tune and Amphitrite sculpted over the village fountain, and, above
all, the plump, jolly, bearded face of a Pan smiling at the entrance
to a grotto festooned with aristolochia and ivy, these were the
household gods who protected this retreat. I admit that they
inspired me at that time with more veneration than did the poor
Christian images in the church and the two battered saints in its
portico, which some learned men asserted to be the Esus and Cer-
nunnos of the Gauls. One day, feeling uncomfortable among all
these different symbols, I asked my uncle what God was.

"God is the sun," he replied.

That was the private belief of an honest man who had lived all
his life as a Christian, had passed through the Revolution, and
who came from a district where many had the same idea of the
Divinity. This did not prevent the women and children from
going to church, and I owed to one of my aunts a certain amount
of instruction that made me realize the beauty and grandeur of
Christianity. After 1815, an Englishman who was in our part of
the world made me learn the Sermon on the Mount and gave me
a New Testament... I only mention these details to point out
the causes for a certain irresolution which with me is frequently
linked with a pronounced religious sentiment.

I want to explain how, after having been far from the true path
for so long, I felt myself led back to it by the cherished memory
of a dead person, and how my need to believe that she was still
alive brought back into my mind a precise feeling for the various
truths which I had not gathered firmly enough into my soul.
Despair and suicide are the result of certain situations fatal for
the man who has no faith in immortality, with all its sorrows and
joys; I shall think I have done something good and useful by
relating clearly the succession of ideas by means of which I re-

covered my peace of mind and a new strength with which to match the future misfortunes of life.

The successive visions of my sleep had reduced me to such despair that I could scarcely speak; the society of my friends gave me only a momentary distraction; my mind was wholly occupied by its illusions and refused to entertain the least different conception; I was unable to read and could not understand ten lines in a row. I said of the most beautiful things: "What do they matter? For me they do not exist."

One of my friends, called George, [13] undertook to overcome this despondency of mine. He took me out to various of the environs of Paris, and was content to do all the talking, while I only replied in a few disjointed phrases. One day his expressive and quasi-monastic countenance seemed to give great import to the eloquence he was calling forth against the years of scepticism and political and social depression that had followed the July Revolution. I had been one of the young men of that period and I had tasted its ardors and bitternesses. An emotion took hold of me; I told myself that such lessons could not be given without the intention of Providence, and that no doubt a spirit was speaking through him . . . One day we were dining in an arbor in a little village near Paris. A woman came and sang close to our table, and something in her worn but sympathetic voice made me think of Aurélia's. I looked at her. Her very features were not unlike those I had loved. She was sent off, and I did not dare to detain her, but I said to myself: "Who knows? Perhaps *her spirit* is in that woman!" And I felt glad I had given her alms.

I said to myself: "I have misused my life, but if the dead forgive, then it is certainly on condition that we forever refrain from evil and repair all we have done wrong. Can that be? . . . From now on I will try to do no more evil and give back the equivalent of everything I owe."

13 Georges Bell (Joachim Hounau) (1824-1899), a doctor's son from Pau, politically active in the 1848 revolution, to whom we are indebted for much editorial work connected with Nerval.

I had recently wronged someone. It was only an act of negligence but I began by going and apologizing. The joy I obtained through act of reparation did me an immense amount of good; from then on I had a reason for living and acting, and I took a new interest in the world.

Difficulties arose. Inexplicable happenings seemed to collaborate to thwart my good resolution. My state of mind made the work I had promised impossible. As they thought me well now, people became more exacting, and, since I had given up telling lies, I found I was at a disadvantage in dealing with those who were not so hindered. The mass of reparations I had to make was crushing in proportion to my impotence. Political events worked indirectly, not only by worrying me but also by removing the means for my putting my affairs in order. The death of one of my friends completed these reasons for despondency. With sorrow I revisited his house, and saw the pictures he had so happily shown me a month before; I passed by his coffin at the moment when it was being nailed down. As he was my age and generation, I asked myself: "What would happen if I died suddenly like that?"

The following Sunday I got up in a fit of deep dejection. I went and saw my father whose maid-servant was ill; he seemed in a bad temper. He insisted on going himself to get wood from the loft, and the only service I could render him was to hand him one log that he needed. I left in dismay. In the street I met a friend who wanted to take me along to dine with him in order to distract me a little. I refused his offer and, without having eaten anything, I made towards Montmartre. The cemetery was closed, which I considered an ill omen. A German poet [14] had given me a few pages of his to translate and had advanced me a sum for the work. I set off for his house to return him the money.

As I went through the Clichy gate, I saw a fight. I tried to separate the combatants but without success. At that moment a big workman crossed the very spot where the fight had been, carrying on his left shoulder a child in a hyacinth-colored dress.

14 Heinrich Heine.

I imagined that it was Saint Christopher carrying Christ and that I was condemned for not having had strength enough in the scene that had just taken place. From that moment on I wandered about in despair through the vague parts that divide the suburb from the city. It was too late to go on with my projected visit. So I went back through the streets towards the center of Paris. Near the rue de la Victoire I met a priest and in my distressed condition I wanted to confess to him. He told me that this was not his parish and that he was going out for an evening with a friend, but that, if I wanted to consult him on the following day at Notre-Dame, I had only to ask for Father Dubois.

In despair I went in tears to Notre-Dame de Lorette, where I threw myself at the foot of an altar to the Virgin, asking forgiveness for my sins. Something within me said: "Our Lady is dead, and your prayers are useless." I went and knelt at the very end of the choir and slipped from my finger a silver ring, whose stone was engraved with the three Arabic words: *Allah! Mohammed! Ali!* Immediately several candles were lit in the choir and a service began in which I tried to join in spirit. When the priest had got to the *Ave Maria*, he interrupted himself in the middle of the prayer and began again seven times, without my being able to remember the words that should have come next. The prayer over, the priest delivered a sermon which seemed to allude to me alone. When all the lights were extinguished, I got up and went out in the direction of the Champs-Élysées.

When I reached the place de la Concorde, I thought of killing myself. Several times I started towards the Seine, but something stopped me from completing my plan. The stars shone in the sky. Suddenly it seemed to me that they were all extinguished like the candles I had seen in the church. I thought that the hour had arrived and that we had come to the end of the world predicted in the Apocalypse of Saint John. I thought I saw a black sun in an empty sky and a red ball of blood above the Tuileries. I said to myself: "The eternal night is beginning, and it will be terrible. What will happen when men find that there is no more sun?"

I returned by the rue Saint-Honoré and pitied the belated country folk whom I met. When I came to the Louvre I walked as far as the square and there a strange sight greeted me. I saw several moons moving swiftly across the clouds, driven rapidly by the wind. I thought that the earth had left its orbit and was wandering through the firmament like a ship that had lost its masts, approaching or receding from the stars which grew alternately larger and smaller. I contemplated this chaos for two or three hours and then set out for Les Halles. The peasants were bringing in their produce, and I told myself: "How astonished they will be to see the night going on . . ." Yet here and there dogs were barking and cocks crowing.

Broken with weariness, I went home and threw myself on my bed. When I woke up, I was amazed to see the light. A kind of mysterious choir chanted in my ears. Childish voices were repeating in chorus: "*Christe! Christe! Christe! . . .*" I imagined they had collected a large number of children in the neighboring church (Notre-Dame-des-Victoires) to invoke Christ. "But Christ is no more!" I said to myself. "And they do not know it yet!"

The invocation lasted for about an hour. At last I got up and wandered under the galleries of the Palais-Royal. I told myself that probably the sun had retained enough strength to light the world for another three days, but that all the while it was using up its substance, and indeed I thought it looked cold and colorless. I stifled my hunger with a small cake in order to give myself strength to get as far as the German poet's house. When I got there I told him that it was all over and that we must be prepared for death. He called his wife who asked me: "What's the matter?"

"I don't know," I said. "I am lost."

She sent out for a cab, and a young girl took me to the hospital Dubois.

V.

There my illness returned and took on various complications. At the end of a month I was better. For the next two months I resumed my wanderings around Paris. The longest journey

I made was to visit the cathedral at Rheims. Gradually I began
writing again and composed one of my best tales. [15] Yet I wrote
with difficulty, nearly always in pencil on odd sheets, and according
to the whim of my reverie or my walk. Correcting gave me endless
trouble. A few days after I had published the work I was attacked
by persistent insomnia. I went and walked about all night on the
hill of Montmartre and there I watched the sun rise. I talked for
hours with peasants and workmen. At other times I went to Les
Halles. One night I dined in a café on the boulevard and amused
myself by tossing gold and silver coins into the air. Then I went
to the market and got into an argument with a total stranger whom
I struck roughly; I do not know why nothing came of this. At
a certain hour I heard the clock of Saint-Eustache strike and I
began thinking of the battles between the Burgundians and the
Armagnacs, and I imagined the ghosts of the warriors of that
era around me. I picked a quarrel with a postman who wore on
his chest a silver badge, and whom I accused of being the Duke
John of Burgundy. I tried to prevent him going into a bar. For
some extraordinary and inexplicable reason his face filled with
tears when he saw me threatening him with death. I felt softened
and let him pass.

I went towards the Tuileries gardens, but they were shut. I then
followed the quays and walked up to the Luxembourg. Then I
returned to eat with one of my friends. After that I went to
Saint-Eustache where I knelt piously at the altar of the Virgin
and thought of my mother. The tears I shed relieved my spirit
and, on my way out of the church, I bought a silver ring. I then
went to see my father and as he was out I left him a bunch of mar-
guerites. I went to the Jardin des Plantes. There were a lot of
people there and I stopped for some time, watching the hippopotamus bathing in its pool. [16] Then I went to the Natural History

15 *Sylvie.*
16 According to Champfleury, Nerval took off his hat and threw it to the hippo.
In a letter dated May 31, 1854, to Georges Bell, Nerval asks Bell to try to find the
man he had struck (mentioned in the lines above) and to offer him "une réparation."

museum. The sight of the monsters there made me think of the flood, and as I walked out a violent shower of rain came down in the gardens.

I said to myself: "What bad luck! All these women and children will get soaked!..." Then I thought: "But it's worse than that. A real flood is beginning." The water rose in the neighboring streets; I ran down the rue Saint-Victor and, with the idea of halting what I believed to be the flooding of the universe, I threw the ring I had bought at Saint-Eustache into the deepest part. At that very moment the storm abated and the sun began to shine.

Hope returned to my soul. I had arranged to meet my friend George at four o'clock, and went to where he lived. Passing an antique shop, I bought two velvet screens covered with hieroglyphic figures. It seemed to me that I was consecrating the forgiveness of heaven. I got to George's house at the right time and told him of my hopes. I was wet through and tired out. I changed my clothes and lay down on his bed. During my sleep I had a marvellous vision. It seemed to me that the goddess appeared to me, saying: "I am the same as Mary, the same as your mother, the same being also whom you have always loved under every form. At each of your ordeals I have dropped one of the masks with which I hide my features and soon you shall see me as I really am." From the clouds behind her there appeared a lovely orchard, and a soft, yet penetrating radiance illuminated this paradise. Although I only heard her voice I felt myself plunged into a delicious intoxication. Soon afterwards I woke up and said to George: "Let's go out."

While we were crossing the Pont des Arts I explained the transmigration of souls to him, and said: "Tonight it seems to me that I have the soul of Napoleon in me, inspiring me and commanding me to do great things." [17]

---

[17] These delusions of grandeur, which occur throughout the poems, follow here logically upon the moment of mystical pardon by the apparition, a moment of supreme reconciliation that proves too much for the poet. He is taken off to Dr. Emile Blanche at Passy (August, 1853).

In the rue du Coq I bought a hat and, while George was waiting for the change from the gold piece I had thrown on the counter, I went on my way and came to the galleries of the Palais-Royal. There everyone seemed to be staring at me. A persistent idea had fixed itself in my mind that there were no more dead; I went through the Galerie de Foy saying: "I have committed a sin," and I could not find out what it was by consulting my memory which I believed to be that of Napoleon. "There is something here for which I have not paid!" With this idea in my mind I went into the Café de Foy and in one of the customers there I thought I could recognize old father Bertin of the *Débats*. [18] Then I crossed the gardens, somewhat interested in the little girls dancing in rings. I then left the galleries and made my way towards the rue Saint-Honoré. I went into a shop to buy a cigar and, when I came out, the crowd was so dense I was nearly suffocated. I was extricated by three of my friends who got me into a café while one of them went in search of a cab. I was taken to the Hospice de la Charité.

During the night my delirium grew worse and more so in the early hours when I found I was tied down. I succeeded in freeing myself from the straitjacket and towards morning walked about the various wards. I had the idea that I had become like a god, possessed of powers of healing, so that I put my hands on some of the patients. Going up to a statue of the Virgin I took off its

---

18 *Le Journal des Débats* was founded after the 18 *brumaire* by Louis-François Bertin, and perpetuated by the Bertin family. After initial difficulties it became a noteworthy opposition organ until 1830 when it was involved, along with the *Globe National*, *Temps*, and *Constitutionnel*, in the revolution. For these papers were prohibited by a police order on Monday July 26th, the day after Charles X had signed ordinances at Saint-Cloud which amounted to a *coup d'état*. It was the issue of freedom of the press that first touched off disturbances. Monsieur Baude published his *Temps* on the Tuesday in defiance of the police order, his offices were broken up by the police, the discharged journeymen printers became turbulent, and barricades were flung up. *Le Journal des Débats* naturally became a staunch supporter of the July monarchy. Nerval probably had in mind here Bertin l'Aîné, who had a striking face and was painted by Ingres in 1832.

crown of artificial fllowers in order to test the power in me. I walked in long strides, talking in an animated way of the ignorance of men who believed they could be cured by science alone, and seeing a bottle of ether on a table I drank it in one gulp. A hospital assistant, with a face I compared to an angel's, tried to stop me, but I was supported by neurotic strength and, just as I was about to overthrow him, I stopped and told him he did not understand my mission. Doctors came along then and I went on with my harangue on the impotence of their art. Then, though I had no shoes on, I went down the stairs and, coming to a garden, I went out and picked flowers there, strolling about on the grass.

One of my friends had returned to fetch me. So I left the garden and, while I was speaking to him, they thrust me into a strait-jacket and made me get into a cab and I was taken away to an asylum outside Paris. As soon as I found myself among the insane, I realized that everything had been an illusion for me until then. However, the assurances that I attributed to the goddess Isis seemed to realize themselves by a series of trials to which I had to submit. So I accepted them with resignation.

The part of the house I was in looked out over a vast exercise-ground, shaded by walnut-trees. In one corner arose a little mound, where one of the inmates walked in a circle all day long. Others, like me, contented themselves with strolling on the platform or the path, which was bordered with grassy banks. On a wall to the west side were drawn figures, one of which represented the shape of the moon with geometrical eyes and mouth; over this face a kind of mask had been painted; the left wall was covered with various drawings in profile, one of which represented a sort of Japanese idol. Further on, a skull was carved in the plaster; on the opposite side, two stones had been sculpted into rather good gargoyles by one of the guests of the garden. Two doors led down to cellars, which I imagined to be subterranean passages like those I had seen at the entrance to the Pyramids.

VI.

At first I imagined that all the people collected in this garden had some influence over the stars, and that the man who was walking in an incessant circle was regulating the movement of the sun. One old man, brought there at certain hours of the day, who spent his time making knots and looking at his watch, seemed to me to be in charge of the task of verifying the passing of the hours. To myself I attributed an influence over the moon's course, and I believed it had been struck by thunder from the Almighty and that this had imprinted on its face the look of the mask I had noticed.

I gave a mystic significance to the conversations of the attendants and to those of my comrades. It seemed to me that these people were the representatives of every race in the world and that together we had to reorganize the courses of the stars and further develop the sidereal system. In my view there had been an error in the general combination of numbers and from that all humanity's ills arose. Further, I believed that the heavenly spirits had taken on human forms and were present at this kind of general congress, although they appeared to be occupied with ordinary affairs. My own role seemed to be to re-establish universal harmony by means of Cabalistic arts and to seek a solution in summoning the occult powers of the various religions.

As well as the walk, there was another room for our use, whose windows with their perpendicular bars opened on a horizon of verdure. As I looked through these panes of glass at the lines of the out-buildings, I saw the facade and windows stand out like a thousand little pavilions ornamented with arabesques, topped with tracery work and spires, that reminded me of the imperial lodges along the shores of the Bosphorus. This naturally led my mind on to Oriental ideas. At about two o'clock I was put in a bath, and I felt as if I were being attended by the Valkyries, the daughters of Odin, who wanted to raise me to immortality by gradually purging my body of its impurities. [19]

In the evening I walked about serenely in the moonlight and, when I looked up at the trees, their leaves seemed to me to curl up capriciously so as to form the figures of knights and ladies borne along on caparisoned steeds. For me they were the triumphant figures of our ancestors. That thought led me to think that there was a vast conspiracy between every living creature to reestablish the world in its original harmony, that communication took place by means of the magnetism of stars, that an unbroken chain around the earth linked the various intelligences devoted to this general communion, and that songs, dances, looks, magnetized from one to another, betrayed the same aspiration. For me the moon was the sanctuary of fraternal souls who had been relieved of their mortal bodies and who were working with greater freedom towards the regeneration of the universe.

Already the length of each day seemed to be increased by hours; so that, by rising at the hour fixed by the institution clocks, I was really only walking in the empire of shadows. My companions around me seemed to be asleep and to resemble specters of Tartarus, until the hour at which the sun rose for me. Then I greeted that luminary with a prayer, and my real life began.

From that moment on, when I felt sure that I was being subjected to the tests of a sacred initiation, an invincible strength entered into my soul. I imagined myself a hero living under the gaze of the gods; everything in Nature took on a new aspect, and secret voices, warning and exhorting me, came from plants, trees, animals, and the most lowly insects. The speech of my companions took mysterious turns, whose sense I alone could understand, and formless, inanimate objects lent themselves to the calculations of my mind; from combinations of pebbles, from shapes in corners, chinks or openings, from the outlines of leaves, colors, sounds, and smells, emanated for me hitherto unknown harmonies.

[19] The picture of the Valkyries washing Nerval's body makes a typical purification ceremony that can be matched in both Dante and *Faust*.

"How have I been able to live so long," I asked myself, "outside Nature without identifying myself with it? Everything lives, moves, everything corresponds; the magnetic rays, emanating either from myself or from others, cross the limitless chain of created things unimpeded; it is a transparent network which covers the world, and its slender threads communicate themselves by degrees to the planets and stars. Captive now upon earth, I commune with the chorus of the stars who share in my joys and sorrows."

Then I shuddered to think that even this mystery might be surprised. "If electricity," I told myself, "which is the magnetism of physical bodies, can be forced in a direction imposed on it by laws, that is all the more reason why hostile and tyrannical spirits may be able to enslave the intelligences of others, and make use of their divided strength for their own purposes of domination. Thus it was that the gods of old times were conquered and enslaved by new gods; and thus," I went on, consulting my memory of the ancient world, "that necromancers dominated entire peoples, whose succeeding generations became captive under their everlasting scepter. Ah misery! Death itself cannot free them! For we live again in our sons as we have lived in our fathers, and the relentless lore of our enemies can pick us out anywhere. The hour of our birth, the exact place on earth where we appear, the first movement, the name, the room, and all the consecrations and rituals imposed upon us, establish a lucky or unlucky series on which the whole of our future hangs. But while, by human reckoning, all this is already a terrible thought, realize what it implies when attached to the hidden formulas that set up the order of worlds. It has been rightly said that nothing is unimportant, nothing powerless in the universe; a single atom can dissolve everything, and save everything! What terror! There lies the eternal distinction between good and evil. Is my soul the indestructible molecule, the sphere inflated by a little air, which yet can find its place in nature, or is it that very void, a reflection of that nothingness which disappears in immensity? Or could it be that fateful particle destined to undergo, through all its transfigurations, the vengeance of powerful beings?" By this I was led to take account of my life and even of my previous existence. By proving to myself that I was good, I proved to myself that I must always have been good. "And if I have been evil," I said to myself, "will not my present life be sufficient expiation?" This thought reassured me, but did not free me from the fear of being forever classed among the unhappy. I felt myself thrust into cold water, and a colder water trickled down my forehead. I turned my thoughts to the eternal Isis, sacred mother and spouse; all my aspirations, all my prayers were mingled in that magic name, and I seemed to live again in her; sometimes she appeared to me in the guise of Venus of the ancients, sometimes as the Christian Virgin. Night made this dear vision clearer to me, and yet I asked myself: "What can she, conquered as she is and perhaps oppressed, do for her poor children?"

Pale and torn the crescent moon thinned each evening and soon perhaps we should never see her again in the sky! Yet it seemed that this celestial body was the refuge of all my sister souls, and I saw it peopled with plaintive shades, destined to be born again one day on earth...

My room lies at the end of a corridor, on one side of which live the insane, and on the other the asylum servants. It has only the privilege of one window, opening towards the courtyard, which is planted with trees and which in the daytime serves as an exercise-ground. I love to gaze at a leafy walnut-tree and two Chinese mulberries. Beyond, a busy street can be seen vaguely through the trellis-work, which is painted green. At sunset the horizon widens; it is like a hamlet with windows clothed in foliage or cluttered with bird-cages and drying rags, from which occasionally appears the head of a young or old housewife, or the pink cheeks of a child. There are shouts, dancing, bursts of laughter; it is either gay or sad to hear, according to what hour it is and how it strikes one.

I found there all the remnants of my various fortunes, the confused remains of several sets of furniture scattered or sold over the past twenty years. It is a junk heap as bad as Doctor Faust's.

A tripod table with eagles' heads, a console table supported on a winged sphinx, a Seventeenth-Century commode, an Eighteenth-Century bookcase, a bed of the same period with an oval-ceilinged baldequin covered with scarlet damask (but this there was no room to erect), a rustic dresser laden with faïence and Sèvres porcelain, most of it somewhat damaged; a hookah brought back from Constantinople, a large alabaster cup, a crystal vase; some wood panelling from the destruction of an old house I had once lived in on the site of the Louvre, covered with mythological paintings done by friends who are today famous; two large canvases in the style of Prudhon, representing the Muses of History and Comedy. For some days I amused myself by rearranging all these things, creating in this narrow attic an odd interior composed of palace and hovel, that aptly summarizes my wandering life. Over my bed I have hung my Arab clothes, my two carefully darned cashmere shawls, a pilgrim's flask, a game-bag. Above the bookshelves stretches an enormous map of Cairo; a bamboo bracket at the head of my bed supports a varnished Indian tray on which I can put my toilet articles. I was overjoyed to rediscover these humble relics of those years alternating in fortune and misery, to which the memories of my whole life are tied. They had put to one side only a little picture on copper, in the style of Correggio, showing *Venus and Love*, some pier-glasses of nymphs and satyrs, and an arrow I had kept in memory of the bowmen of Valois to whom I used to belong in my youth; since the new laws had come in, the weapons had been sold. On the whole I found nearly everything I had previously possessed there. My books, an odd assortment of the knowledge of all ages, history, travels, religion, the Cabala, astrology, enough to gladden the shades of Pico della Mirandola, the sage Meursius, and Nicholas of Cusa—the Tower of Babel in two hundred volumes—they had left me all that! They were enough to drive a wise man mad; let us try to ensure that there is enough to make a madman sane.

With what delight have I been able to file away in my drawers the mass of my notes and letters, correspondence both public and

private, famous or obscure, as a chance meeting made them so,
or a distant country I visited.   In rolls, better wrapped than the
others, I find Arabic letters, relics of Cairo and Stamboul.   Oh
joy! Oh mortal sorrow! These yellowed characters, these faded
drafts, half-crumpled letters, these are the treasures of my only
love . . . Let me read them again . . . Many of them are missing,
others torn or scratched out; here is what I find: [20]

. . . .

One night I was talking and singing in a kind of ecstasy. One
of the warders came and fetched me from my cell, and made me
go down to a room on the ground-floor, where he shut me up.
I went on with my dream and, although I was standing up, I imagined myself enclosed in a sort of Oriental pavilion. I felt all the
corners and found it to be octagonal.   A divan ran around the
walls, which seemed to me to be of thick plate-glass, beyond which
I could see shining treasures, shawls, and tapestries.   Across a
street, a landscape was visible through the latticed door, and it
seemed to me that I could distinguish the shapes of trees and rocks.
I had already lived there in some other existence, and I thought

---

[20] Owing to this reference, early editors, like Gautier and Houssaye, felt invited
to insert at this particular lacuna in the manuscript ten of the *Lettres d'Amour à Jenny
Colon*. Many of these are fragmentary redactions, some apparently intended for another use than in the *Aurélia* by Nerval, although in another moment he seemed to
have disliked the idea of their appearing before the public at all.   In a case of this
kind an editor, or translator, has to act as an interlocutor and, however sincerely
previous editors may have felt they were serving Nerval by inserting these letters
to Jenny here, Mlle de Rossi stands with those who have excised them. She is fully
confirmed by Béguin/Richer, who are fairly exhaustive in their paraphernalia and conclude, "Mieux vaut laisser la lacune." The text I translate, that of the original, is
surely the one Nerval himself would have preferred in the circumstances. Not only
is the artistic unity now undisturbed by this long interpolation, but we have a better
balance in the manuscript, and one that reflects Nerval's intentions more faithfully.
For suddenly to be confronted with a lengthy reminiscence of Jenny at this point
overemphasizes what was for Nerval only one aspect of his womanhood creation
in *Aurélia*. The letters to Jenny have frequently been published apart, and they can
be consulted in the Béguin/Richer edition of the *Oeuvres*, along with the rest of
Nerval's *Correspondance*.

I recognized the deep grottos of Ellora. [21] Gradually a bluish light penetrated the pavilion and brought out strange apparitions inside. I thought I was in the midst of some vast charnel-house where the history of the universe was written in characters of blood. [22] Opposite me was painted the body of an enormous woman; but various parts of her had been sliced off, as if by a sword; on the other walls, other women of different races, whose bodies dominated me more and more, made a bloody jumble of limbs and heads, ranging from empresses and queens to the humblest peasants. It was the history of all crime, and I only had to keep my eyes on any one spot to see depicted there some tragic scene.

"There," I told myself, "is what has resulted from power bestowed on man. Man has little by little destroyed and cut up the eternal type of beauty into a thousand little pieces, so that his races are more and more losing strength and perfection . . ." And indeed, on a line of shadow creeping in through a chink in the door, I saw the descending generations of future races.

At last I was torn from these macabre reflections. The kind and compassionate face of my excellent doctor brought me back to the living world. He allowed me to witness something that interested me intensely. Among the patients was a young man, once a soldier in Africa, who had refused to take food for six weeks. By means of a long rubber tube introduced into one of his nostrils, they poured a quantity of semolina and chocolate into his stomach.

This sight made a deep impression on me. Until then I had been given up to the monotonous circle of my own sensations or moral sufferings, and here I met an unaccountable creature, patient and taciturn, seated like a sphinx at the last gates of existence. I began to love him because of his misfortune and abandonment, and I

21 In the Deccan, supposedly the site of Aureng-zebe's tomb.
22 Audiat finds this idea borrowed from Cazotte's *Ollivier,* in a passage to which Nerval alludes in his preface to *Le Diable amoureux.* The point of noting this is to show that apparently not all Nerval's dreams in *Aurélia* were his own hallucinations, or, rather, that some of these dreams were as much literary memories as the play of his own imagination.

felt uplifted by this sympathy and pity. He seemed to me a sublime interpreter, placed between death and life, a confessor predestined to hear the soul's secrets which words dared not utter or could not succeed in expressing. It was the ear of God unsullied by another's thought. I spent hours in examining him mentally, my head bowed over his, and holding his hands. It seemed that a certain magnetism united our two spirits, and I was delighted the first time a word came from his mouth. No one would believe me, but I attributed this commencement of cure in him to my ardent will-power. That night I had a marvellous dream, the first for a long time. I was in a tower, so deep in the earth and so high in the heavens, that all my life seemed to be passed in going up and down it. Already my strength was spent, and my courage failing, when a door in the side opened, a spirit appeared and said: "Come, brother! . . ."

I do not know why but I had the idea that he was called Saturninus. He possessed the features of the poor sick man, only transformed and intelligent. We were in a countryside lit with the glow of the stars and, as we stopped to look at them, the spirit figure placed his hand upon my forehead, as I had done, the night before, when I had endeavored to magnetize my companion. Immediately one of the stars I could see in the sky began to grow larger, and the divinity of my dreams appeared, smiling, in a somewhat Indian robe, as I had seen her before. She walked between us, and the meadows grew green, flowers and leaves sprang up from the earth in her footsteps . . . She said to me: "The ordeal you have undergone is coming to an end; these countless stairways which wore you out so going up and down are the bonds of old illusions that impeded your thoughts; now remember the day when you implored the Holy Virgin and, thinking her dead, were possessed of a frenzy of the mind. Your vow must be carried to her by a simple soul, one free from the ties of the earth. She is near you and that is why I myself have been permitted to come and encourage you."

This dream filled my spirit with joy and brought with it a wonderful awakening. Day was breaking. I wanted some material sign of the vision which had consoled me, and so I wrote these words on the wall: "This night you came to me."

Here, under the title of *Memorabilia*, I will put down the impressions of certain dreams which followed the one I have just described.

MEMORABILIA

. . . .

The song of the shepherds has re-echoed about a slender peak in Auvergne. *Poor Mary!* Queen of the heavens! It is you they are invoking so piously. The rustic melody has reached the ears of the corybants. They emerge, singing also, from the secret caves where love gave them shelter. Hosannah! Peace on earth and glory in heaven!

In the Himalayas a little flower is born. Forget-me-not. The glittering gaze of a star plays on it for an instant, and an answer is heard in a soft foreign tongue. *Myosotis!*

A silver pearl shone in the sands; a golden pearl sparkled in the sky... The world was created. Pure loves, divine sighs! Inflame the sacred mountain... for you have brothers in the valleys and in the bosom of the woods shy sisters are hiding.

Perfumed arbors of Paphos, you mean less to me than those places where the life-giving air of one's own country can be breathed in deeply. Over there, on the mountain tops, the world dwells content. The wild nightingale creates contentment!

Oh, how beautiful is my dear friend! She is so dear that she has pardoned the world, so kind she has pardoned me. The other night she was sleeping in some palace and I could not join her. My dark chestnut stallion slipped from beneath me. The broken reins streamed along its sweating flanks, and it required enormous efforts on my part to keep it from lying down on the ground.

That night Saturninus came to my assistance and my dear friend took her place at my side on her white mare caparisoned with silver. She said to me: "Courage, brother! This is the last stage of the journey." And her great eyes consumed space, and her long hair, full of the perfume of Yemen, floated in the air.

I recognized the beloved features of ***. We flew to our triumph and our enemies fell at our feet. The messenger hoopoe led us to the summit of the skies, and the bow of light shone in the sacred hands of Apollo. The enchanted horn of Adonis echoed through the woods.

Oh Death, where is thy victory, now that the all-conquering Messiah has ridden between us? His garment was of the color of hyacinth, and his wrists and ankles sparkled with diamonds and rubies. When his light switch touched the pearly gates of the New Jerusalem, we were all three bathed in light. It was then that I came down among men to give them the glad tidings.

I have come out of a very sweet dream. I saw the woman I loved, radiant and transfigured. Heaven opened in all its glory and I read the word *forgiveness* written in Christ's blood.

A star shone suddenly and revealed the secret of the world of worlds to me. Hosannah! Peace on earth and glory in heaven!

From the depths of the silent shadows two notes rang out, one low, one shrill,—and the eternal orb immediately began to turn. Blessed be the first octave of the divine hymn! From Sabbath to Sabbath, let it enfold each day in its magic net. The hills sing of you to the valleys, the springs to the streams, the streams to the rivers, and the rivers to the sea; the air thrills, and light gently bursts the budding flowers. A sigh, a shiver of love comes from the swollen womb of earth, and the choir of stars unfolds itself in infinity; it parts and returns again, contracts and expands, sowing in the remoteness of space the seeds of new creations.

On the crest of a bluish mountain a little flower is born. Forget-me-not. The glittering gaze of a star plays on it for an instant, and an answer is heard in a soft foreign tongue. *Myosotis!*

Woe to you, God of the North,—who with one hammer blow broke the holy table, made of the seven most precious metals! For you could not break the *Rose Pearl* which reposed in its center.

It rebounded under your iron,—and here we are, armed for it . . .
Hosannah!

The *macrocosm*, or greater world, was constructed by Cabalistic
art; the *microcosm*, or smaller world, is its image reflected in every
heart. The Rose Pearl has been stained with the royal blood of
the Valkyries. Woe to you, God of the Forge, for attempting
to break the world!

But Christ's pardon was pronounced for you also.

Therefore blessed be thou, O giant Thor, Odin's most powerful
son! Be blessed in Hela, your mother, for often death is sweet,
and in your brother Loki, and in your hound Garnur!

The serpent which surrounds the world is itself blessed, for
it is slackening its coils, and its yawning jaws breathe in the anxoka,
the sulphurous flower, the bursting flower of the sun!

May God preserve sacred Balder, son of Odin, and the beautiful Freya!

. . . .

I found myself *in spirit* at Saardam, which I visited last year.
Snow lay on the ground. A little girl was walking and sliding
over the icy surface towards, as I thought, the house of Peter the
Great. Her proud profile had a Bourbon look. Her dazzlingly
white neck slightly emerged from a cape of swan's feathers. With
her little pink hand she sheltered a lighted lamp from the wind,
and was about to knock on the green door of the house when a
lean cat came out, entangled itself in her legs, and upset her.

"Why!" said the girl, getting up. "It's only a cat."

"Well, a cat is something after all," answered a soft voice.

I was present at this scene and I had in my arms a little grey
cat which began to mew.

"It's that old fairy's child!" said the little girl. And she went
into the house.

That night my dreams took me first to Vienna. Everyone
knows that on each of the squares of this city there is one of those
tall columns called *pardons*. Marble clouds are gathered to typify
the order of Solomon, and to uphold the globes where seated di-

vinities preside. Suddenly—oh, wonder!—I began to think of that august sister of the Emperor of Russia, whose imperial palace at Weimar I had seen. A fit of tender melancholy showed me the colored mists of a Norwegian landscape lit by a soft grey daylight. The clouds became transparent, and in front of me there opened an abyss into which rushed in tumult the frozen waves of the Baltic. It seemed that the whole of the Neva with its blue waters were to be swallowed up in this crack in the world. The ships of Cronstadt and Saint Petersburg bobbed at anchor, ready to break away and vanish in the gulf, when a divine radiance from above lighted up this scene of desolation.

In the bright beam of light piercing the mist, I saw the rock on which stands the statue of Peter the Great. Above this solid pedestal clouds rose in groups, piling up to the zenith. They were laden with radiant, heavenly forms, among which could be distinguished the two Catherines and the Empress Saint Helen, accompanied by the loveliest Princesses of Muscovy and Poland. Their gentle expressions, directed towards France, lessened the distance by means of long crystal telescopes. By that I saw that our country had become the arbiter of the old quarrel of the East, and that they were awaiting its solution. My dream ended in the sweet hope that peace would at last be granted us.

In this way I urged myself on to a bold undertaking. I resolved to fix my dream-state and learn its secret. "Why should I not," I asked myself, "at last force those mystic gates, armed with all my will-power, and dominate my sensations instead of being subject to them? Is it not possible to control this fascinating, dread chimera, to rule the spirits of the night which play with our reason? Sleep takes up a third of our lives. It consoles the sorrows of our days and the sorrow of their pleasures; but I have never felt any rest in sleep. For a few seconds I am numbed, then a new life begins, freed from the conditions of time and space, and doubtless similar to that state which awaits us after death. Who knows if there is not some link between those two existences and if it is not possible for the soul to unite them now?"

From that moment on I devoted myself to trying to find the meaning of my dreams, and this anxiety influenced my waking thoughts. I seemed to understand that there was a bond between the external and internal worlds: that only inattention or spiritual confusion distorted the outward affinities between them,—and this explained the strangeness of certain pictures, which are like grimacing reflections of real objects on a surface of troubled water.

Such were the inspirations of my nights; my days were spent quietly with the poor patients whom I had made my friends. The consciousness that henceforth I was purified from the faults of my past life gave me infinite mental delight; the certainty of immortality and of the co-existence of everyone I had loved was, as it were, a material reality for me now, and I blessed the fraternal soul who had brought me back from the depths of despair to the clear paths of religion.

The poor lad from whom intelligent life had been so strangely withdrawn was so well cared for that gradually his torpor was overcome. I learnt that he had been born in the country and so spent whole hours singing him old village songs, which I tried to make as moving as possible. I had the happiness of seeing that he heard them, and he repeated certain parts of the songs. At last, one day, he opened his eyes for a second, and I saw that they were as blue as those of the Spirit who had appeared to me in my dream. One morning, some days later, he kept his eyes wide open and did not shut them. Then he began to speak, though only at intervals, and he recognized me and addressed me in a familiar way, calling me brother. However, he still could not get himself to eat. One day, coming in from the garden, he said to me: "I am thirsty."

I went and got him something to drink; the glass touched his lips but he could not swallow.

"Why," I asked him, "don't you want to eat and drink like other people?"

"Because I am dead," he answered. "I was buried in a certain graveyard, and in a certain place there . . ."

"And where do you suppose you are now?"

"In Purgatory. I am undergoing my expiation."

Such are the odd ideas that come with that sort of sickness;
I recognized that I myself had not been far from just such a strange
belief. The way I had been cared for had already brought me
back to the affection of family and friends, and I was able to judge
with greater sanity the world of illusion in which I had lived for
a little while. All the same, I feel happy over those convictions
I have acquired, and I compare this series of trials I went through
to that ordeal which, for the ancients, represented the idea of a
descent into hell.

POETRY[1]

[1] The text used for this translation is the one established by Albert Béguin, and published as Gérard de Nerval, *Poésies*, texte établi et présenté par Albert Béguin, Lausanne, Mermod, 1944, a fuller edition than that contained in the Béguin/Richer *Oeuvres* of 1952. An attempt has been made to give here the dates of first publication in each instance; fuller details may be obtained by recourse to the bibliographical volume, prepared by Aristide Marie, in the Champion *Oeuvres Complètes*. Mention has been made of the more important collections of poetry Nerval himself published during his lifetime in the Introduction, and the poems have generally been taken in the way he himself assembled them. Owing to the physical limitations imposed on this volume, however, the selection of the poetry had to be rigorous. The *Poèmes de Jeunesse* and *Lyrisme et Vers d'Opéra* were not drawn from at all. Within the very small compass permitted it was hard to strike a representative balance, but the leaning was always towards the more mature poetry, and towards those poems which are close to the prose selections offered. It is even more difficult to please all tastes in the matter of the translation, of course, and the English facing the French texts is meant simply to give a reasonably literal rendering, with something of Nerval's feeling, which will refer the reader to the original, and in which the personality of the translator intrudes as little as possible. The English translations are not intended to stand as poems in their own right. The intention of this whole volume, in fact

is to divert the reader to, rather than from, Nerval's original writings. On the whole it will be seen that Nerval's French is accessible, a fact that does not, alas, make him any easier to translate. Perhaps one might turn Nerval's compliment to Heine on himself, when he told the German poet that there was only one man capable of translating him, and that was Heine.

CHAMBRE DE MARGUERITE.

Faust, 1828. I thought it might interest some readers to provide one example of Nerval's art of German translation. I chose this song, not only because it matches Nerval's own sentiments so well, but also because he reduced it to prose in the 1840 edition of his *Faust*. Both versions are given here, against Goethe's German. While it can be seen how beautifully Nerval translates this love lament—the verse sigh at the end of stanza 7 is delightfully caught—it will at once be seen that he took liberties with his original no modern critic would allow. This is an altogether different tradition of translation from our own.

CHAMBRE DE MARGUERITE

Une amoureuse flamme
Consume mes beaux jours;
Ah! la paix de mon âme
A donc fui pour toujours!

Son départ, son absence,
Sont pour moi le cercueil;
Et loin de sa présence
Tout me paraît en deuil.

Alors, ma pauvre tête
Se dérange bientôt;
Mon faible esprit s'arrête,
Puis se glace aussitôt.

Une amoureuse flamme
Consume mes beaux jours;
Ah! la paix de mon âme
A donc fui pour toujours!

Je suis à ma fenêtre,
Oh dehors, tout le jour,
C'est pour le voir paraître,
Ou hâter son retour.

Sa marche que j'admire,
Son port si gracieux,
Sa bouche au doux sourire,
Le charme de ses yeux;

La voix enchanteresse
Dont il sait m'embraser
De sa main la caresse,
Hélas! et son baiser...

D'une amoureuse flamme
Consumant mes beaux jours;
Ah! la paix de mon âme
A donc fui pour toujours!

Mon coeur bientôt se presse,
Dès qu'il le sent venir;
Au gré de ma tendresse
Puis-je le retenir?

O caresses de flamme!
Que je voudrais un jour
Voir s'exhaler mon âme
Dans ses baisers d'amour!

GRETCHENS STUBE
Gretchen am Spinnrade allein

Meine Ruh ist hin,
Mein Herz ist schwer;
Ich finde sie nimmer
Und nimmermehr.

Wo ich ihn nicht hab',
Ist mir das Grab,
Die ganze Welt
Ist mir vergällt.

Mein armer Kopf
Ist mir verrückt,
Mein armer Sinn
Ist mir zerstückt.

Meine Ruh ist hin,
Mein Herz ist schwer;
Ich finde sie nimmer
Und nimmermehr.

Nach ihm nur schau' ich
Zum Fenster hinaus,
Nach ihm nur geh' ich
Aus dem Haus.

Sein hoher Gang,
Sein' edle Gestalt,
Seines Mundes Lächeln,
Seiner Augen Gewalt,

Und seiner Rede
Zauberfluss,
Sein Händedruck,
Und ach! sein Kuss!

Meine Ruh ist hin,
Mein Herz ist schwer;
Ich finde sie nimmer
Und nimmermehr.

Mein Busen drängt
Sich nach ihm hin;
Ach, dürft' ich fassen
Und halten ihn!

Und küssen ihn,
So wie ich wollt',
An seinen Küssen
Vergehen sollt'!

(GOETHE, *Faust*, Erster Teil.)

CHAMBRE DE MARGUERITE

Le repos m'a fuie! hélas! la paix de mon coeur malade,
  je ne la trouve plus, et plus jamais!

Partout où je ne le vois pas, c'est la tombe! Le monde
  entier se voile de deuil!

Ma pauvre tête se brise, mon pauvre esprit s'anéantit!

Le repos m'a fuie! hélas! la paix de mon coeur malade,
  je ne la trouve plus, et plus jamais!

Je suis tout le jour à la fenêtre, ou devant la maison,
  pour l'apercevoir de plus loin, ou pour voler à sa rencontre!

Sa demarche fière, son port majestueux, le sourire de
  sa bouche, le pouvoir de ses yeux,

Et le charme de sa parole, et le serrement de sa main!
  et puis, ah! son baiser!

Le repos m'a fuie!... hélas! la paix de mon coeur
  malade, je ne la trouve plus, et plus jamais!

Mon coeur se serre à son approche! ah! que ne puis-je
  le saisir et le retenir pour toujours!

Et l'embrasser à mon envie! et finir mes jours sous ses baisers!

ODELETTES

NOBLES ET VALETS

Ces nobles d'autrefois dont parlent les romans,
Ces preux à fronts de boeuf, à figures dantesques,
Dont les corps charpentés d'ossements gigantesques
Semblaient avoir au sol racine et fondements;

S'ils revenaient au monde, et qu'il leur prît l'idée
De voir les héritiers de leurs noms immortels,
Race de Laridons, encombrant les hôtels
Des ministres, — rampante, avide et dégradée;

Êtres grêles, à buscs, plastrons et faux mollets: —
Certes ils comprendraient alors, ces nobles hommes,
Que, depuis les vieux temps, au sang des gentilshommes
Leurs filles ont mêlé bien du sang de valets!

NOBLEMEN AND LACKEYS

Those noblemen of old days you read of in books,
Mighty men with faces like beef and figures out of Dante,
Their bodies fashioned from huge bones,
Seemed to stem, root and stock, from the soil.

If they came back to earth and took into their heads
To see who had inherited their immortal names,
A Laridon progeny, cringing, greedy, and degraded,
Who clutter the mansions of our ministers today,

Frail fellows, corsetted, wearing chest-pads and false calves:
Surely then those noble men would know
That since their days their daughters had mingled much
Of the blood of lackeys with that of aristocracy.

LE RÉVEIL EN VOITURE

Voici ce que je vis: — Les arbres sur ma route
Fuyaient mêlés, ainsi qu'une armée en déroute;
Et sous moi, comme ému par les vents soulevés,
Le sol roulait des flots de glèbe et de pavés.

Des clochers conduisaient parmi les plaines vertes
Leurs hameaux aux maisons de plâtre, recouvertes
En tuiles, qui trottaient ainsi que des troupeaux
De moutons blancs, marqués en rouge sur le dos.

Et les monts enivrés chancelaient: la rivière
Comme un serpent boa, sur la vallée entière
Etendu, s'élançait pour les entortiller...
— J'étais en poste, moi, venant de m'éveiller!

AWAKENING IN THE CARRIAGE

This is what I saw—On the road the trees fleeing,
All intermingled, like a defeated army:
Underneath the ground swaying in the high wind
Like rolling waves of clod and paving-stone.

Among the green plains the steeples seemed to lead
Hamlets of plaster houses, tile-roofed,
Which trotted along like flocks
Of white sheep, marked in red on their backs.

And the drunken mountains tottered: the river,
Like a boa constrictor stretched over
The whole valley, darted out to wrap itself around them . . .
I was in the carriage, having just awoken!

LE RELAIS

En voyage, on s'arrête, on descend de voiture;
Puis entre deux maisons on passe à l'aventure,
Des chevaux, de la route et des fouets étourdi,
L'oeil fatigué de voir et le corps engourdi.

Et voici tout à coup, silencieuse et verte,
Une vallée humide et de lilas couverte,
Un ruisseau qui murmure entre les peupliers, —
Et la route et le bruit sont bien vite oubliés!

On se couche dans l'herbe et l'on s'écoute vivre,
De l'odeur du foin vert à loisir on s'enivre,
Et sans penser à rien on regarde les cieux...
Hélas! une voix crie: " En voiture, messieurs!"

FRESH HORSES

You stop on the way, get down from the carriage,
And by chance pass between two houses
Horses standing stunned after the hard-driven journey,
Their eyes tired of seeing and their bodies benumbed.

And then suddenly you see a valley,
Humid, silent, and green, covered in lilacs, a stream
Murmuring between poplars—and very soon
The roar of the road is quite forgotten.

Lying in the grass you listen to yourself living,
Leisurely you get drunk on the scent of green hay,
Watching without a thought the sky overhead . . . then
Unfortunately a voice calls out, "All aboard, gentlemen!"

UNE ALLÉE DU LUXEMBOURG

Elle a passé, la jeune fille
Vive et preste comme un oiseau:
À la main une fleur qui brille,
À la bouche un refrain nouveau.

C'est peut-être la seule au monde
Dont le coeur au mien répondrait,
Qui venant dans ma nuit profonde
D'un seul regard l'éclaircirait!

Mais non, — ma jeunesse est finie...
Adieu, doux rayon qui m'as lui, —
Parfum, jeune fille, harmonie...
Le bonheur passait, — il a fui!

A LANE IN THE LUXEMBOURG

And now the girl has passed me by,
Quick and nimble as a bird:
In her hand a dazzling flower,
On her lips a song unheard.

Perhaps she is the only one
Whose heart would answer mine,
Who with a single look would shine
And light my lonely night.

But no—my youth has gone . . .
Farewell, soft and illuminating ray,
Perfume, young girl, harmony . . .
Fortune fades,—has fled away.

NOTRE-DAME DE PARIS

Notre-Dame est bien vieille; on la verra peut-être
Enterrer cependant Paris qu'elle a vu naître.
Mais, dans quelque mille ans, le temps fera broncher
Comme un loup fait un boeuf, cette carcasse lourde,
Tordra ses nerfs de fer, et puis d'une dent sourde
Rongera tristement ses vieux os de rocher.

Bien des hommes de tous les pays de la terre
Viendront pour contempler cette ruine austère,
Rêveurs, et relisant le livre de Victor...
— Alors ils croiront voir la vieille basilique,
Tout ainsi qu'elle était puissante et magnifique,
Se lever devant eux comme l'ombre d'un mort!

NOTRE-DAME

Notre-Dame is very old; yet eventually perhaps
We shall see her bury the city she saw born, Paris.
Still, in some millenium, time will make her topple,
This heavy carcass, like a wolf makes an ox,
It will twist her iron sinews and with insensible tooth
Sadly corrode her old bones of rock.

Many men of every country on earth will come
To contemplate this austere ruin,
Dreaming, reading again that book by Victor...
—Thus they will think to see the old basilica,
Just as she used to be, powerful and splendid,
Rising before them like the shade of one dead!

AVRIL

Déjà les beaux jours, la poussière,
Un ciel d'azur et de lumière,
Les murs enflammés, les longs soirs;
Et rien de vert: à peine encore
Un reflet rougeâtre décore
Les grands arbres aux rameaux noirs!

Ce beau temps me pèse et m'ennuie.
Ce n'est qu'après des jours de pluie
Que doit surgir, en un tableau,
Le printemps verdissant et rose,
Comme une nymphe fraîche éclose,
Qui, souriante, sort de l'eau.

APRIL

Already there are fine days and dust,
Already a blazing,˙ azure sky,
The walls are on fire, the evenings lengthening,
And the green going; little by little
A reddish reflection decorates
The towering trees with their black branches.

This fine weather weighs me down and wearies me.
It is only after rainy days
That spring should surge up,
A picture going green and rose-colored,
Brought out like a new nymph
Who steps from the water, smiling.

FANTAISIE

Il est un air pour qui je donnerais
Tout Rossini, tout Mozart et tout Weber,
Un air très-vieux, languissant et funèbre,
Qui pour moi seul a des charmes secrets.

Or, chaque fois que je viens à l'entendre,
De deux cents ans mon âme rajeunit:
C'est sous Louis treize... Et je crois voir s'étendre
Un coteau vert que le couchant jaunit,

Puis un château de brique à coins de pierre,
Aux vitraux teints de rougeâtres couleurs,
Ceint de grands parcs, avec une rivière
Baignant ses pieds, qui coule entre des fleurs.

Puis une dame, à sa haute fenêtre,
Blonde aux yeux noirs, en ses habits anciens...
Que, dans une autre existence peut-être,
J'ai déjà vue! — et dont je me souviens!

FANTASY

There is a melody for which I would surrender
All Rossini, all Mozart, all Weber,
An ancient, langorous, funereal tune,
With hidden charms for me alone.

And every time I hear that air,
Suddenly I grow two centuries younger.
I live in the reign of Louis the Thirteenth . . . and see stretched out
A green slope yellowed by the sunset,

Then a brick castle with stone corners,
Its panes of glass stained by ruddy colors,
Encircled with great parks, and a river
Bathing its feet, flowing between flowers.

Then I see a fair-haired, dark-eyed lady
In old-fashioned costume, at a tall window,
Whom perhaps I have already seen somewhere
In another life . . . and whom I remember!

LA GRAND'MÈRE

Voici trois ans qu'est morte ma grand'mère,
— La bonne femme, — et, quand on l'enterra,
Parents, amis, tout le monde pleura
D'une douleur bien vraie et bien amère.

Moi seul j'errais dans la maison, surpris
Plus que chagrin; et, comme j'étais proche
De son cercueil, — quelqu'un me fit reproche
De voir cela sans larmes et sans cris.

Douleur bruyante est bien vite passée:
Depuis trois ans, d'autres émotions,
Des biens, des maux, — des révolutions, —
Ont des coeurs sa mémoire effacée.

Moi seul j'y songe, et la pleure souvent;
Depuis trois ans, par le temps prenant force,
Ainsi qu'un nom gravé dans une écorce,
Son souvenir se creuse plus avant!

GRANDMOTHER

It is three years now since grandmother died,
The dear soul: and when she was buried,
Everyone, parents and friends, wept for her,
With a sorrow that was very real and very bitter.

Only I wandered through the house,
Feeling surprise rather than sadness; and as I went close
To her coffin, they told me I ought not to see it
Without wanting to cry.

Vociferous sorrow is soon over:
For three years, other emotions,
Good and evil, even revolutions,
Have erased this memory from the minds of men.

Only I think of it and weep for her.often;
For three years now, taking strength from time,
Like a name engraved in the bark of a tree,
Her memory sinks more deeply into me.

POLITIQUE

1832

Dans Sainte-Pélagie,
Sous ce règne élargie,
Où, rêveur et pensif,
   Je vis captif,

Pas une herbe ne pousse
Et pas un brin de mousse
Le long des murs grillés
   Et frais taillés!

Oiseau qui fends l'espace...
Et toi, brise, qui passe
Sur l'étroit horizon
   De la prison,

Dans votre vol superbe,
Apportez-moi quelque herbe,
Quelque gramen, mouvant
   Sa tête au vent!

Qu'à mes pieds tourbillonne
Une feuille d'automne
Peinte de cent couleurs
   Comme les fleurs!

POLITICS

1832

In Saint Pélagie prison,
Under this liberal regime,
Where, dreaming and thoughtful,
  I languish a captive,

Not a blade of grass,
And no moss grows,
Along the recently constructed,
  Barred walls!

O bird cleaving space . . .
And breeze passing over
The narrow horizon
  Of our prison,

In your proud flight
Bring me some weed,
Or blade of grass that has stirred
  Its head in the wind!

Let an autumn leaf
Whirl at my feet
Painted with hundreds of colors
  Like the flowers!

Pour que mon âme triste
Sache encor qu'il existe
Une nature, un Dieu
    Dehors ce lieu,

Faites-moi cette joie,
Qu'un instant je revoie
Quelque chose de vert
    Avant l'hiver!

So my unhappy soul
May know there still are
Nature and God
  Beyond this prison,

Permit me this pleasure,
Let me see for a moment
Something that is green
  Before winter!

LES CYDALISES

Où sont nos amoureuses?
Elles sont au tombeau:
Elles sont plus heureuses,
Dans un séjour plus beau!

Elles sont près des anges,
Dans le fond du ciel bleu,
Et chantent les louanges
De la mère de Dieu!

O blanche fiancée!
O jeune vierge en fleur!
Amante délaissée,
Que flétrit la douleur!

L'éternité profonde
Souriait dans vos yeux...
Flambeaux éteints du monde,
Rallumez-vous aux cieux!

THE CYDALISES

Where are our lovers?
They are in the grave:
They are far happier,
In a more beautiful region.

They are close to the angels,
In the depths of the sky,
Singing the praises
Of the Mother of God!

O white betrothed!
O virgin in flower!
Forsaken beloved,
Faded by sorrow.

Deep eternity
Smiled in your eyes...
May you relight in heaven
The dead torches of this world.

LES CHIMÈRES
CHIMERAS

EL DESDICHADO

Je suis le ténébreux, — le veuf, — l'inconsolé,
Le prince d'Aquitaine à la tour abolie:
Ma seule *étoile* est morte, — et mon luth constellé
Porte le *soleil* noir de la *Mélancolie.*

Dans la nuit du tombeau, toi qui m'as consolé,
Rends-moi le Pausilippe et la mer d'Italie,
La *fleur* qui plaisait tant à mon coeur désolé,
Et la treille où le pampre à la rose s'allie.

Suis-je Amour ou Phébus?... Lusignan ou Biron?
Mon front est rouge encor du baiser de la reine;
J'ai rêvé dans la grotte où nage la sirène...

Et j'ai deux fois vainqueur traversé l'Achéron:
Modulant tour à tour sur la lyre d'Orphée
Les soupirs de la sainte et les cris de la fée.

EL DESDICHADO

I am the dark man, the disconsolate widower,
The prince of Aquitania whose tower has been torn down:
My sole *star* is dead,—and my constellated lute
Bears the black *sun* of *Melancolia.*

In the darkness of my grave, you who have consoled me,
Give me back Posilipo and the Italian sea,
The *flower* so dear to my tormented heart,
And the arbor of vines where the rose twines the branch.

Am I Amor or Phoebus? . . . Lusignan or Biron?
My forehead is still red with the kiss of the queen;
In the grotto where the siren swims I have had a dream . . .

And twice I have crossed and conquered the Acheron:
On Orpheus' lyre in turn I have sent
The cries of faery and the sighs of a saint.

MYRTHO

Je pense à toi, Myrtho, divine enchantcresse,
Au Pausilippe altier, de mille feux brillant,
A ton front inondé des clartés d'Orient,
Aux raisins noirs mêlés avec l'or de ta tresse.

C'est dans ta coupe aussi que j'avais bu l'ivresse,
Et dans l'éclair furtif de ton oeil souriant,
Quand aux pieds d'Iacchus on me voyait priant,
Car la Muse m'a fait l'un des fils de la Grèce.

Je sais pourquoi là-bas le volcan s'est rouvert...
C'est qu'hier tu l'avais touché d'un pied agile,
Et de cendres soudain l'horizon s'est couvert.

Depuis qu'un duc normand brisa tes dieux d'argile,
Toujours, sous les rameaux du laurier de Virgile,
Le pâle hortensia s'unit au myrte vert!

MYRTO

It is of you, divine enchanteress, I am thinking, Myrto,
Burning with a thousand fires at haughty Posilipo,
Of your forehead flowing with an Oriental glare,
Of the black grapes mixed with the gold of your hair.

From your cup also I drank to intoxication,
And from the furtive lightning of your smiling eyes,
While I was seen praying at the feet of Iacchus,
For the Muse has made me one of Greece's sons.

Over there the volcano has re-opened, and I know
It is because yesterday you touched it with your nimble toe,
And suddenly the horizon was covered with ashes.

Since a Norman Duke shattered your gods of clay,
Evermore, beneath the branches of Virgil's laurel,
The pale hydrangea mingles with the green myrtle!

HORUS

Le dieu Kneph en tremblant ébranlait l'univers:
Isis, la mère, alors se leva sur sa couche,
Fit un geste de haine à son époux farouche,
Et l'ardeur d'autrefois brilla dans ses yeux verts.

" Le voyez-vous, dit-elle, il meurt, ce vieux pervers,
Tous les frimas du monde ont passé par sa bouche,
Attachez son pied tors, éteignez son oeil louche,
C'est le dieu des volcans et le roi des hivers!

" L'aigle a déjà passé, l'esprit nouveau m'appelle,
J'ai revêtu pour lui la robe de Cybèle...
C'est l'enfant bien-aimé d'Hermès et d'Osiris!"

La déesse avait fui sur sa conque dorée,
La mer nous renvoyait son image adorée,
Et les cieux rayonnaient sous l'écharpe d'Iris.

HORUS

Trembling, God Kneph shuddered the universe:
Then Isis, the mother, lying on her bed, arose,
Made a gesture of hatred at her savage spouse,
And the fire of old shone in her green eyes.

"Do you see him," she said, "he is dying, the old
Pervert, all the frosts of the world have passed by
His mouth, tie up his crook foot, put out his squint eye,
He is lord of volcanoes and king of winter's cold!

Already the eagle has gone, the new spirit calls me,
I have put on for him the robe of Cybele...
He is the beloved infant of Hermes and Osiris!"

On her gilded shell the goddess had gone,
The sea gave us back the image of this adorable one,
And the heavens flamed under the scarf of Iris.

ANTÉROS

Tu demandes pourquoi j'ai tant de rage au coeur
Et sur un col flexible une tête indomptée;
C'est que je suis issu de la race d'Antée,
Je retourne les dards contre le dieu vainqueur.

Oui, je suis de ceux-là qu'inspire le Vengeur,
Il m'a marqué le front de sa lèvre irritée,
Sous la pâleur d'Abel, hélas! ensanglantée,
J'ai parfois de Caïn l'implacable rougeur!

Jéhovah! le dernier, vaincu par ton génie,
Qui, du fond des enfers, criait: " O tyrannie! "
C'est mon aïeul Bélus ou mon père Dagon...

Ils m'ont plongé trois fois dans les eaux du Cocyte,
Et, protégeant tout seul ma mère Amalécyte,
Je ressème à ses pieds les dents du vieux dragon.

ANTEROS

You ask me why my heart is raging so,
Why I carry an unflinching head upon my supple neck,
It is because I come from the race of Antaeus
That I hurl back the darts against the all-conquering god.

Yes, I am one of those whom the Avenger drives,
He has scarred my forehead with his angry lip,
And sometimes, alas, Abel's pallor is covered in blood,
For I carry from Cain that inexorable red.

Jehovah! the last man, conquered by your genius,
From the depths of hell, cried out: "O tyranny!"
It is Belus, my ancestor, or my father Dagon...

Three times they have plunged me in the waters of Cocytus,
Now alone I protect my mother Amalek,
Sowing again at her feet the old dragon's teeth.

DELFICA

La connais-tu, Dafné, cette ancienne romance,
Au pied du sycomore, ou sous les lauriers blancs,
Sous l'olivier, le myrte, ou les saules tremblants,
Cette chanson d'amour qui toujours recommence?...

Reconnais-tu le TEMPLE au péristyle immense,
Et les citrons amers où s'imprimaient tes dents,
Et la grotte, fatale aux hôtes imprudents,
Où du dragon vaincu dort l'antique semence?...

Ils reviendront, ces Dieux que tu pleures toujours!
Le temps va ramener l'ordre des anciens jours;
La terre a tressailli d'un souffle prophétique...

Cependant la sibylle au visage latin
Est endormie encor sous l'arc de Constantin
— Et rien n'a dérangé le sévère portique.

DELFICA

Do you know that old tale, Daphne,
That love song that always begins again,
At the foot of the sycamore or under white laurels,
Beneath the olive tree, myrtle or quivering willow? . . .

Do you remember the TEMPLE with the huge peristyle,
The bitter lemons in which you sank your teeth,
And that grotto, fatal to rash visitors,
Where sleeps the conquered dragon's ancient seed? . . .

They will return, those gods you still weep for!
Time will bring back the order of old days;
Earth has trembled with a sigh of prophecy . . .

But still the sibyl with the Latin countenance
Is sleeping under the arch of Constantine
—And nothing has disturbed the stern portico.

ARTÉMIS

La Treizième revient... C'est encor la première;
Et c'est toujours la seule, — ou c'est le seul moment;
Car es-tu reine, ô toi! la première ou dernière?
Es-tu roi, toi le seul ou le dernier amant?...

Aimez qui vous aima du berceau dans la bière;
Celle que j'aimai seul m'aime encor tendrement:
C'est la mort — ou la morte... O délice! ô tourment!
La rose qu'elle tient, c'est la *Rose trémière*.

Sainte napolitaine aux mains pleines de feux,
Rose au coeur violet, fleur de sainte Gudule:
As-tu trouvé ta croix dans le désert des cieux?

Roses blanches, tombez! vous insultez nos dieux,
Tombez, fantômes blancs, de votre ciel qui brûle:
— La sainte de l'abîme est plus sainte à mes yeux!

ARTEMIS

The Thirteenth returns ... Once more she is the first;
And she is still the only one, or this the only moment;
For you are surely queen, first and last?
For you are surely king, O first and last lover? ...

Love the one who loved you from the cradle to the grave;
The one alone I love loves me dearly still:
She is death—or the dead one ... Delight or torment!
And the rose she holds is the *hollyhock*.

Saint of Naples with your hands full of fires,
Mauve-hearted rose, flower of Saint Gudule:
Have you discovered your cross in the desert of the skies?

White roses, fall! you offend our gods,
Fall, white phantoms, from your burning heaven:
—The saint of the pit is stronger in my eyes!

VERS DORÉS

Eh quoi! tout est sensible!

PYTHAGORE.

Homme, libre penseur! te crois-tu seul pensant
Dans ce monde où la vie éclate en toute chose?
Des forces que tu tiens ta liberté dispose,
Mais de tous tes conseils l'univers est absent.

Respecte dans la bête un esprit agissant:
Chaque fleur est une âme à la Nature éclose;
Un mystère d'amour dans le métal repose;
"Tout est sensible!" Et tout sur ton être est puissant.

Crains, dans le mur aveugle, un regard qui t'épie:
A la matière même un verbe est attaché...
Ne la fais pas servir à quelque usage impie!

Souvent dans l'être obscur habite un Dieu caché;
Et comme un oeil naissant couvert par ses paupières,
Un pur esprit s'accroît sous l'écorce des pierres!

GILDED VERSES

Everything is sentient.
PYTHAGORAS.

Do you think that you alone can think, free-thinking man,
In this world where life bursts out in everything?
In your liberty you dispose those forces at your command,
But the universe is far from all your plans.

Honor in each animal an active spirit;
Each flower is a soul blossoming in Nature;
In metal there dwells a mystery of love;
"Everything is sentient!" And everything has power upon you.

Fear then, in the blind wall, the prying glance:
A voice is attached to matter itself...
Do not therefore put matter to impious use!

Often in an obscure being lives a hidden God,
And, like a new-born eye covered by its lids,
A pure spirit grows under the covering of stone!

AUTRES CHIMÈRES
MORE CHIMERAS

LA TÊTE ARMÉE

Napoléon mourant vit une *Tête armée*...
Il pensait à son fils déjà faible et souffrant:
La Tête, c'était donc sa France bien-aimée,
Décapitée, aux pieds du César expirant.

Dieu, qui jugeait cet homme et cette renommée,
Rappela Jésus-Christ; mais l'abîme, s'ouvrant,
Ne rendit qu'un vain souffle, un spectre de fumée:
Le demi-dieu, vaincu, se releva plus grand.

Alors on vit sortir du fond du purgatoire
Un jeune homme inondé des pleurs de la Victoire,
Qui tendit sa main pure aux monarques des cieux;

Frappés au flanc tous deux par un double mystère,
L'un répandait son sang pour féconder la terre,
L'autre versait au ciel la semence des dieux!

THE ARMED HEAD

As he died, Napoleon saw an armed head . . .
He thought of his already weak and suffering son:
So the head was his beloved France,
Decapitated, dying at its Caesar's feet.

God, who judged that man and his renown,
Recalled Jesus Christ; but the pit opened up
And gave only an empty breath, a specter of smoke:
Conquered, the demi-god raised himself higher.

Then, emerging from the depths of purgatory, was seen
A youth wet with the tears of Victory,
Holding out his unsullied hand to the rulers of the skies.

Both their sides were struck by a double dilemma,
One poured out his blood to fertilize the earth,
The other spilt to heaven the seed of the gods!

A MADAME IDA DUMAS

J'étais assis chantant aux pieds de Michaël;
Mithra sur notre tête avait fermé sa tente;
Le Roi des rois dormait dans sa couche éclatante,
Et tous deux en rêvant nous pleurions Israël,

Quand Tippoo se leva dans la nuée ardente...
Trois voix avaient crié vengeance au bord du ciel;
Il rappela d'en haut mon frère Gabriel,
Et tourna vers Michel sa prunelle sanglante:

" Voici venir le loup, le tigre et le lion...
L'un s'appelle Ibrahim, l'autre Napoléon
Et l'autre Abd-el-Kader qui rugit dans la poudre;

" Le glaive d'Alaric, le sabre d'Attila,
Ils les ont... Mon epée et ma lance sont là;
Mais le César romain nous a volé la foudre."

TO MADAME IDA DUMAS

I was sitting singing at the feet of Michael;
Mitra had closed his tent overhead;
The King of Kings slept on his dazzling bed,
And both of us in our dreams wept for Israel,

When Tippoo arose in the burning cloud ...
At the sky's edge three voices had demanded revenge;
He called back from on high my brother Gabriel,
And turned his bloody pupil towards Michael:

"Here comes the wolf, the tiger and the lion ...
The first is called Ibrahim, the second Napoleon
And the last Abd-el-Kader roaring in the powder-smoke;

"The blade of Alaric, the saber of Attila,
Such men carry them ... My own sword and spear are there;
But the Roman Caesar has stolen our thunder."

A MADAME AGUADO

Colonne de saphir, d'arabesques brodée,
Reparais! Les ramiers s'envolent de leur nid.
De ton bandeau d'azur à ton pied de granit
Se déroule à long plis la pourpre de Judée.

Si tu vois Bénarès, sur son fleuve accoudée,
Détache avec ton arc ton corset d'or bruni,
Car je suis le vautour volant sur Patani,
Et de blancs papillons la mer est inondée.

Lanassa! fais flotter ton voile sur les eaux,
Livre les fleurs de pourpre au courant des ruisseaux.
La neige du Cathay tombe sur l'Atlantique.

Cependant la prêtresse au visage vermeil
Est endormie encor sous l'arche du soleil,
Et rien n'a derangé le sévère portique.

TO MADAME AGUADO

O sapphire column, embroidered with arabesque designs,
Come back again! The ring-doves are flying from their nests.
The purple of Judaea unfolds itself in each long pleat
From your azure head-band to your granite feet.

If you see Benares leaning on her river,
Loose with your bow your corset of burnished gold,
For I am the vulture flying over Patani,
And the sea is soaked in butterflies of white.

Lanassa! let your veil float on the waters,
Deliver the purple flowers to the ripple of the streams.
The snow of Cathay falls on the Atlantic.

Yet still the priestess with the ruddy countenance
Is sleeping under the archway of the sun,
And nothing has disturbed the stern portico.

POÉSIES DIVERSES
VARIOUS POEMS

STANCES ÉLÉGIAQUES

Ce ruisseau, dont l'onde tremblante
Réfléchit la clarté des cieux,
Paraît dans sa course brillante
Étinceler de mille feux;
Tandis qu'au fond du lit paisible,
Où, par une pente insensible,
Lentement s'écoulent ses flots,
Il entraîne une fange impure
Qui d'amertume et de souillure
Partout empoisonne ses eaux.

De même un passager délire,
Un éclair rapide et joyeux
Entr'ouvre ma bouche au sourire,
Et la gaîté brille en mes yeux;
Cependant mon âme est de glace,
Et rien n'effacera la trace
Des malheurs qui m'ont terrassé.
En vain passera ma jeunesse,
Toujours l'importune tristesse
Gonflera mon coeur oppressé.

Car il est un nuage sombre,
Un souvenir mouillé de pleurs,
Qui m'accable et répand son ombre
Sur mes plaisirs et mes douleurs.
Dans ma profonde indifférence,
De la joie ou de la souffrance

ELEGIAC STANZAS

This stream, whose quivering wave
Reflects the brilliance of the skies,
Seems in its sparkling course
To shine with a thousand fires;
While at the bottom of its peaceful bed,
Where the waves flow slowly
Down an imperceptible slope,
It drags an impure slime,
And this everywhere poisons its waters
With a bitter filth.

In the same way a passing frenzy,
A rapid, joyous flash
Half-opens my mouth in a smile,
And laughter shines in my eyes;
Yet my soul is like ice,
And nothing will erase the mark
Made by depressing misfortune.
My youth will pass in vain,
Insistent sadness shall always
Swell my oppressed heart.

For the cloud is a dark one,
A memory soaked in tears,
It bears me down and spreads its shadow
On each pleasure and each sorrow.
In this deep indifference
I am unmoved by any sting

L'aiguillon ne peut m'émouvoir;
Les biens que le vulgaire envie
Peut-être embelliront ma vie,
Mais rien ne me rendra l'espoir.

Du tronc à demi détachée
Par le souffle des noirs autans,
Lorsque la branche desséchée
Revoit les beaux jours du printemps,
Si parfois un rayon mobile,
Errant sur sa tête stérile,
Vient brillanter ses rameaux nus,
Elle sourit à la lumière;
Mais la verdure printanière
Sur son front ne renaîtra plus.

Of either joy or suffering;
Wealth which the crowd envies
Will perhaps adorn my life,
But nothing will give me back hope.

Half-severed from its trunk
By the black breath of south winds,
The dry branch sees once more
The lovely days of spring
And smiles at the light,
As now and then a lively ray
Wandering on its sterile head,
Makes its naked branches glitter;
But never will its face be seen
Clad again in springtime's green.

MÉLODIE IRLANDAISE
(*Imitée de Thomas Moore.*)

Le soleil du matin commençait sa carrière,
Je vis près du rivage une barque légère
Se bercer mollement sur les flots argentés.
Je revins quand la nuit descendait sur la rive:
La nacelle était là, mais l'onde fugitive
Ne baignait plus ses flancs dans le sable arrêtés.

Et voilà notre sort! au matin de la vie
Par des rêves d'espoir notre âme poursuivie
Se balance un moment sur les flots du bonheur;
Mais, sitôt que le soir étend son voile sombre,
L'onde qui nous portait se retire, et dans l'ombre
Bientôt nous restons seuls en proie à la douleur.

Au déclin de nos jours on dit que notre tête
Doit trouver le repos sous un ciel sans tempête;
Mais qu'importe à mes voeux le calme de la nuit!
Rendez-moi le matin, la fraîcheur et les charmes;
Car je préfère encor ses brouillards et ses larmes
Aux plus douces lueurs du soleil qui s'enfuit.

Oh! qui n'a désiré voir tout à coup renaître
Cet instant dont le charme éveilla dans son être
Et des sens inconnus et de nouveaux transports!
Où son âme, semblable à l'écorce embaumée,
Qui disperse en brûlant sa vapeur parfumée,
Dans les feux de l'amour exhala ses trésors!

IRISH MELODY
(*After Thomas Moore.*)

When the morning sun began its course,
Beside the bank a slender boat was softly
Cradled on the silvery waves.
It was night when I came back;
The little boat was there, but now the tide no longer
Bathed its sides, and it stood locked in the sands.

Such is our own fate! In the morning of life
Our spirits are hunted by hopeful dreams,
And balance a while on the surges of good luck;
But when evening extends its somber veil,
The swell that supported us retires, and in the shadow
Soon we become a lonely prey to sorrow.

In the fading of our days we are told that our head
Should find repose beneath a stormless sky;
But no calm of night is any use to my desires!
Give me morning again, freshness and charm,
For I still prefer its mists and tears
To the softest lights of a disappearing sun.

Oh! Who has not wished to see suddenly reborn
That moment of delight that awakens his whole being,
Creating unknown senses and new raptures,
When his soul, like embalmed bark,
Scattering, as it burns, its scented vapors,
Breathes out its treasures in love's first ardors!

LAISSE-MOI

Non, laisse-moi, je t'en supplie;
En vain, si jeune et si jolie,
Tu voudrais ranimer mon coeur:
Ne vois-tu pas, à ma tristesse,
Que mon front pâle et sans jeunesse
Ne doit plus sourire au bonheur?

Quand l'hiver aux froides haleines
Des fleurs qui brillent dans nos plaines
Glace le sein épanoui,
Qui peut rendre à la feuille morte
Ses parfums que la brise emporte
Et son éclat évanoui?

Oh! si je t'avais rencontrée
Alors que mon âme enivrée
Palpitait de vie et d'amours,
Avec quel transport, quel délire
J'aurais accueilli ton sourire
Dont le charme eût nourri mes jours!

Mais à présent, ô jeune fille!
Ton regard, c'est l'astre qui brille
Aux yeux troublés des matelots,
Dont la barque en proie au naufrage,
A l'instant où cesse l'orage,
Se brise et s'enfuit sous les flots.

LEAVE ME

No, leave me, I implore you;
Young and pretty as you are, it is in vain
You try to awaken my heart:
Do you not see from my sadness
That my pale and ageing forehead
May no more smile at happiness?

When the cold breath of winter
Freezes the blossoming breast
Of the flowers that shine in our valleys,
Who can give back to the dead leaf
Its perfumes carried off in the wind
And its vanished brilliance?

Ah! if only I had met you in those old days
When my intoxicated soul
Trembled with life and loves,
With what ecstasy and what delight
Would I have welcomed your smile
Whose charms might have nourished my days!

But now, O young girl,
Your look is like that star which shines
In the troubled eyes of sailors,
Whose ship is a prey to wreck,
The moment the storm ceases,
And breaks and scatters under the waves.

Non, laisse-moi, je t'en supplie;
En vain, si jeune et si jolie,
Tu voudrais ranimer mon coeur:
Sur ce front pâle· et sans jeunesse
Ne vois-tu pas que la tristesse
A banni l'espoir du bonheur?

No, leave me, I implore you;
Young and pretty as you are, it is in vain
You try to awaken my heart:
Do you not see that sadness
Has banished all hope of fortune
From this pale and ageing forehead?

UNE FEMME EST L'AMOUR

Une femme est l'amour, la gloire et l'espérance;
Aux enfants qu'elle guide, à l'homme consolé,
Elle élève le coeur et calme la souffrance,
Comme un esprit des cieux sur la terre exilé.

Courbé par le travail ou par la destinée,
L'homme à sa voix s'élève et son front s'éclaircit;
Toujours impatient dans sa course bornée,
Un sourire le dompte et son coeur s'adoucit.

Dans ce siècle de fer la gloire est incertaine:
Bien longtemps à l'attendre il faut se résigner.
Mais qui n'aimerait pas, dans sa grâce sereine,
La beauté qui la donne ou qui la fait gagner?

A WOMAN IS LOVE

A woman is love, fame and expectation;
To the children she brings up, to the consoled man,
She lifts the heart and calms all suffering,
Like a spirit of heaven exiled on the earth.

Bent by labor or again by destiny,
Man rises at her voice and his face brightens;
Always impatient in his trammeled course,
A smile subdues him and his heart softens.

In this iron century fame is uncertain:
One has to be resigned to waiting for it long.
But who should not love, in its serene charm,
The beauty that gives it or lets it be won?

ÉPITAPHE

Il a vécu tantôt gai comme un sansonnet,
Tour à tour amoureux insoucieux et tendre,
Tantôt sombre et rêveur comme un triste Clitandre,
Un jour il entendit qu'à sa porte on sonnait.

C'était la Mort! Alors il la pria d'attendre
Qu'il eût posé le point à son dernier sonnet;
Et puis sans s'émouvoir, il s'en alla s'étendre
Au fond du coffre froid où son corps frissonnait.

Il était paresseux, à ce que dit l'histoire,
Il laissait trop sécher l'encre dans l'écritoire.
Il voulait tout savoir mais il n'a rien connu.

Et quand vint le moment où, las de cette vie,
Un soir d'hiver, enfin l'âme lui fut ravie,
Il s'en alla disant: Pourquoi suis-je venu?

EPITAPH

At times he lived gaily as a starling,
Amorous, careless and tender in turn,
At times he was somber, dreaming like some sad Clitandre,
One day he heard a knocking at his door.

It was Death! So he asked her to wait
Until he had completed his last sonnet;
And then calmly he went to be laid out
At the bottom of the cold coffin, in which his body shivered.

He was lazy, so they say,
He let the ink dry too often in the well.
He wished to know all things but discovered nothing.

And when the moment came when, tired of this life,
One winter evening at last his soul was torn from him,
He went away asking: Why did I come?

NOTES TO THE POEMS

ODELETTES

NOBLES ET VALETS.

Almanach des Muses, 1832. Line 7 refers in Laridon to the name of the dog in La Fontaine's *l'Éducation* typifying degeneracy: "Oh! combien de Césars deviendront Laridons!"

LE RÉVEIL EN VOITURE.

Almanach des Muses, 1832.

LE RELAIS.

Almanach des Muses, 1832.

UNE ALLÉE DU LUXEMBOURG.

Almanach des Muses, 1832.

NOTRE-DAME DE PARIS.

Almanach des Muses, 1832.

AVRIL.

Almanach dédié aux Demoiselles, 1831.
Annales romantiques, 1835, under the title, *Le Vingt-Cinq Mars.*

FANTAISIE.

Annales romantiques, 1832. In 1843, when Nerval published this poem under the title *Vision* in *La Sylphide,* he dedicated it to Théophile Gautier. There is more than a hint of the Mortefontaine château, mentioned in *Sylvie,* in the last two stanzas of this poem. Jeanine Moulin believe that it was principally addressed to Adrienne, in which case it is possible that Nerval saw Madame de Feuchères at a tall window in the château of Saint-Leu, near Pontoise. S. A. Rhodes, in his excellent biography of Nerval, suggests that the air referred to at the beginning may be the evocatory hymn Nerval sings in *Aurélia,* as he follows the star to what he believes to be death. It but remains to add that a variant of the second line ends "tout Wèbre." In the poem as we have it here, Nerval clearly wished this pronunciation to be used.

LA GRAND'MÈRE.

Annales romantiques, 1835.

POLITIQUE.

Le Cabinet de Lecture, 4 décembre 1831, under the title *Cour de Prison.* This refers to Nerval's brief "political" imprisonment, mentioned in the Introduction. Line 8 recalls that Sainte-Pélagie was built in the rue du Puits-de-l'Ermite in 1792, about forty years before Nerval was lodged within its walls. During the 1830 revolution the debtors imprisoned there constructed a battering-ram and broke out, but once outside they at once appointed several of their number to help guard the real criminals left behind, an incident that well characterizes the mood of this bourgeois revolution. The prison was demolished in 1899.

LES CYDALISES.

Petits Châteaux de Bohème, 1852.

LES CHIMÈRES

Twelve sonnets were grouped under this head by Nerval, as an appendix to *Les Filles du Feu* of 1854. Seven of them had previously been collected, under the head "Mysticisme," in his *Petits Châteaux de Bohème.* They must remain the despair of those who wish to add *brief* exegetical notes; in those I have given I would like to acknowledge indebtedness to Jeanine Moulin's study, *Les Chimères de Gérard de Nerval,* of 1937. It is as well to approach these poems through Nerval's statement: "La femme est la Chimère de l'homme ou son démon, comme vous voudrez."

EL DESDICHADO.

Le Mousquetaire, 10 décembre 1853. A manuscript in the possession of Paul Eluard* carries the title, *Le Destin.* This poem is a cornerstone of Nerval's work and has drawn out innumerable commentaries. One of the most helpful for a newcomer to Nerval is that provided by S. A. Rhodes:

The poem is autobiographical, like most of his verses, but every personal allusion in it, real or imagined, has been transmuted into a myth. He dubbed himself 'widowed' and 'Prince of Aquitania,' for he fancied himself a scion of the fabled Brunyer de la Brunie, whose towers in old Aquitania had, indeed, long since been destroyed: and he was 'widowed' by the death of his only star, Aurélia, or Jenny Colon—all of which means symbolically that he had been excluded from the earthly paradise as a divine punishment, since that is the cabalistic significance of the 'torn down tower,' and the name '*Broun* or *Brunn* means *tower*,' Gérard himself indicated on his genealogical tree. The sun on his star-studded lute was therefore black, like that in Albert Dürer's engraving... but the sonnet evokes also memories of his Italian journeys, visits with Octavie to the Posilipo and the grotto underneath, and promises of bliss that he never reaped, for the flower that delighted his heart was *the other.* Hence his complaint in the tercet.

To this admirable general commentary one may add that Nerval really imagined himself descended from the old Labrunie family whose ruined castle still stands on

---

* This was written before Eluard's death.

the banks of the Dordogne. The second line was lifted and used as line 429 of *The Waste Land* by T.S. Eliot who suggests Richard Coeur-de-Lion by the prince, owing to his association in the poem with Arnaut Daniel, "il miglior fabbro" as Guido Guinicelli calls him in the *Purgatorio*. The Biron family, including the famous Marshal of France under Henry IV, and his treacherous son, came principally from the Périgord, while the Lusignans held Cyprus between 1192 and 1475, Amalric and Guy de Lusignan playing notable parts in the history of the Latin East. As Audiat puts it: "Like Biron a traitor to his fatherland, like Lusignan the toy of a delicious siren, is he not at the same time guilty and abandoned?"

MYRTHO.

L'Artiste, 15 février 1854. This poem is clearly part of the same vision that inspired *Delfica* and another poem, not included here since two stanzas are the same as those of *Delfica*, namely *A J.Y. Colonna*. This latter title is an obvious Italianate of Jenny Colon, comprising also Francesco Colonna whose love for Lucrezia Ippolita Nerval likened to his own for Adrienne. The Norman Duke mentioned in line 12 is Duke Roger who took Naples in 1130. The poem is surely addressed to Octavie, the young English girl he took to Posilipo and whom he liked to invest with the attributes of Isis. Under this aspect of eternity (Virgil's laurel symbolizing art) the imagery of the last line unites Octavie, epitomized by the Christian flower, "Le pâle hortensia," of the north, with the pagan and dark beauty of the "myrte" of Sylvie.

HORUS.

Les Filles du Feu, 1854. Again Nerval invokes Isis. Line 11, as well as linking in with the erotic imagery, makes an apt alchemical analogy. Horus, Egyptian God of Light, was the child of Isis and Osiris, and a symbol of life produced by an heroic mother, similar in this to Christ, son of the Blessed Virgin. In contrast to these suggestions the attribute of Kneph was the serpent. Line 9 varies when the tercet recurs in *A Louise d'O., Reine* as follows:

"L'aigle a déjà passé ... Napoléon m'apelle;"

Nerval imagines himself the universal "révolté," son of demi-gods like Napoleon or Horus (cf. *La Tête Armée*).

ANTÉROS.

Les Filles du Feu, 1854. Anteros, son of Aphrodite (Venus) and Ares (Mars), typifies tragic love. Antaeus was the giant son of Poseidon and Gé; he drew his strength from contact with the earth, eventually being squeezed to death in Hercules' arms, and thus opposes the heavens, just as paganism (Anteros) is here heroically contrasted with inhibiting religion (Jehovah). Anteros-Nerval stands beside the Syrian Baal and Phoenician Dagon against Jewish monotheism. Nerval, in fact, is again the accursed outcast, of the tribe of Antaeus, Cain, and Amalek. Line 12 refers to his own plunges into the "river of lamentation." In the last line, which should be compared with line 8 of *Delfica*, we are reminded of another Phoenician, Cadmus, who sowed the teeth of the famous dragon slain by Jason. The imagery is closely knit, Antaeus suggesting the earth, the cult of Dagon, and agriculture.

DELFICA.

L'Artiste, 28 décembre 1845, under the title *Vers dorés* and dated Tivoli 1843, an attribution challenged by Audiat. This poem was subsequently published by Nerval under the title *Daphné*, while the poem presented in this selection as *Vers dorés* was first titled *Pensée antique*. This sonnet is obviously saturated with memories of Octavie and indeed celebrates their visit to the Temple of Isis at Pompeii in 1834. In her flight from Apollo Daphne was transformed into a laurel, which then became Apollo's favorite tree. Nerval accordingly evokes the Delphic oracle, delivered by the priestess of Apollo. Lines 12 to 13 remind us that the sibyl of Delphi has been sleeping since the advent of Christianity (Constantine); the "ancienne romance," or "chanson d'amour," is that of Phoenician paganism which in line 9 the poet promises will return. The rewriting of the final tercet in *A Madame Aguado* should be remarked. The imagery, meanwhile, is almost perfectly harmonious—a laurel, a temple, a grotto, a blue sky overhead and a blonde sinking her teeth into a lemon ("elle imprimait ses dents d'ivoire dans l'écorce d'un citron" Nerval tells us in *Octavie*). The structural simplicity is beautifully in keeping with this imagery.

ARTÉMIS.

Les Filles du Feu, 1854. Another complicated and arcane poem, this has attracted many attempts at elucidation. Nerval first called his *Aurélia* by the name of *Artémis*, the twin sister of Apollo who lived in celibacy and was associated with the Roman Diana. The ideas of celibacy and the moon are predominant in the imagery of the poem, which evokes yet again Aurélia, under various forms. Indeed the poem epitomizes what Jeanine Moulin calls Nerval's erotic syncretism. Thirteen, for Nerval, was a number symbolizing eternity and the return of his love, i.e. Aurélia-Isis. In the midst of the poem the white rose of Christianity is opposed by the hollyhock of hell (*Althaea rosea*), to which there is a reference in *Aurélia* and which reflects the paganism of Nerval's femininity ideal. Time is annihilated by the criss-crossing of the associations drawn from differing poetic ages. Line 2 probably means that only one woman, Aurélia, can create for the poet the moment of ultimate bliss. Line 3 addresses Jenny-Adrienne (here the aristocratic emphasis predominates): line 4 addresses the poet himself (the "prince d'Aquitaine" once more). Line 5 refers to Nerval's mother. The difficult line 7 takes us to a Jenny-Aurélia personification, for her death was death itself for Nerval. Diana, Jenny, and Saint Rosalie (the personification of line 9, though Nerval confuses the color of Saint Gudule's flower), the last figure taken from Hoffmann's *Die Elixiere des Teufels*, are now the three principals, the trinity, and it is interesting to note that Maxime du Camp tells us that Nerval once showed him a colored drawing he had done with just these three personages together. Line 12 returns us to Nerval's literary beginnings, with the need for the purifying roses of *Faust II*. "La sainte de l'abîme," or Aurélia, is the apex always of this trinity and here she is clearly anti-Christian. But in this poem, which Aristide Marie calls hermetic and lapidary, Audiat observes how the central idea of woman remains constant, despite the succession of images assumed by woman.

VERS DORÉS.

L'Artiste, 16 mars 1845, under the title, *Pensée antique*.

AUTRES CHIMÈRES

LA TÊTE ARMÉE.

Poésies complètes, Paris, Michel-Lévy, 1877. Béguin helpfully points out that this poem is illuminated by the note Nerval appended to *La Mort de l'Exilé* in *Napoléon et la France guerrière*, as follows:

Napoleon's last words were: "My God" and "the French nation . . . My son! Armed head! . . ." No one knows what these last words signified. Shortly afterwards he was heard to cry out: "France! France!"

Napoleon died on St. Helena in March 1821. Général Bertrand, who with his family had followed his Emperor into exile, knew of Napoleon's love of his son and had once, on his birthday, presented him with a portrait of this son, Nerval's supposed relation. Napoleon is said to have replied: "Must this dear child, born French and heir to the noblest crown in the world, be now deprived of his father's affection and brought up in an Austrian Court!" In his last moments in the bedroom at Longwood Napoleon was shown a bust of his son and uttered the words quoted by Nerval. By now the reader will have noticed one recurrent contrast in Nerval's poetry, that between the symbols of Caesar and Christ. Yeats, who had more affinity with Nerval than any other English poet, was equally haunted by this dichotomy. In *A Vision* Yeats writes, "Caesar and Christ always stand face to face in our imagination."

A MADAME IDA DUMAS.

Poésies, 1924. As Ida Ferrier, Mme Dumas had acted in *l'Alchimiste*, as well as in other Dumas-Nerval collaborations, and Nerval maintained a correspondence with her. Line 2 refers to the Hindu deity believed to rule over the day. Lines 5, 10, and 11 collect three strong leaders, two of them bitter rebels with whom Nerval, in the penultimate line, throws in his lot. Ibrahim Pasha was Viceroy of Egypt from 1844 to 1848, the son of Mohammed Ali who is mentioned in *Aurélia*. Tippoo Sahib,

Sultan of Mysore in the Eighteenth Century, fought strenuously against the British until his defeat at Seringapatam by Cornwallis. Abd-el-Kader, Amir of Mascara and Arab hero *par excellence*, was a vigorous opponent of French rule in Algeria and surrendered to the Duc d'Aumale, "Adrienne' s" protégé on December 23rd, 1847. He was freed at Amboise by Napoleon III in 1852, as an act of clemency on establishing the Empire. "You have been an enemy of France," Napoleon is reported to have said, "but in all justice I must recognize your courage, your integrity, your fortitude in misfortune." In July 1860 Abd-el-Kader, passing his retirement in Damascus, intervened on behalf of Christianity in the famous "Syrian massacres."

A MADAME AGUADO.

Poésies, 1924. The last tercet should be compared with that of *Delfica*. In 1941 another poem, *Érythréa*, was published for the first time from an Eluard manuscript and turned out to be a variant of *A Madame Aguado*. The new poem, however, has notes attached to it, two of which are worth appending here. For "vautour" in line 7 Nerval noted "*Typhon*," who was the god of evil and sterility in ancient Egypt. For "prêtresse" in line 12, Nerval noted "*Amany*," which is the name of a range of mountains (Giaour Dagh in the North) in Asia Minor. The Vicomtesse Aguado was a *dame d'honneur* to the Empress Eugénie and can be seen in Winterhalter's famous picture *L'Impératrice Eugénie et ses dames d'honneur*, frequently reproduced. Frederic Loliée devotes a passage to her in his *Les Femmes du Second Empire*. It was Madame Aguado who delivered Napoleon III's first fateful invitation to the Comtesse de Castiglione.

POÉSIES DIVERSES

The 1877 edition of Nerval's poetry gave this title to those poems of his which he had never grouped himself, some of which, of course, were only posthumously published.

STANCES ELÉGIAQUES.

Almanach des Muses, 1829, and signed M. Louis Gerval. The reader should remember that this date was before Nerval's meeting with Jenny Colon (although she herself had been on the stage by this time), so that the third stanza refers perhaps to a boyhood love.

MÉLODIE IRLANDAISE.

La Psyché, janvier, 1830, under the title *Imitation de la 57e Mélodie de Thomas Moore*, and signed Gérard. Nerval seems to have maintained a steady interest in Thomas Moore, which is worth representing here. In the *Almanach des Muses* for 1828 he published a similar poem, inspired by Moore's *Believe me if all those endearing young charms,* called *A Auguste H ... Y* and which he reprinted in 1854. Amusingly enough, Albert Dubeux has discovered that in 1849, when Nerval was travelling with Gautier in England, he wrote this latter poem in the album of a lady he had met in the steamer crossing over, falsely assuring her that it was "jusqu'à présent inédit."

LAISSE-MOI.

Almanach des Muses, 1831, signed L. Gerval. Again it should be remembered that this poem does not, therefore, refer to Jenny.

UNE FEMME EST L'AMOUR.

L'Artiste, 13 mai 1855.

ÉPITAPHE.

Petite Revue internationale, 30 mai 1897; published by the Vicomte de Tressère, a pseudonym for Mme de Solms (see note 14 to the Introduction above).

Selected Ann Arbor Paperbacks
Works of enduring merit

For a complete list of Ann Arbor Paperback titles write:

THE UNIVERSITY OF MICHIGAN PRESS ANN ARBOR